A PUZZLING PICKLE

A MULBURY MYSTERY

JUNO HARVEY

First published by Mandurang Press 2025

Book cover by Melissa Williams Design

ISBN: 978-0-6456511-5-7 (ebook)

ISBN:978-0-6456511-6-4 (paperback)

To Mel, in our 90th year

ONE

Rosemary Exeter sped towards her hometown of Mulbury, her foot slipping slightly on the unfamiliar accelerator. The little car was quieter than any she'd driven before and it was odd although somehow worthy. Being rid of her long-gone husband Alasdair's blue sedan and replacing it with this hatchback was the final shedding of a long-held skin.

The road from Ken Cooper's car yard in Birdton passed through Big Town. Saturday afternoons were closed from shopping, and most of the buildings were dark. A few offices had their lights on and, as she whizzed past, Rosemary glimpsed a spiky-haired man silhouetted at his desk at the front of the rural insurance company, and a few cleaners vacuuming the community centre.

She cleared town and accelerated through the country-side. Sheep and horses grazed contentedly on short autumn grasses as she went by. Sunshine lit the ground, beaming from a vast cloudless blue sky. The beautiful scenery was only marred by an ugly billboard in the paddock before Mulbury, declaring the takeover of the pristine paddocks by a housing company called D-Day Development promising

Sophisticated town houses with landscaped common areas so no need for a garden! Rosemary averted her gaze, her lip curling at the thought of a housing estate rammed up beside the quaint miners' cottages and carefully tended vegetable patches of Mulbury.

It was six minutes to two o'clock when she finally drove into the tourist town. She turned into Goldmarket Road and continued past the shops under the veranda—Honey's tearoom, Jasper's bookshop, her own preserves shop, and Mrs Lionel's green cleaning products—to High Road, raising her hand at Mrs Lionel and Jasper as they walked across Goldmarket Square. By the time Rosemary pulled up, they'd entered The Leftover Restaurant, which the owners, Roman and Jules, had kindly offered as the venue for the first aid course starting soon. Rosemary clambered out of the car and fiddled with the unfamiliar key to lock the door.

'Nice.'

The voice behind her made her startle. 'What is, Robert?'

'Your purchase. Very nice. The colour is...special.'

'Right.'

Robert grinned and indicated the bonnet. 'The sun really makes it look bright but what would you call that colour?'

'Mauve.'

'Okay.' He ran a hand through his cinnamon-coloured hair. 'I'd say purple.'

'Think what you like, Robert Sparkling. I like it.'

'And, although the colour is questionable, you have a good vehicle there.'

'If it turns out not to be, I have my mechanic to blame for a poor inspection. It won't, though. Ken is as trustworthy as they come.' Rosemary eyeballed the oil stain on the front of Robert's shirt. 'Didn't *my mechanic* have time to change?'

'Like you, I'm running late.' He glanced down. 'Is it that obvious I've come straight from the garage?'

'Yes.' Rosemary straightened her jacket and smoothed the braid hanging over her shoulder. 'Right. Come on. We'll be last in.'

The entrance to the restaurant faced Goldmarket Square although the old two-storey bank building was set a little way back and wasn't as prominently placed as the other businesses nearby. Only Franco's Patisserie remained open, its entrance shaded by the enormous eucalyptus branches of The Exceptional Tree dominating the Square. The two cafes—Kelly's Mullings of Mulbury and Rakisha's The Sweet Potato—had their doors firmly shut and their outdoor settings packed away. Most of the business owners needed to refresh their first aid training, which meant Mulbury was practically a ghost town for the afternoon. As Rosemary and Robert stepped inside, they saw Kelly and Rakisha already seated in the circle of chairs around the instructor, with Mrs Lionel and Jasper signing in at the front of the room. Rosemary looked for Honey Blossom, but only saw her son-in-law, Ronnie, and not her daughter. Running a tearoom with a baby in tow was a lot of work, and Rosemary suspected Honey was catching up on her baking while Honey B's Teas was closed.

Roman Capriccio hurried over. 'Ah, Rosemary, so wonderful you came back in time. And Robert. You are ready to do the first aiding?'

'As ready as I'll ever be,' said Robert, reaching over to where Jules was standing by the door to give her a cheek kiss. 'Do you need a hand with anything?'

Roman shook his head. 'No, thanking you. I helped the

instructor carry his equipment in.' He held his arms out and struck a body builder stance. 'He is lucky I am a strongman. The big case was as heavy as a coffer.'

'Coffin, I think you mean, my love, and it was on a trolley so not really that heavy.' Jules smiled at her husband.

Roman's moustaches twitched as he grinned at his wife. 'Perhaps not.'

'Still, it was kind to help,' said Jules, turning her smile to Rosemary. 'Good of you to come along. If you could please sign the attendance sheet and write your name on a sticky label.'

'I had to come along.' Rosemary finished writing her name and straightened to watch the instructor at the front of the room unpack a box of bandages. 'Mandatory every three years if you want to keep your certification.'

'Yes.' Jules capped the pen and put it on the table. 'And very useful to have when our clientele consists of mainly older people, many of whom are not nearly as fit as Mrs Lionel.'

Rosemary glanced over to her good friend chatting amiably to Rakisha. Mrs Lionel had her share of arthritic complaints but they were hardly ever on display. She accepted help with the heavier work of creating products for The Green Mulbury, relying a little more on Robert over the last few months than she used to. Despite running the garage and renovating his house, Robert always had time for Mrs Lionel. Everyone always had time for Mrs Lionel. 'Correct,' said Rosemary, turning back to Jules. 'Let's hope we include ourselves in the fit category when we catch up to Mrs Lionel in a couple of decades time. Is anyone else coming?'

'No. Franco says he's too busy. Milly and the Hubbard sisters are waiting on a load of bark chips.'

'Right. Just us then.'

Jules smiled and put out her arm to indicate the chairs as if she was seating guests for a dining experience. Rosemary made her way to where Jasper sat next to Mrs Lionel, his head down over a book he hastily stuffed in his jacket pocket when he saw her.

'And how is Miss Ruby?' she asked, settling in a chair.

Jasper's face colour deepened into a warm red. 'She has finally made her choice.'

'Was it the Colonel or the blacksmith?'

'Who would you have chosen?'

Rosemary tapped her finger on the side of the chair. 'Let me think. If I was Miss Ruby, I'd go for the Colonel to lift her from servitude and to occupy his mansion.'

Jasper shook his head. 'But she doesn't love the Colonel.'

'So, she chose the blacksmith. Very unwise but undoubtedly more romantic.' She frowned. 'Regency romances are rather predictable.'

'Not always.' Jasper stared wistfully over Rosemary's shoulder. 'There's a moment when you think it's not going to work out, but it does. My bet is that the blacksmith is actually the heir to the mansion.'

'Right.' Rosemary tossed her braid over her shoulder. 'Perhaps we're lucky these days that mansions can be bought rather than waiting to be inherited.'

Jasper gave a brief nod. 'Like Robert bought Ravenshome.'

Rosemary watched as Robert stepped around the practice mannikin's large case and took a seat across from them. 'Yes. Exactly.'

'There's still luck involved.'

Rosemary twisted to face Jasper. His face was its

normal healthy hue. He tucked a strand of his lengthening hair behind an ear. 'Luck. Or hard work?'

'I didn't mean Robert doesn't work hard. But you've got to admit it's also lucky for him he comes from a wealthy family. Otherwise, he probably wouldn't have been able to afford his garage, Ravenshome and Mulbury Feeds.' Jasper shrugged. 'It was lucky for the Hubbard sisters he could buy the animal produce business from them when they most needed him to.'

'Are you bitter about Robert's wealth?'

Jasper took a moment to reply, pushing hair back behind his other ear. 'No, I'm not. He's a good person.'

Rosemary studied Jasper before nodding. There was no sourness tainting Jasper's kind features, nor was there any trace of sadness. The last year or so had not been nice to the bookseller, but he seemed recovered from both his illness and the impact of someone impersonating his father. In fact, Rosemary noted with satisfaction, Jasper Lu looked like his old, happy, bookish self, even if that meant he'd regained his love of hopelessly impractical fiction.

The first aid instructor, a sprightly fellow dressed in red scrubs, clapped his hands together and the room fell quiet. 'Now,' he said. 'My name is Bern. Not Bernard or Bernie or Berno. Please address me by my proper name.'

From across the room, Robert raised his eyebrows at Rosemary.

'In my workshops,' Bern continued, 'we start on time. Mobile phones are off. Questions are kept to the end of the section we're completing. We will cover bandaging and splinting, wound first aid, and cardiopulmonary resuscitation, also known as CPR. You must demonstrate all activities as if performing them on a live person even though...' he pointed at the mannikin case on the floor '...we are *simulating* a real experience.'

Rakisha raised her hand, the many bangles on her wrist jangling as they slid down her arm. 'It's difficult, darling, don't you think?'

Bern leaned over to peer at Rakisha's name tag. 'Is that a question, Rachael?'

Rakisha's bangles clashed again as she lowered her hand. 'Pardon?'

'You asked a question and I specifically said no questions until the end of a section.'

Rakisha's mouth opened slightly.

'It was more of a comment,' said Rosemary, staring at Bern.

'Even so. If we could wait until I finish a section before comments.' Bern cleared his throat.

'She has a point, dear.' Mrs Lionel smiled at the instructor. 'For some of us, it will be difficult to pretend the situation is real.'

'Nonetheless, this is how we must tackle the situation.' Bern rubbed his hands together. 'And I can assure you...' he peered at Mrs Lionel's tag '...Mrs Lentil, this mannikin we use for demonstration of CPR is very lifelike and easy to imagine as a real person.' He stood straight and pushed his chest out. 'I headed the fundraising committee to purchase this training item and we exceeded our expectations, enabling us to not only buy a high-fidelity model but a transport trolley *and* a mobile van.'

'Well done, Bernard,' said Rosemary.

Bern scowled and stared at Rosemary's tag. 'As I said before, Roseanne, I would appreciate being called by my proper name.'

Rosemary smiled, feeling Mrs Lionel's hand on hers. 'As would we.'

Before Bern could respond, Robert stood up, his phone in his hand. 'My apologies, Bernie. I need to go.'

'People who leave the course for other reasons will not be able to return,' said Bern loudly.

'I understand.' Robert glanced at Rosemary, his face grim. 'I will not be returning today.'

'I guess he's had enough of Bern already,' said Jasper quietly as Robert hurried away and the instructor started handing out first aid manuals.

Rosemary shook her head. 'No. Something's up.'

'He'll let us know soon enough,' said Mrs Lionel. 'Leave it for now.'

'Let's begin,' said Bern with a stern look at his students.

Rosemary couldn't remember a first aid training session more boring than the one Bern was unravelling slowly before them. The first thirty minutes consisted of Bern's unspectacular journey to become a trainer after an incident in which he encountered the sharp lid of a dog food can, leading to his discovery of large home first aid kits. Among the plasters, cotton wool pads and saline solutions, Bern found his true direction in life. As he fondly patted the rolled practice bandages lying neatly side by side on the table, he said, 'There's nothing like the smell of a clean swab now, is there?'

Before Rosemary could point out his question and that it should be kept until the end of the section, Mrs Lionel spoke up. 'You have a lovely array of teaching paraphernalia, dear. We are going to learn a lot today.'

Bern grinned. 'Thank you, Mrs Lentil. A good trainer makes sure he has the correct equipment to deploy maximum teaching practice. Let me show you the pièce de résistance!' He rubbed his hands together again and knelt next to the mannikin case.

'A retired nurse like you is going to learn a lot,' said Rosemary quietly.

'Shush, dear.' Mrs Lionel lightly elbowed her friend. 'A refresher will do me, and you, good. It wouldn't hurt to look impressed when he opens that case.'

Bern finished unclipping the case and sat back on his heels. 'I can dress this fellow up to represent an average person by using different clothing and wigs, so he's a very valuable asset.' He bent forward, hands on the hard case. 'Here he is, Cecil the CPR dummy!' Bern flung back the lid and gasped.

'Goodness, darling,' said Rakisha. 'Cecil is rather life-like, isn't he?'

Every Mulburian was suddenly on their feet, staring in the mannikin's case. Cecil was hunkered awkwardly in the confines of the case wearing a flannelette shirt, dirty trousers, and thick socks. His eyes were slightly open, revealing a glimpse of blue, but it was the cold purple of his lips that told Rosemary the true story.

'I'm answering your question, Rakisha, even if it isn't time.' Rosemary looked at Bern, who had his hand covering his mouth and horror etched on his face. 'I'd say this isn't Cecil and, whoever it is, is not lifelike at all. This fellow is *death*like.'

TWO

It didn't take long for the hush that had fallen over Mulbury when businesses closed for the first aid training to dissipate. Three police cars, two with lights and sirens, barrelled into the little town, making the few tourists eating Franco's pies under The Exceptional Tree look up so quickly pastry fell from their open mouths. A broad man in a dark suit exited from the last car, shooting a stern look at the younger constables driving the patrol cars who shut the noise off smartly. Rosemary stepped forward from her spot outside The Leftover Restaurant to greet him. 'Hello, Geoffrey.'

'Rosemary.' The detective dipped his head at her. 'What puzzling pickle is happening in Mulbury today? The bodies are piling up.'

'Body. So far only one.'

Geoffrey raised one eyebrow. 'So far? Are you expecting more?'

'No. But never say never.'

'Hmmm.' Geoffrey looked over her shoulder. 'In the restaurant, is it?'

'Yes.'

'But not a diner.'

'No. More a piece of training equipment.'

Geoffrey nodded his head slightly. 'Nothing astounds me anymore.'

Rosemary moved aside to let him study the old bank. 'I bet.'

'Righto.' Geoffrey moved to go inside but stopped. 'Before I get too carried away, how are you? Ronnie and Honey? Little Tallulah?'

Rosemary smiled. 'We're all fine, thank you. Honey B's Teas is going very well. Honey is back to occasionally baking special cakes, and Ronnie has a bit of private investigator work still although he seems to only take on small insurance jobs.'

'Well, they have the baby now.'

'Tallulah is six months old.'

'How time flies.' Geoffrey walked on for a few stops and halted again. 'And Pearl? Any news on how she's going?'

'Your sister-in-law has nearly finished her therapy.' Rosemary eyed the tall man. 'They say she has post-traumatic stress disorder from the robbery in her own café decades ago. That might explain her exacting behaviour all these years.'

'Yes, it might indeed.' Geoffrey frowned. 'And I should have known to give her the benefit of the doubt. After all, she was married to my brother for thirty years.'

'You weren't to know.' Rosemary thought back to the erratic behaviour of Ronnie's mother when last she visited. 'None of us knew and we feel guilty we weren't nicer to her. We can make it up when she returns to Mulbury. I suspect Ronnie will want her to live closer to him eventually.'

'I will make an effort to visit her soon, as I will to see the baby.' He tipped his head to Rosemary and strode to the crime scene.

Rosemary glanced across Goldmarket Square at the row of shops under the veranda on Goldmarket Road. They remained shut, although she could see the silhouette of Jasper in The Read Mulbury, pottering among his towering bookcases of second hand books. The Green Mulbury remained dark as Mrs Lionel was visiting Mulbury Feeds, probably to check that Heather was not being too affected by the discovery of Cecil. Although *Cecil* was undoubtedly not the man's name. Rosemary pursed her lips as she walked toward the bookshop. She'd never seen the dead man before and neither, she suspected, had any of her friends.

The Read Mulbury had a sign that read *Grab a book from your TBR pile until I open* but the heavy door swung inwards as she pushed on it. Jasper looked up from a pile of books on his counter and smiled. 'Rosemary.' The smile dropped from his face. 'Does Geoffrey know what happened?'

'He knows there's a dead body in a mannikin's case.'

'I meant, does he know why there's a dead body in a mannikin's case?'

Rosemary shook her head. 'He's a detective, Jasper, not a clairvoyant.' Jasper's cheeks reddened, and she felt mean. 'But he's a clever man. He'll work it out soon enough.'

'He often needs your help.' Jasper held up one of the books in front of him. 'Have you read this series, *Spectre Season*?'

Rosemary took the book from him. 'No. Should I?'

'I'm not sure. I've just finished the last one and thought

it well-written. This one...' he shook the book '... is about a man who thinks his dog is a ghost.'

She handed the book back. 'Let's give it to Mrs Lionel.'

Jasper frowned. 'Why?'

Rosemary bit the inside of her cheek. 'No reason. I hear she's looking for something to read.'

He indicated a shelf nearby. 'She came in yesterday and bought two historical fictions. I think she'll be okay for a while.'

'Right. I didn't know she'd done that.' She ran her hand over the rest of the books in front of her. 'Any other treasures in these?'

'No, pretty standard.' Jasper balanced the ghost dog book on top of the others. 'Tea?'

'Always.'

She followed Jasper through the doorway that led to his living quarters, pausing to pat Snowy who was in his usual place upside down on the couch. The old dog thumped his tail on a cushion, smiling happily as Rosemary stroked the grey hairs on his tummy. She left him to it, and by the time she got to the kitchen, gentle dog snores filtered through from the loungeroom.

Jasper's kitchen was a jumble of dirty plates and half-read books. He put the kettle on, and hastily picked up crockery from the table to dump in the sink. She let him fuss for a bit, politely staring out the glass door to Jasper's scrubby back yard and the fence dividing all their places from old Mr Cameron's. When he stopped clanking crockery, she sat, not before lifting a dictionary from the chair and bookmarking the open books in front of her with old receipts before stacking them in a pile. Jasper plonked a teapot into the empty space, followed by two mugs. 'Earl Grey okay?'

'Yes.'

She waited until he'd poured the tea and sat down opposite her. 'Jasper, what are your plans over the autumn?'

His hand stilled on his mug. 'What do you mean?'

'It's a simple question.'

He tapped one finger. 'Okay, well, I've got a simple answer. I'll be working in my bookshop.' He grimaced. 'I've still got to make up for what I didn't earn when I was away. Jules was great selling my books online but it didn't make up for lost income. My wild goose chase after my father-who-wasn't cost a bit.'

'I see.' Rosemary sipped her tea, noting the delicate bergamot infusion.

'Do you?' Jasper smiled suddenly, his face relaxing. 'Why do I never trust you to ask random questions? You have a reason for checking what I intend to do.'

She paused before nodding. 'You're correct. I do. I want to know you're settled.'

'I'm settled.' He hooked a stray wavy strand of hair back. 'I'm not going anywhere, I'm not sick, and I'm not chasing lost fathers or speculating about famous mothers. I'm not even thinking about my curse. It's done its worst for now.'

Rosemary studied him but saw nothing but sincerity. She sat back and drank her tea. 'Good,' she said. 'You can help out here, then.'

'Help?'

'We have a mystery to solve.'

'A mystery? Oh, you mean Cecil.'

'Unless he climbed into that case and died of his own accord.'

Jasper gulped his tea. 'I don't imagine that he did. But you said it yourself: Geoffrey will work it out.'

'And you said it as well: often he needs help.'

'We'll keep our eyes and ears open.'

'Yes.'

'Talking about ears…' Jasper stood and went to the kitchen door. 'Do you hear that?'

Rosemary listened. A din reached her, shouts and car revving from further away than the road in front of them. 'Yes.'

'Tourists grumpy that our shops are closed?'

'Our tourists are usually milder than that.' Rosemary slipped past him and wound her way through his lounge room and the dark bookshop to the front windows. A car parked diagonally across Goldmarket Square, its passenger door open. The noise came from a little woman with short-cropped fair hair struggling in the arms of two uniformed police officers with pained expressions on their faces. A heavily built, grim-faced man stood behind her, running his hands in agitation through his sleek pompadour. 'I sense that Cecil has been identified.'

Jasper peered over her shoulder. 'Oh, that woman is so distressed! Will we see whether we can help?'

'Yes.'

Jasper opened the door and they crossed the road to the Square. Rosemary glanced in the abandoned car but it was empty. They stopped a few metres from the woman who now had Geoffrey in front of her. 'I understand this could be a terrible shock, Mrs Brownlee. If you could take a moment to calm yourself.'

'Calm?' The woman pulled her arms free of the officers and took a step toward Geoffrey. 'And what's to be calm about, sir? I want to see Bob and I want to see him now.'

'It is not recommended you see the body at this stage. You will need to prepare yourself.'

'I am prepared!' The woman stopped, squared her shoulders, and stared up at Geoffrey. 'I am prepared,' she said more quietly. 'I would like to see my husband now.'

Geoffrey nodded slowly. 'Okay, Mrs Brownlee, although we have a crime scene here and I will have to ask you to respect that. The deceased looks quite normal, with no obvious signs of how he died.'

'Yes, yes.' Mrs Brownlee shivered. 'He's been away with work this week so I haven't seen him for days. I just want to confirm he's dead.' She took a step forward. 'Now, if you don't mind.'

Geoffrey directed the uniforms to follow Mrs Brownlee. He saw Rosemary and gave her a curt nod before striding past Mrs Brownlee to the entrance of The Leftover Restaurant.

'Goodness,' said a voice behind Rosemary. 'Short, isn't she?'

'Kelly.' Rosemary didn't bother to turn around. 'Not very sympathetic of you.'

'Well, you know, Rosemary.' Kelly walked around Jasper, trailing her hand on his arm, to stop in front of them. 'I have other skills and leave the sympathy to better people than me.' She smiled thinly. 'Jasper, for instance.'

'Right.' Rosemary studied Kelly, noting the high colour on her checks and the glint of something cunning in her eyes. 'Remind me. What are your talents?'

'Ah, Rosemary, you well know what my talents are. They include serving great coffee while asking innocent questions of naïve police officers.' Kelly swung around to look at the restaurant where the dark shapes of Mrs Brownlee and her entourage gathered in the doorway, making her dark bob swing around her shoulders. 'And so people tell me things. Such as the identity on the driver's license of the man stuffed in a dummy's case.'

'Mr Brownlee,' said Jasper. 'Because that poor woman is Mrs Brownlee.'

'You're adorable, Jasper.' Kelly stroked his arm again. 'You're correct but you don't know any more, do you?'

'No.'

'No. I didn't think so. Let me tell you about Mr Brownlee.' Kelly smoothed her bob and kept her gaze on Jasper's face. 'Mr Bob Brownlee is a fifth-generation sheep farmer, now specialising in coloured wool. Married to Bunnie Brownlee, he was the darling of the spinners and weavers club, supplying them with fleece at cost price with a new batch delivered just this week. By all accounts, he was an overly cheerful man, always willing to lend a jolly hand, loved practical jokes and pranks like dressing up as a sheep to scare the lady weavers and putting whoopee cushions under seats. He was the clown at many social events, even if those social occasions didn't want a clown.'

Rosemary waited but Kelly had paused. 'Right. Apart from the fact he liked joking around, Bob Brownlee fits the profile of many farmers in our district, Justin Gentleman as an example.'

Kelly rolled her eyes. 'Justin Gentleman is quite a nice man but he's no Bob Brownlee. When was the last time Justin joined into any social function?'

'He comes to our Monday dinners occasionally,' said Jasper.

'As do I, and that doesn't mean I'm a social butterfly.' Kelly twirled a short length of her hair around a finger before letting it bounce back into its sharp-edged position. 'Monday dinners are a free feed for people like Justin.'

Rosemary felt her lip curl, as it often did when talking

to Kelly. She counted to three as Mrs Lionel was always telling her to do and, by doing so, let Jasper steal in.

'I get what you're saying, Kelly,' he said. 'Mr Bob Brownlee was fun to be around and had no enemies.'

'That's it, Jasper, love.' Kelly put her hand on his. 'And...?'

Jasper glanced at Rosemary who shrugged one shoulder. 'And so why was he stuffed into a resus dummy's case?'

THREE

The police took the rest of the day to investigate the crime scene. Finally, the forensic investigators finished and the dead man was driven away, Bunnie Brownlee following closely, driven by the grim-faced man. Rosemary kept her eyes on things from her shop, patiently cleaning and restacking her shelves of autumnal preserves. As the sun lowered, the beams from the skylight in the middle of the shop angled in to hit the rich pinks and reds of her quince jam and pear chutney. If there hadn't been frenetic activity just across the Square, the quiet time spent in her little shop would have been perfect.

The last of the police cars left with Geoffrey in the passenger's seat. He held a hand up in farewell to the shops under the veranda but Rosemary didn't think he could see her or any of the shop owners. It was more a homage to Mulbury, a gesture to include them in the ongoing police activity. She packed the step ladder away, swooping to pat her ginger tabby as she passed. 'Back to normal, Sunny.'

Sunny sat in the kitchen, tail wrapped around her paws,

and stared unblinkingly at her mistress. *What is normal in Mulbury?* her gaze seemed to say.

'You've got me there.' Rosemary offered Sunny her dinner. 'You might be the only essence of normality in the place.'

Sunny gave her a derisive look before delicately licking at her meal.

'My apologies. I meant you're consistently nonchalant.'

The slight flick of her tail was the only indication Sunny had heard.

Rosemary put the kettle on, looking out the window to the gum trees lining the back fence as she waited. Either she was lost in reflection or the kettle was too loud, but as she went to take a cup from the cupboard, her phone flashed a missed call from Robert Sparkling. She called him straight back, moving to open the glass balcony door so she could be closer to the trees. 'Hello Robert. Sorry I didn't pick up.'

'Of course, I expect you to always answer my calls straight away.'

It was a common joke but Rosemary didn't hear any mirth in Robert's low voice. 'What's wrong?'

He sighed, a whoosh of air down the phone. 'Is it that obvious?'

'Yes.'

'Okay.' He sighed again, making Rosemary move the phone slightly way from her ear. 'My father has died.'

'Right.' Rosemary put a hand to her chest. 'I'm sad to hear that. It was unexpected?'

'Yes, and no. He was ninety-two.' Robert gave a short chuckle. 'Thank you for being you.'

'What do you mean?'

'Thank you for not pulling out that horrible line, *sorry for your loss* as if my father is a sock.'

'It's not my favourite expression, either. But I am sad for you. No matter what your relationship was with your father, his death is confronting.'

'Yes. Good word that. I have been, and continue to be, confronted.'

'You want to talk about it. That's why you called.'

Robert was quiet for a moment. 'I actually called to see whether you'd lock up the garage for me. I'll be away until after the funeral.'

'Of course. And Ravenshome?'

'Patti and Gerry will take care of the house.'

Rosemary chuckled.

'What's the matter?'

She swapped the phone to her other ear so she could take up a broom in her hand to sweep the leaf-clad balcony as she talked. 'Ravenshome is hardly a *house*.'

'Well, maybe not a house in conventional terms, but *my* house. Home, I should say.'

'You've become increasingly fond of it.'

'Yes.' His voice was warm. 'I know it had a dark past, but now that Patricia's is at the front, it's taken on a kind of softness. When I come downstairs in the morning, I have to push my way through racks of frocks made from abandoned tablecloths. It's very homely.'

Rosemary smiled at the image of Patti's bespoke upcycled garments crowding the old ballroom. 'I suspect every room you walk into downstairs is full of something Patti has created or is in the process of creating. And now Heather has joined her as an apprentice seamstress.'

'The pair of them often huddle together over piles of jumpers they've found in an op shop like they're Christmas presents. I'm just amazed at their creativity. There wouldn't be a need for anyone to buy new clothes made in a factory if they shopped at Patricia's.'

Rosemary glanced down at the jacket she was wearing. It was indeed one of Patti's items, an upcycled pair of Rosemary's favourite jeans that had been too holey to wear as trousers. As a jacket, it was perfect. 'Kudos to her.'

'Yes.' Robert fell quiet again. 'Anyway, that was why I rang.'

'Any idea when the funeral will be?'

'Soon, I imagine. My father had organised it before he... well, he was always very organised. We're waiting for family members to fly into the city. I'll be back as soon as I can.'

'We can hold the fort here if you need more time. I can cancel any work you have at the garage.'

'It's okay, I only had a couple of jobs booked in for this coming week. Locals, you know. I've already rung them.'

'Right.' Rosemary waited but the silence stretched on. 'Are you alright, Robert?'

He sighed once more. 'I am. As you know, my father and I weren't particularly close. I guess it's the end of an era I'm adjusting to. And the fact that city life does not appeal to me, not one bit.'

'Ah. You've discovered the pleasures of being a Mulburian. Well, it's not all pleasurable, as I'm sure Bob Brownlee would say if he was alive.'

'Who?'

Rosemary leaned the broom against the rail and swapped her phone back. Evening was approaching and the lights were on in both Mrs Lionel's and Jasper's living areas. She pulled her jacket closer. 'You didn't hear.'

'Hear what?'

'The first aid training was cancelled because there was a body in the CPR mannikin's case.'

'*Sorry?* You mean, a *real* body? Not a mannikin?'

'A real body. The fellow's name was Bob Brownlee.'

'And he was in the case *why?*'

'Your guess is as good as anyone's.'

'Wow.' The phone rustled as if Robert was shaking his head. 'Unbelievable.'

'Yes, but it happened. We don't know anything else.'

'Okay, well, keep me informed.'

'Will do. Bye for now.'

'Bye.'

Rosemary ended the call and tucked the phone into her pocket. She went back inside and hunted for the Mulbury keys, the collection of everyone's shop and business keys she was currently the custodian of. The garage office key was the newest. When Robert bought the mechanic's from its previous owner, he thought it wise to change the locks. Rosemary separated the key and kept it in her hand as she made her way down the street.

The air was cooling. Rosemary buttoned her jacket up as she walked under the veranda towards Low Road. The Read Mulbury was dark, although a rectangle of light from deep inside signalled Jasper's presence. Honey B's Teas was similarly dim, but its blinds were still up revealing Ronnie dancing around the lounge room beyond the café with Tallulah laughing in his arms and Cuddles the Golden Retriever prancing at his feet. Rosemary paused, but Honey was probably busy elsewhere. She smiled as Ronnie swept into view again, the baby clutching at his shoulders, her face lit with delight. A stealthy warmth crept into Rosemary and her smile stayed as she crossed the road to the garage.

Robert had done little to modernise the business, save for the computer accounting system and the means to service cars with electronic needs. Rosemary pushed her way into the office, taking in the acrid odour of oil and cement cleaner, so different to the usual fragrances of fruit and vinegar she spent each day with. She checked the computer was off, pulled down the little blind at the front of the office, and switched on the night light Robert had installed in case he needed to come in early or late. It was hard to resist tidying the desk a little, so she did, stacking car manuals into a neat pile and putting some pens back into their holder. As she did, she knocked over a photo frame partially hidden by a bag of rags left haphazardly across the in-tray. She picked it up and wiped it with one of the rags to better see what it was.

A stony-faced man stood with his arms across the shoulder of two boys who stared wide-eyed into the camera. One boy was clearly Robert, identified by his dark eyes and dusky coloured hair but also by the way he stood tall and straight as if holding the man's arm up. The other boy was smaller with a wavy ash blond cut and a slouch. It was if he was ducking away from the man who had similar light hair parted meticulously to one side. It was a family portrait, no doubt, and so Rosemary was looking at Robert's now deceased father and a younger brother.

She sat the frame back on the desk carefully, hesitating before pulling the bag of rags across it. When Robert spoke of his father, it was with no affection, but he'd never spoken of a brother. Families were tricky things, Rosemary knew, so she had never asked for more than had been offered. She slipped out the door and locked it.

A glare of lights, and a white car hurtled up Low Road. It continued toward the cemetery before braking noisily. Rosemary crossed the road and stood on the corner near Honey B's Teas, watching. For a full two minutes, the car chugged unhappily in the middle of the street before its reversing lights came on and it went backwards down the hill until it was alongside Goldmarket Square. After some zig zagging, it parked near Franco's Patisserie, and a group of people stepped out.

Now that the car was stationary, quiet fell over Mulbury. Rosemary counted five people, three men of various sizes, and two women. One of the women was a tiny thing compared to her tall companion, and seemed familiar but it was too dark to see her clearly. Each person wore a large jacket that dangled to mid-calf, or in the small woman's case, to her ankles. They started across the Square, the first man holding something in front of him while the man beside him carried what appeared to be an old-fash-ioned TV antenna. A larger man straggled behind the group, puffing heavily as he tried to keep up, and waving his hands as if wanting them to stop.

Rosemary glanced into the tearoom. Ronnie was nowhere to be seen but she could hear faint laughter from the back of the residence. It was dinner time, and eating was what any sensible Mulburian would be doing. Rosemary decided she wasn't yet hungry and crept across the road to follow the small crowd.

They walked stealthily, eerily quiet except for the heavy breathing of the last man. Rosemary ducked under a bough of The Exceptional Tree and waited until they'd gone past The Sweet Potato. Antenna Man held it higher and someone whispered something which was followed by a 'Shhhhh!' from someone else. As Rosemary followed them, keeping to the shadows around Mullings of Mulbury, she realised where they were going.

The Leftover Restaurant was as dark as the rest of the businesses around it. Blue and white tape across its doorway waved lightly in the slight breeze. The small crowd stopped, fanning out so they stood in a line. Rosemary went as close as she could without revealing herself and crouched down behind a rubbish bin.

'Anything?' Antenna Man asked.

'Nothing,' said the man holding the object.

'A flicker?' asked the small woman.

'No. Nothing.'

The small woman shook her head. 'That's not right.'

'It doesn't lie,' said the man. 'If there's anything-'

'Bob!' screamed the small woman. 'Bob! I'm here!'

Scuffles and mumbling erupted from the small crowd as they surrounded the tiny woman and hurried her back across the Square. Rosemary made herself as compact as she could but they didn't glance her way. The man with the object threw it into a backpack so he could scoop his arm around the small woman's back as the other woman tried to take her arm. Antenna Man stormed ahead to open the car.

They passed Rosemary in a flurry of gravel. There were loud bangs as car doors opened and closed. Rosemary ran, crouched awkwardly, to the wall of Franco's Patisserie, and watched the car stutter before taking off. It turned sharply to head back down the road and the illumination from Franco's inside light lit the front seat occupant. The small woman's face, twisted in distress as it had been when she'd been bundled away, was suddenly recognisable. It was Bunnie Brownlee.

FOUR

'And she was calling out to him? In the dark?'

Rosemary passed the plate of ginger biscuits to her friend and nodded. Mrs Lionel took one and held it in her fingers. 'She called out his name. Twice.'

'Poor dear.' Mrs Lionel dunked the biscuit into her tea and took a quick bite. 'Perhaps she doesn't quite realise he's dead.'

'I believe she identified him.'

'Goodness. It sounds like she's in complete denial. I hope she has access to a counsellor.'

Rosemary poured herself more tea and rested her chin in her hand. It was late afternoon, the first real chance she'd had to talk to Mrs Lionel or anyone about the previous evening. The day had been filled with gawking tourists, their main mission in visiting to see the cordoned off restaurant. Rosemary was at first disgusted and then run off her feet as the dark tourists realised there wasn't much to the crime scene but that the rest of Mulbury was very interesting. Having made their way there, it was like they couldn't leave until they'd spent all their money and been in every shop and eaten Franco's entire display of pies. She was, frankly, relieved they were gone so she could do the other chores she'd listed for the day, including buying more cat food. 'I dare say counselling will be offered.' Rosemary toyed with a biscuit. 'How do these taste?'

'Absolutely delicious. New recipe?'

'It was in the back of Aunt Lilibeth's book hidden under a dried flower which finally crumbled away.'

'That recipe book reveals continuous treasures.'

Rosemary nodded. 'It does.' She nibbled at the biscuit.

Mrs Lionel put her cup down. 'Penny for your thoughts, dear?'

'Not sure they're worth that much.' Rosemary grimaced. 'I was wondering about two things. Why Bunnie Brownlee called out to her dead husband, but also why Robert Sparkling chose Mulbury to live.'

'I see.' Mrs Lionel stretched down to pat Sunny who rubbed against her leg. 'I don't think the latter is a mystery. Robert found a place he could settle. Mulbury takes in people and holds them in its arms.'

'Very poetic.'

'Probably but I believe it.' Mrs Lionel helped herself to more tea. 'I imagine that what Robert was missing in his life before he came here was support of one kind or another. He's found friends here, a lovely home, good businesses to invest in. There is no enigma to his actions. I'd be more worried about poor Bunnie Brownlee.'

'Right.' Rosemary shook her head slightly. 'Let's focus on her.'

'You think it was more than a woman crying out in her loss?'

'It wasn't that sort of plea. She called him as if he was late for dinner and she'd spent hours slaving over a hot stove.'

Mrs Lionel shrugged. 'Could still be shock?'

'Yes.'

'Something else bothering you?'

Rosemary pushed her cup away and leaned forward so her elbows were on the table. 'The people she was with. They were furtive.'

'It does sound like they were sneaking around at night, not wanting to be seen. Perhaps they were protecting Bunnie?'

'With a TV antenna?'

Mrs Lionel smiled. 'That could be all they had at hand.'

'It's the sort of thing you keep in the boot of a car.' She glanced at Mrs Lionel. 'Sorry.'

'Perfectly fine because you're right. I have no idea why they would be wandering around in the dark with appliances best suited to a lounge room.' Mrs Lionel scraped back her chair. 'Anyway, I must go. The shop needs a tidy after that lot went through.'

'How are your stocks?'

'Much depleted. I need to bring some more soap up from the cellar.'

Rosemary stood. 'Let me help you. The ladder is very steep.'

'I will admit it does hurt my knees.' Mrs Lionel leaned on the table to help her stand. 'My joints have been quite stiff lately. It's a warning that winter is on its way.'

Rosemary slid the remaining biscuits into their tin, put the lid back on, and followed Mrs Lionel through The Preserved Mulbury to the fresh air outside. The street was empty. Only Rakisha's outdoor setting conveyed a sense that Mulbury was still open for business. Honey's sandwich board was packed away, as was Jasper's trolley full of display books that normally sat outside his shop. 'Looks like we've all given up early today.'

'No harm in that every now and then.'

Rosemary pushed open the door to The Green Mulbury, setting off the electronic frog sensor motion. She gritted her teeth at the continual croaking and shut the door as soon as the proprietor was inside. The shelves of the shop were indeed decimated, with gaps not only in soap but in all of Mrs Lionel's green cleaning products. Rosemary set to work bringing more products up from the cellar while her friend arranged them neatly about the shop.

Rosemary's phone rang as she was shutting the cellar's trapdoor. 'Hello, Robert.'

'Rosemary. All good?'

'Depends on what you mean by that.'

He chuckled but it sounded forced. 'The garage?'

'Locked up.'

'Dead body mystery solved?'

'No.'

'Ah, okay.' He stopped talking and Rosemary heard the whooshes of a busy city street. 'I'll be coming home on Tuesday after the funeral.'

'That soon?'

'My father made sure his service was also prepaid to be prioritised. It was a condition of his contract with the funeral parlour. He left nothing to chance.'

There was no fondness in Robert's voice. Rosemary walked into The Green Mulbury and signalled to Mrs Lionel, putting the phone on speaker. 'Mrs Lionel's here, too. Are you alright, Robert?'

'Yes, thank you.'

Rosemary bristled. 'I'm not asking whether you'd like a slice of cake. I'm genuinely asking after you.'

Robert paused. 'I know what you're asking, Rosemary. I'm not sure how to answer. You see...' He fell quiet.

'No, I don't see. What is it?'

The noise through the phone changed to something more like hushed café conversation. 'We're talking to the solicitors tomorrow about my father's will but I already know what's in it. We've always known as he shared it with us. I know what's coming.'

'And you don't like it.'

'Not really. It will complicate matters.'

'Right.' Rosemary waited but the only sound was the distant clink of coffee cups. 'You don't want to talk about it.'

'Not right now.'

'Rosemary's correct, dear,' said Mrs Lionel, brushing a grey curl from her face. 'We are genuinely concerned for you. It's tough, losing your father. It doesn't matter how old he was or how old you are. It's a changing of the guard.'

'It is, Mrs Lionel. That's just it. You are very perceptive.'

'No, just experienced. Please look after yourself.' Mrs Lionel glanced at Rosemary. 'Mulbury looks forward to having you home.'

The phone crackled, as if he was shifting it around. 'Thanks. I'll see you in a couple of days. Bye for now.'

'Well,' said Rosemary, putting her phone away. 'That doesn't sound good.'

'Whatever it is, it'll work out.' Mrs Lionel dabbed the back of her hand on her forehead. 'And I've had enough of restocking. Tea?'

'Thanks, but I'll go and fix up my stocks before I get dinner.'

'Oh. You've spent all this time with me. I could help you now.'

Rosemary considered her friend's tired face. 'No, you won't. You need a sit down and a chat to Percy.'

Mrs Lionel looked down at the floor. Rosemary couldn't see anything but she knew Mrs Lionel could. Even if he was an imaginary dog, he was great comfort to the older woman. 'Alright then, we will,' Mrs Lionel said. 'But please call on me if you need a hand.'

'Of course.' Rosemary moved toward the door. 'I'll see you tomorrow.' The frog let rip as it caught sight of her and she hurried to close the door behind her.

'Just the person I wanted to see.'

Rosemary jumped slightly. A large man in a dark grey suit stood on the pavement. 'Geoffrey. I didn't expect you here on a Sunday.'

'It isn't really a business visit. I hadn't seen the kids for a while and Honey asked me to afternoon tea. The tearoom was very busy but I did the great-uncle tasks of holding that beautiful baby and patting the dog while Tallulah's parents scurried around serving people.' He smiled and Rosemary could see a faint line of drool on his lapel. 'They're going well, aren't they, Ronnie and Honey, I mean?'

'Yes. The tearoom is very successful.' Rosemary indicated her shop front. 'Tea, Geoffrey? Although you've probably just had a teapot full.'

'Several, actually.' The detective put a hand on his stomach. 'So, no thanks, Rosemary. I'll go.' He turned to Goldmarket Square and pointed. 'Nothing to report on that front, either, as nothing happened today. Everything remains locked up although I suspect the restaurant can start up again very soon. We'll continue our investigations in Big Town, starting where the first aid training equipment was stored.'

'Where is that?'

'They rent an area in one of the office buildings on the main street. It was an old gymnasium, if I recall. We'll look into it, see what we can find.'

'Bunnie Brownlee was here last night.'

Geoffrey's eyes narrowed. 'Was she? What was she doing?'

'Visiting the crime scene, albeit in the dark and with a group.'

'I see. Interesting.' Geoffrey tapped a hand on his pocket, making his car keys jingle. 'It's early days. Keep me informed, Rosemary, if anything else comes up.' He dipped his head in farewell.

Rosemary watched as he got in his car and drove away, noting the awkward way he bent to slide into his sedan and the moment he took to settle in his seat. Geoffrey was close to retirement, but each year he put it off for a little longer. His dedication was admirable.

She looked back at her shop. 'Talking about dedication.'

Sunny sat in the windowsill of The Preserved Mulbury, looking quite offended. Her tail twitched as Rosemary stepped inside. She gave her mistress a long look.

'Right. Cat food.'

Rosemary spun and went back outside, leaving Sunny to stare after her as she walked briskly down the pavement and across the road to Mulbury Feeds.

It was right on closing time. Rosemary ran the last few metres to where Hannah Hubbard was rolling down the large shed door. 'Hannah, wait!'

The middle Hubbard sister dropped her hands and the

door stilled. 'What's up, Rosemary? Any more dead people in town?'

'Not that I've noticed although it could be me if I don't get Sunny some dried food.'

Hannah rubbed her head, making her blonde spikes stand up all over her head. 'Why do I find that so easy to imagine? I wouldn't get on Sunny's bad side if you paid me.' She beckoned. 'Come on in.'

Rosemary slipped under the gap and stopped. 'It's clear I haven't been here for a while.'

The front of the shed was full of terracotta and glazed pots, while watering cans and artfully arranged packets of seeds sat on racks nearby. Packaged secateurs and gleaming shovels stacked against the shed wall and a line of bright gumboots decorated a hay bale.

'Isn't it great?' Hannah grinned, putting her hands on her hips. 'It's all Milly's doing. I didn't think I'd like anyone else but family working here, but she's been a godsend.'

'Talking about me?' Milly emerged from behind a stack of potting mix. She pulled off her leather gardening gloves and looked around with pride. 'Holly had the idea before she drove away to join Christopher. I just took over and went with it.'

Rosemary nodded. 'You're enjoying working in Mulbury?'

The older woman's face creased as she smiled. 'Very much so.'

'And living with Rakisha? How are you going there?'

Milly's pleasant face suddenly morphed into concern. 'Oh, I'm so glad you asked, Rosemary. I really shouldn't be talking about this but...'

'Hey, Milly,' said Hannah. 'It's okay. We know Rakisha is eccentric. It must be tricky sometimes.'

Milly twisted her gloves. 'I've found her quite delightful. Until now.'

Rosemary tilted her head to better judge Milly's distraught face. 'What's happened?'

'Poor Rakisha.' Milly let her arms drop to her sides. 'I think she's got a nasty secret.'

FIVE

Rosemary had a strong urge to say to Milly that Rakisha probably had many secrets. Rakisha was, as Mrs Lionel said, a *character*. Jasper had once described the tie-died-clad woman of the many bangles as warm-hearted and wildly wondersome. Rosemary had her own descriptive words for Rakisha, most of which, if not affectionate, were supportive. 'Right,' she said now, studying Milly. 'You've had a few months of sharing the house with Rakisha. What's different now?'

'That's just it, I'm not sure.'

'Did she get a letter or phone call from Silkie, her sister?' asked Hannah. 'They don't really see eye to eye. Something like that might have rattled her.'

Milly shook her head. 'Not recently. I do remember a phone call from Silkie a month or so ago but Rakisha didn't seem upset by it. She told me Silkie was a chameleon, whatever that means, but Silkie was happier than she'd ever been.'

'It's not Silkie then.' Rosemary perched herself on a bale

of lucerne. 'What makes you say it's a secret? And what makes it nasty?'

'The way she's behaving. It's as if she's walking on glass the whole time.'

'Since before the events at The Leftover Restaurant?'

'No. I noticed it yesterday evening.'

'What is she doing, Milly?' Hannah pulled a strand of hay from the bale and chewed its end. 'What did you notice?'

'Well.' Milly tucked her gloves into her back pocket. 'It was after I came home from work yesterday. Remember I didn't go to the training afternoon. She was twitchy. Jumpy. Burning an unusual amount of incense. I heard her chanting in her bedroom. I mean, I usually don't mind her chanting, it's sort of soothing, but it changed. It's more like she's reciting something rather than meditating. She's sort of...' She waved her hands around. '...wild-eyed.'

Rosemary pursed her lips. 'She could be disturbed by our discovery in the mannikin case. Is she eating?'

'Yes, we had dinner together last night like we do every night. Typically, lots of tofu and vegetables.' Milly patted her stomach. 'I'm rather enjoying it.'

'What about the café? Do you know how it's going?'

'Well, I think it's fine. You know, she has her fans of organic tuber coffee and carob nut brownies. And, of course, there are always those customers who get taken by surprise and probably never come back.' Milly smiled. 'The café is charming, really, isn't it? Sometimes I think Rakisha is one of Mulbury's main attractions.'

'Bohemia can be attractive.'

'The allure of incense.' Hannah chuckled. 'Just like the fragrance of dog food pellets brings people in here.'

'Talking about dogs...' Rosemary raised her eyebrows at Milly.

'Oh, do you mean Rufus?' Milly turned around and crouched down. 'Rufus! Come here.'

A moment passed before a little tan dog crept out from behind a pallet of chicken feed. It paused as it saw the group but Milly clicked her fingers and it ran to her. She swept it up. 'Who's a good boy then?'

'Rufus spends all day with us,' said Hannah. 'Or, should I say, some of the day with us and some of it with Heather when she goes to Patricia's.'

'Rufus is very fond of Heather,' said Milly, stroking the dog's head.

'What about Rakisha? Does she mind Rufus?'

'No. She knew I had him when she asked me to stay with her. I don't think Rufus has caused a problem.' Milly set the dog down and he wandered off toward the office. 'Although she doesn't always remember his name. It's always like it's on the tip of her tongue and then gets lost, which I think she finds quite distressing. Last night she called him Salty.'

'Weird.' Hannah stuck her hands in her pockets. 'Why did she do that?'

Milly shook her head. 'No idea. I just figured it was a Rakisha quirk.'

Hannah huffed. 'Yep, that could be it.'

'Rakisha is not equipped to handle anything nasty so we need to keep an eye for changed behaviour, no matter how odd she is on a normal day.' Rosemary straightened. 'Now, can I have some cat food, Hannah?'

While Hannah organised a bag of cat food and Milly hung more seed packets on the display tree, Rosemary watched Rufus as he trailed around the shed, nose to the ground and tail up. He was no bigger than Sunny, a funny mix of terrier and hound with a head slightly larger than needed for his body and a muddy-coloured curly coat of fine hair. Hardly a dog to cause offence. No, something else was under Rakisha's skin.

'Here you are, Rosemary.' Hannah dumped the bag into Rosemary's arms. 'I'll put it on your account.'

'Thanks, Hannah. Any word from Holly and Christopher?'

'My big sister is living the dream.' Hannah rubbed her head again. 'Not that she says that. Toffee is working hard and moving up the police ranks, and she's found a job managing the local thrift store. There's no sign they're coming back for a while.'

'You miss her.'

Hannah's lively face saddened briefly. 'Yep. I do. But she rings regularly and we do the video thing so we can see the beach behind her.' She shook her head and brightened. 'Good on her, really. She's happy. We're happy. It's all good.'

Rosemary nodded, raised the bag slightly in farewell, and left Milly and Hannah to lock up. As she went back across the road, she spotted the youngest Hubbard sister coming home from spending the day at Patricia's where her bespoke upcycled garments were beginning to rival Patti's. Heather skipped a few steps and twirled in circles before continuing, and Rosemary heard the faint sounds of singing. She smiled. Heather was happy and when Heather was happy the rest of Mulbury felt at ease.

Except for Rakisha.

The café owner stood in front of The Preserved Mulbury, staring in the window. Rosemary juggled the bag more comfortably in her arms and went to call out, but

Rakisha turned suddenly in a flurry of cotton layers and hurried off over Goldmarket Road, long greying curls swirling about her and bangles clashing as she went.

Rosemary stopped in front of her shop, trying to see what Rakisha had been looking at but only Sunny sat in the window bay looking sternly at her mistress and the bag of food. The sternness continued until Rosemary filled her bowl with a dribble of the dried food which Sunny sniffed before stalking off as if to say, *Thank you but I'm not hungry.*

Rosemary chuckled as she stowed the bag in the laundry, the chuckle sticking in her throat as she turned back to see a man standing in her kitchen. 'Jasper. Don't you know how to knock?'

'Oh.' Jasper craned his head to look through the doorway to the shop's front door. 'I thought you'd hear the bell jangling.'

'I had my head in a cupboard.'

'Oh, sorry. Anything I can help with?'

'Are you talking about my head or the cupboard?'

Jasper's face reddened and he hooked a length of hair behind one ear. 'Well, neither, really, I was just-'

'It's okay, Jasper. I don't need your help with anything.'

'Oh. Right. Okay.' He moved back to let her pass. 'Well, I need your help.'

'With what?'

'Dinner tomorrow.' His lips twisted. 'It's my turn to host everyone.'

'Yes.' Rosemary waited.

'I'd forgotten.'

'No, you haven't. It's Sunday and you've remembered. Plenty of time.'

'Yes, you'd think so. It's just...'

'Just what?'

He picked up a quince from her fruit bowl and bounced it up and down in his hand. 'I've made previous arrangements.'

Rosemary shook her head. 'Why do I think this conversation is going to take a while?' She indicated her dining table. 'Sit down. I'm making mushroom risotto for dinner so you might as well stay for it. You don't seem to know what to say about what you're up to tomorrow night.'

'It's really not that secret.'

'Then spit it out.'

'I'm taking tango lessons and they start tomorrow night.'

Rosemary stopped at the fridge. 'You're doing *what?*'

'Don't laugh.'

'Do you hear me laughing?'

'No.' Jasper's chair squeaked against the floor as he wriggled. 'You just don't see me wanting to learn the tango.'

Rosemary opened the fridge door and fished out mushrooms before saying more. 'I remember having difficulties getting you to walk around the block when you were trying to get fit. Exercise isn't really your thing.'

'Well, it isn't exercise, is it? It's dancing.'

Rosemary placed the mushrooms on a board and started chopping.

'Well, okay, it *is* exercise but it's more than that.'

Rosemary held her knife up. 'It's a social activity.'

'Yes, that's it.'

She lowered the knife. 'You need a partner for tango.'

Jasper's face warmed again right to the tip of his nose. 'Apparently, there are more women than men in a normal class and you dance with a range of women.'

'Right. You're going there to meet women.'

'No, no, that's not it!'

Rosemary started on an onion, the vapour making her eyes sting. 'Okay, so you've suddenly decided to take up dancing because...?'

'Ken asked me to.'

Rosemary blinked back onion teas and put the diced vegetable into a pan before answering. 'Ken.'

'Yes, Ken. You know, the car salesman.'

'Yes, of course I know Ken. Among other things, he sold me my car.' Rosemary stirred, picking her next words carefully. 'You've been catching up with Ken.'

'Yes, at least once a week. He's a nice fellow. I think he's a bit lonely.' Jasper leaned his chair back on two legs, earning a glare from Rosemary. He let the chair drop. 'I take some books with me and we talk about them.'

'I haven't seen him here.'

'We usually meet halfway.'

Rosemary nodded. The car yard in Birdton was a decent drive, one of the reasons she was almost late for the first aid class yesterday. The other reason she was running behind was because she'd been chatting to Ken. He *was* a decent man, a good listener and knowledgeable about many topics. They'd struck on a common love of olives, and he'd explained his experiments with ash and seawater as preserving methods. He used to have olive trees, decades ago in another part of Australia when he was young. The wistfulness he'd spoken of them kept Rosemary a little longer, but he'd not said anything more about that time. Rosemary had the impression Ken's life had many episodes, finally leading to coming out of retirement to carry on his dead brother's car yard. 'I can imagine Ken liking the tango.'

Jasper gave a short laugh. 'Easy, isn't, to see him zipping around the floor? He may be a good twenty years older than me but he's about twenty times as fit. All that cycling.'

Rosemary stirred the onion and added rice. 'You get on with him well.'

'Yeah.' Jasper put his forearms on the table and stretched his arms out. 'He's like a-'

Both their phones rang at once, but Jasper was quicker to answer. 'Gerry? What's up?'

Rosemary wiped her hands on a cloth and answered the call from Honey. 'Is there something I should know about?'

'You bet.' Honey's voice was urgent. 'There's been another body found in The Leftover Restaurant.'

SIX

Rosemary and Jasper hurried across the dim Square to where Honey and Gerry stood with Jules, Ronnie and Tallulah. The baby was alert in her father's arms, pulling at his jumper and chewing on her hand. Teething, thought Rosemary, before Jules caught at her arm. 'Rosemary, Roman's in there by himself.'

The door to the restaurant was closed but Roman was visible in one of the small front windows, his form bent over something out of sight.

'I've tried the door and it's locked.' Jules held her phone up. 'He says he doesn't want us to see what it is, that it's too horrible.'

'Has he rung the police?'

'I did.' Jules put the phone to her ear. 'Roman, Rosemary is here. Yes. Alright.' She put the phone on speaker.

'Roman,' said Rosemary, leaning over the screen. 'You'd be best to leave everything so the police can deal with it.'

'I have, so no fear, Rosemary. I just roll him over to check he is not alive.'

'Who is it? Someone we know?'

Roman straightened, looked out the window at the crowd, and spoke into his phone. 'I do not know who it is. A man. He is so transparent.'

'He means pale,' Jules interpreted. 'Roman said his face was unusually pallid.'

'The man is definitely dead?' asked Rosemary.

'Yes, sadly so.' Roman looked down again. 'He has fallen quickly and is a big, big man. His arm is broken, he fell on it, I believe. He looks twisted.'

Jules shook her head. 'The poor man.'

'Erk,' said Honey. 'Thanks for not letting us in, Roman.'

'I know. It is quite dreadful but I still had to check the fellow for life.'

'We understand,' said Jules. 'Can you come out now? I hear sirens.'

Roman's call clicked off and a moment later he was at the restaurant's door. His face under his bushy dark moustaches was white and he trembled a little as he stepped down to join the others.

'How did you know he was there, Roman?' asked Rosemary as Jules rubbed her husband's back.

'I went to rearrange the restaurant back to its usual configuration. The room he is in, we keep the chairs. There is a chance we are to reopen tomorrow.'

'I don't think that's going to happen.'

Roman smoothed his moustaches. 'No, indeed, Rosemary. I entered the storeroom looking for chairs and found a man. It is not a room I use for anything but the chairs.'

'How did he get in, Roman?' asked Rosemary. 'Is the window open?'

'No. I could not see anything on him to indicate how he entered.'

'Here are the police, Mum,' called Honey. 'I can't see Geoffrey, though.'

Two police cars arrived and uniformed officers got out. They had clearly been given a job and shooed the Mulburians away from the scene to question Roman and cordon off the area until further instructions. The small crowd watched for a moment until Tallulah grumbled and Ronnie took her back to the tearoom, Honey going with them.

Rosemary nodded at Roman. 'He's going to need a strong cup of tea with a teaspoon of sugar, Jules.'

Jules put a hand to her cheek. 'Yes. I'll take him home when I can. What a shock for my lovely man.'

The activity had drawn Rakisha and Milly from their home. They joined the others and Jules filled them in. Rosemary watched Rakisha carefully, but the woman, while stunned, seemed as ignorant as the rest of them as to what had happened. Two deaths in the same restaurant were very coincidental and Rosemary did not believe in coincidence. Bob Brownlee's death was no doubt linked to the man lying in the storeroom.

'WARWICK JONES,' said Jasper as he sat at the table with Rosemary to finally eat his risotto.

'Sorry?'

'The dead man. The second dead man, that is. His name was Warwick.'

Rosemary pushed the cheese mill toward Jasper. 'How do you know that?'

'When you went home to continue making dinner—

delicious by the way—the police found his wallet on him. I overheard his name.'

'Right.' Rosemary ate a forkful of rice. 'Do we know any Warwicks?'

Jasper shook his head. 'I certainly don't.'

'Did you hear, or see, anything else?'

'No. They shut the door and did their investigation inside.'

'And Roman?'

'He went home with Jules to get that cup of tea.' Jasper chewed thoughtfully. 'This isn't good for The Leftover Restaurant. Who'll want to go to a place where two people have died?'

'You watch.'

'Really?' Jasper shivered. 'People are macabre.'

'You know that already. What's your top selling genre?'

Jasper gave a wisp of a smile. 'Crime fiction.'

'There you have it.'

'But those stories are made up. This is real!'

Rosemary shrugged. 'In some people's mind, reality and fiction go hand in hand.'

They ate in silence for a while, Sunny taking the opportunity to leave her balcony windowsill and perch on the back of the couch behind Jasper to stare at his head.

'Anyway,' Jasper said finally. 'I actually came to ask if you wouldn't mind hosting dinner here tomorrow night so I can...go out.'

'Of course I can.'

'I bought chicken thighs if you want them. I was going to do a slow-cooked chicken and potatoes.'

'Right. I'll take them and do the same.' Rosemary put her fork down and leaned back. 'I'll leave some for you. I take it you'll have to eat once you've finished dancing.'

Jasper helped himself to more dinner. 'Yes, although I've got other arrangements.'

Rosemary pushed her bowl away and tried to catch Jasper's eye but he was concentrating on his meal. 'Have you?'

'Yes.'

'Ken's making dinner?'

'No.' Jasper poked his rice with his fork. 'We're going to the pub afterwards.'

'Right.' Rosemary watched as he took a large mouthful. 'It's okay, you know.'

'Wha'?'

'Don't talk with your mouth full. I mean, it's okay to go tango dancing with Ken and then go to the pub afterwards. He is, as you said, a very nice man.'

Jasper swallowed noisily. 'You don't think I'm... compensating?'

'For what?'

'For all that business looking for my father, finding someone who said he was, and then finding out that he wasn't.'

'You should have known that a man who's never read a book in his life wasn't going to be your father.'

'Harsh.' Jasper finished eating and set his fork down. 'Possibly true.'

Rosemary sighed. 'I don't think you're compensating. I think you've found a friend, albeit of the age to be your father.'

Jasper nodded vigorously. 'That's how I feel. Ken is a friend.'

'Okay, I'll take your chicken thighs and do dinner for you.'

She stood to take their plates away. Through the door of the shop, the police activity was winding up. She glimpsed a van driving away, no doubt with poor Warwick inside, followed by one police car. The night was dull, with no glimpse of a moon, and the rest of the investigation team were operating by strong searchlights pointed at the restaurant.

It was an unexpected flash of light through the window that made her put the plates down and go into the shop. While the main action focused on the area around the restaurant, a small torch beam flashed out from under The Exceptional Tree before switching off. Rosemary strained to see who it was, but it was too dark. By the reflected light coming from the crime scene, she glimpsed four people-shapes walking slowly out from the shadows to a car on Low Road. It chugged as it started before being drive carefully away, turning its lights on only after it had climbed the hill to the cemetery.

Rosemary ran back into the dining area and swept up her car keys from the kitchen bench. 'Feel like a drive, Jasper?'

She didn't wait for an answer but heard Jasper running after her as she yanked the door open, sending the bell above it into an unmelodious clanking. They reached the mauve car at the same time and jumped in. 'Where are we going?' asked Jasper, pulling his seat belt firmly across his chest.

'We're following that car.' Rosemary spun the car around as she spoke and turned sharply up Low Road.

'What car?'

'That one.'

The shadowy car was now a mere two dots of lights on the road kilometres ahead. It followed the curve of the asphalt and disappeared. Rosemary accelerated, noting the smoothness of her new car and smiling despite herself.

'Why?'

'Why what?'

'Rosemary, why are we following that car?'

She glanced at Jasper. He clung to the door arm with white-knuckled alarm. 'You really don't have to do everything I suggest.'

He kept his eyes on the road. 'In case you haven't noticed, I don't. But you sounded like you were on to something.' He pointed. 'Is that the car?'

They'd gone around the bend and faint lights appeared in the distance. There was no way of knowing whether they were from the mysterious car but Rosemary nodded. 'Must be. No one else is about.'

'True enough. Sunday nights are the quietest of the whole week.'

Rosemary accelerated again, aware they were heading into an area thick with gum trees and shrubs where kangaroos were likely grazing. As well as keeping her eyes on the car, she swept her gaze back and forth in case a grazing kangaroo turned into a hopping kangaroo and she needed to stop. The car in front didn't have the same concern. It pushed on faster than Rosemary, its lights getting smaller. 'I'm going to lose them.'

'Looks like it.' Jasper was also watching out for wildlife. 'You might have to let them go.'

Rosemary muttered a word she didn't want Jasper to hear and slowed down. 'Yes.'

'Now we're driving at a normal speed, do you want to tell me why we were following an unknown car along a dark road at a hectic pace?'

'It sounded like the same car as last night.'

'Last night?'

'I saw Bunnie Brownlee and friends outside the restaurant.'

'At night?'

'It was dark. They were acting oddly. And tonight, I see another group of people near the restaurant acting oddly. Too many *odd*lies.'

'You think it's Bunnie Brownlee in the car up front?'

'I don't know for sure, but I am thinking one mysterious car plus one mysterious car adds up to one mysterious car.'

'Okay.' Jasper nodded a little. 'But what were they doing?'

The car rounded another bend. 'No idea. That's why-' Rosemary slammed on the brakes. 'That's them.'

A car had run off the road, black marks on the asphalt lit by their headlights showing its trajectory. It was nose down in a ditch, back wheels spinning. Rosemary pulled her car over, flicking on her hazard lights before jumping out. Through the dimness on the other side of the road, she heard a kangaroo jump away through the undergrowth. She ran to the car.

The driver was already pushing his way out of the rumpled car, his knee hitting a bunch of keys on a stone keychain left dangling in the ignition, making him grunt and clutch at his leg. A man and a woman hammered at the back window while a little woman in the passenger's seat sat silently. Rosemary pulled at the front door while Jasper let the others out of the back. 'Mrs Brownlee,' she said as she tried to open it. 'Are you alright?'

The woman turned her head but didn't look at Rosemary directly. The angle of the car meant she was leaning forward into her locked seatbelt. Her arms flayed once before resting on her lap.

Jasper took over trying to get the door open. 'Can she open it from the inside?'

'She's not in a state to do that. I'll go around the other side.'

Rosemary stepped gingerly around the car. The driver had left the door open so she knelt inside to turn the car off, tangling her hand in the heavy keychain ornaments. Once the car was quiet, she stretched across to grip Bunnie Brownlee's arm. 'Mrs Brownlee. Are you hurt?'

The woman shook her head slowly.

'Nonetheless, I think you'd better stay there until the ambulance arrives.'

At this, Bunnie Brownlee stared over Rosemary's shoulder and smiled. 'Bob.'

Rosemary frowned. 'Are you dizzy at all? Does your head hurt?'

The woman shook her head again.

'You said *Bob*.'

'Yes.' At last Bunnie looked straight at Rosemary. 'Bob.' She lifted one arm to point back down the road. 'I can feel him. He's there.'

SEVEN

Roman set his fork down and dabbed at his moustaches with a linen napkin. 'That was magnificent, Rosemary. I tasted the subtle aromas of basil and thyme among the sharpness of the olive. I could have you show me the recipe.'

'There's no need for that,' said Rosemary. 'The recipe came from you in the first place.'

Roman waved a hand dismissively. 'But you have added something.'

'Salt from the Pink Lake.'

'Ah! I knew it.'

'You could really pick that out, old fellow?' Gerry peered into his dish. 'I mean, I knew it was delicious but I have no idea why. Is there more?'

Patti laughed and touched her husband's hand. 'Sweetie, you don't need any more.'

'Oh, I know I don't *need* any more.' Gerry grinned and patted his stomach. 'But I would *like* more.'

Rosemary ladled the remainder of the casserole on to Gerry's plate. 'When will you be able to reopen, Roman?'

'Yet another day or two.'

Jules shook her head. 'Two bodies. Can you imagine what that's going to do for our reputation?'

'I don't think you'll have to worry about that, dear.' Mrs Lionel sipped her wine. 'The number of people I've had in today prying about these terrible events and asking whether the restaurant is open was eye-opening.'

'Maybe they think Bob is there just like his widow said.'

Rosemary eyed Kelly. The café owner wouldn't normally attend Monday dinner if she knew it was at Rosemary's but all Jasper had done before he headed to dancing lessons was to place a small sign on his door pointing to the right. The change in venue was a surprise for everyone except Mrs Lionel who had helped prepare the chicken. 'Bunnie Brownlee didn't say Bob was in the restaurant.'

'Well, not exactly. What else could she mean, though? She thinks his dead body lays in state on top of Roman's preparation table.'

Roman shook his head. 'Such a horrible thought, Kelly. It is no joke to have the dead ones in a kitchen area.'

Kelly shrugged. 'Can't think it would be very hygienic.'

'I think Bunnie's in shock.' Gerry finished his chicken and leaned back with a sigh. 'She's in denial, of course. I bet she begged her friends to drive her to Mulbury to try and find him. They would have done that because they felt sorry for her.'

'The poor thing,' said Milly, wiping her plate with a piece of focaccia. 'Is she alright after that nasty accident?'

'No idea,' said Rosemary. 'But she didn't seem to be in too much pain when the ambulance put her on the gurney.'

'Terrible for her.' Milly shook her head, making the beads in her hair rattle. 'Can't imagine what it would be like to have your husband discovered that way.'

Rosemary studied the beads. Milly was obviously

enjoying living with Rakisha as well as liking the work at Mulbury Feeds. A long, felt scarf in muted bush colours draped around her neck with distinct traces of woven leaves among the wool. The beads were a new touch, dangling as they did from long bobby pins, but were identical to those tied to the ends of Rakisha's spiralling grey curls. Despite that, Milly remained sensible and logical, unlike Rakisha whose gaze darted from Milly to Rosemary to Kelly as if she was worried what might be said next.

'Upsetting ordeal for Mrs Brownlee,' said Mrs Lionel. 'I do hope she's okay.'

'Do you know her, Mrs Lionel?' asked Hannah as she took Heather's unfinished dinner and tucked into it.

'No, not at all. It sounds like Bob was quite jolly but I've hardly heard anything about Bunnie.'

'And Bunnie's friends? Does anyone know about them?'

Most people around the table shook their heads. Hannah just shrugged and Heather was distracted from the conversation by patting Sunny who sat behind her. Only one person sat perfectly still.

'Rakisha?'

At the sound of Rosemary's voice, Rakisha jumped. She grabbed a bead-less length of her hair and twirled it around her finger. 'Hmmm, darling?'

'Do you know Bunnie or her friends?'

'Bunnie, darling?'

'Bunnie Brownlee.'

'Bunnie Brownlee.' Rakisha tossed the strand over her shoulder and started plucking at the end of her sleeve. 'I don't know a Bunnie Brownlee.'

'Or her friends?'

'Or her friends.' Rakisha finished with her sleeve and

started turning her fork over and over. 'Delicious, darling. The...' She waved her hand over her plate.

'Tofu and olives.'

'Yes. That. And the...' Another wave.

'Bread.'

'The bread, darling. Yes. Lovely and light, darling.'

Rosemary glanced at the heavy loaf of rye she had on the table. She went to say more but felt Mrs Lionel's hand on her arm. Rakisha was now tying her napkin in knots, looking too pale for someone who'd just eaten a hearty plate of vegan casserole.

'It was lucky you turned up, Rosemary.' Hannah stacked Heather's empty plate on her own. 'They could have been stuck in that ditch for a long time.'

'No luck involved.' Rosemary finished her wine. 'We were following them.'

'What?' Hannah stared for a moment then started laughing. 'You were following the dead man's wife?'

'Yes.'

'Why?'

'This is the second time I'd seen a group in the shadows of Goldmarket Square. All four were very stealthy. I decided to be the same. Jasper and I followed them out of town.'

'Stealthy, do you think, Rosemary?' Gerry folded his hands across his tummy. 'Maybe they were embarrassed. I mean, if they were bringing Bunnie Brownlee back to the scene of Bob's death for the second time in a row to help in her grief, maybe they were trying to be secretive about it.'

'That's a good thought, Gerry,' said Mrs Lionel. 'That could be the case.'

'Odd, though,' said Jules, placing her napkin neatly on the table. 'They didn't have to come at night.'

'Maybe that's the time of day Mrs Brownlee feels the worst,' said Heather. 'I did when Mum died.'

The table went quiet. Hannah reached for her sister but Heather patted her sister's arm distractedly and went back to stroking Sunny.

'Yes, dear,' said Mrs Lionel sadly. 'Nighttime is tough when you've lost someone.'

Another moment of silence and then Milly sighed. 'But the night passes and a new day dawns.' She smiled slowly. 'I remember Graham most now during the day, especially when I get my chocolate digestives from the biscuit tin.'

'Really?' Hannah tipped her head on one side. 'Why?'

Milly laughed. 'My husband had a chocolate digestive every day of our marriage. It was his after-dinner snack. We used the same biscuit tin all that time. I've brought it to Rakisha's, haven't I, love?'

Rakisha nodded vigorously. 'The tin glows.'

Hannah shook her head. 'It's not radioactive, is it, Milly?'

'No.' Milly shook her head. 'I think Rakisha means something else.'

Rakisha shrugged. 'The tin glows with love.'

Mrs Lionel leaned forward. 'How beautiful you are, Rakisha, dear. You say such lovely things.'

Rakisha face relaxed. 'Oh no, Mrs Lionel, darling. I only say the truth. Milly's biscuit tin is warm and wonderful. It is imbued with the strength of their marriage.'

'Goodness, Rakisha.' Patti dabbed at the corner of her eye with a white handkerchief. 'You are such a sweetie.'

Several conversations about special things started at once. Gerry leaned to the right to tell Jules about his mother's apron he kept in mothballs in a special wooden box. Roman spoke to Mrs Lionel of his sister's eggbeater hanging on his kitchen wall at home. Even Kelly started on about a jigsaw puzzle of her cousin's, a soldier who didn't return home from Vietnam. Rosemary stood as the conversations leapt around her, clearing the plates. The old blue sedan recently traded for the mauve car was the last reminder of Alasdair's presence, and all she felt was a sense of relief but this was something she didn't want to share with the nostalgic table.

After bread-and-butter pudding for dessert, the guests gathered in Rosemary's lounge area for one last cup of tea. She opened the balcony door a little to let the cool evening air in just as Jasper's kitchen light went on. She stepped out and leaned over the rail. 'Jasper? Jasper!'

The door scraped open. 'I'm home,' he said, leaning out. 'Should I come over?'

'Everyone is still here.'

'Okay, that's good. Maybe I can get some recruits?' He grinned briefly and came over to the rail, climbing it a little awkwardly before jumping down to stand beside her.

Close up, Rosemary caught a snatch of spicy cologne and the faint fragrance of hard exercise. She studied him. 'What are you wearing?'

'Tango gear.' He tugged as the waist band of his wide-legged trousers. 'These were my father's, the father that raised me, that is.'

'He danced tango?'

'No, but wide legs were more fashionable in his day. What do you think?'

Rosemary plucked at his casual T-shirt. 'You need a more appropriate shirt if you're going back. Did you like it?'

Jasper stared down at his shirt. 'It was great, Rosemary.' He smiled. 'A lot of fun. But you're right. I need a better shirt.'

'Jasper!' called Gerry. 'Come in and tell us what you've been doing!'

Rosemary held the door open. 'You'd better fill everyone in. I didn't say where you were.'

Jasper went in and sat next to Gerry on the couch, explaining with large hand gestures and an upheld chin what he'd been doing. Rosemary packed the dishwasher as quietly as she could, leaving the empty casserole dish in the sink to soak. Mrs Lionel brought some cups over and held them out to her. 'I haven't seen Jasper sparkle quite so much for a long time.'

'Yes.' Rosemary loaded the cups. 'It is good to see.'

'He went dancing with Ken?'

'Yes.'

Mrs Lionel nodded. 'A lovely activity for an older friend to introduce someone to.'

'Yes.'

'Any reason, do you think, that Ken invited Jasper and not, for example, you.'

'Possibly.'

'You aren't giving away much, dear.'

'I've nothing to give away. At least, not yet.'

Mrs Lionel took a cloth and wiped the bench. 'Then I'll have to wait and see. But I would like your immediate thoughts on one thing.'

Rosemary shut the dishwasher and leaned against it. 'What would that be?'

'Mrs Bunnie Brownlee. There's something bugging you, isn't there?'

'What makes you think that?'

'Oh.' Mrs Lionel folded the cloth over the edge of the sink. 'Just a hunch. Or maybe it was your complete omission of one fact while telling the story of Bunnie's car accident to the others.'

'You make me sound very secretive.'

'No, you aren't secretive. More...' Mrs Lionel laid a finger against her lips and tapped them once. '...tactical.'

'Right. So, what tactical fact did I leave out that you noticed?'

'You said that on Saturday night there were five people in the group making their way across the Square.'

'That's correct.'

'Tonight, you mentioned four people.'

'I did.'

'They may not be the same group as before. Or one person was missing.'

'I suspect no one was missing.'

Mrs Lionel raised her eyebrows. 'Really? But you said-'

'There were four people in the car.'

'And the fifth?'

Rosemary came closer to Mrs Lionel and lowered her voice. 'I think the fifth person was the one lying dead and twisted in Roman and Jules restaurant.'

EIGHT

The cars started arriving early Tuesday morning. Rosemary watched through the shop window as the first two pulled up alongside Goldmarket Road, followed quickly by another two. Each one was full, so within minutes, twenty people stood on the pavement outside The Preserved Mulbury but not one person looked her way. They all stared across the road to where the double lots of crime scene tape wrapped around The Leftover Restaurant flapped slightly from a soft wind. 'Eerie,' said Rosemary to Sunny. 'It's like they're in thrall.'

Sunny twitched her tail as if to say *They can't be in thrall if there is no cat involved.*

Rosemary waited for a few minutes before resuming her stacking of the window display. The huddle of people, although various shapes and sizes, wore similar maroon tops, making them look like a community football team. She watched them from the corner of her eye as she balanced pale jars of apple jelly on one of Patti's runners made from upcycled curtains. As a woman turned slightly to see passed a slow-moving tourist bus, Rosemary glimpsed embroidered writing on her shirt. 'BTPI,' she muttered to Sunny but the ginger tabby was dozing.

The crowd still hadn't changed position by the time she'd gone back into her kitchen, made tea in her tea-for-one ceramic teapot, and brought it back to the shop. It was almost opening time, and tourists spilled from a bus ready for some buying action, but still the crowd waited. She heard Jasper trundle his book barrow onto the pavement, calling out 'Excuse me, sorry' and getting a slow forward shuffle of people in response. A moment later and he pushed his way through the jangling door, half looking over his shoulder. 'What is going on?'

'No idea.' Rosemary offered him her untouched tea and he took it absently, gulping the hot liquid down and coughing. 'They've been there for a while.'

'Are they waiting for something?'

'It appears that way.'

'Have you seen what that guy has?'

'What guy?'

Jasper took his tea to the window and pointed. 'That guy.'

Rosemary went around him to get a better view. A man stood at the end of the bunch of people holding an object out in front of him. She looked harder and saw what she'd expected. Another man held a wire device like an antenna, only it was hidden down by his side. 'Right. I've seen that before.'

'What about the man?'

'No, I don't think so. Hard to tell because it was night but similar devices were what they were carrying the first time I saw Bunnie Brownlee.'

Jasper stepped forward to look at more of the crowd. 'She isn't there.'

'She might be still recovering from the accident. I imagine she must be bruised.'

He indicated the object another man held. 'What is *that* gadget?'

'I don't know. It looks like it has dials on it.

'Hang on. They're moving.'

The crowd moved together to step off the pavement and walk across Goldmarket Road as if they'd received some secret signal. Rosemary glanced at Jasper to see if he had the same idea as she did. He nodded, and they left The Preserved Mulbury to follow the maroon-shirted group, keeping a respectable but informed distance. As the crowd crossed Goldmarket Square, they mingled briefly with the chatting tourists from the bus, pushing through rudely, making the tourists' noise levels rise. They walked around The Sweet Potato and stopped in front of the crime scene tape bordering The Leftover Restaurant. The man with the antenna raised it high, and the other man switched something on the object he held. A short squeal echoed around the Square.

Rosemary and Jasper stopped at the corner of Rakisha's café. 'What was that?' asked Jasper.

'Something electronic.'

'What's he doing now?'

The man with the device was pacing the length of the tape, followed closely by a man waving the wire contraption in the air. The rest of the crowd looked nervously at him but after a few minutes he stopped and shook his head. 'Nothing extraordinary,' he said loudly. 'A few beeps in mid-range.'

'Could be them,' said a man with sleek, black hair.

'Not enough,' said a woman with a thin, white ponytail.

'Could be one?' asked another woman, her hands on her hips.

'No.' The man with the gadget shook it a little. 'We need to get closer to make sure we're okay.' He started to duck under the tape.

The door of the restaurant opened, and Geoffrey came out. Rosemary frowned. She hadn't noticed his car, or the detective, this morning. He must have parked closer to the restaurant without time for greetings or even coffee. He crossed his arms as he spotted Gadget Man's movement. 'Sorry, sir, you'll have to move back. This is still a crime scene.'

The man halted, the device clutched in front of him. 'For how long?' He glanced back at his friends. 'We're keen to, er, have dinner at the restaurant.'

The amount of nodding heads was almost comical although Geoffrey clearly didn't see anything funny. 'The restaurant will resume operations...' he looked back through the doorway where Roman's silhouette stood '...tomorrow night.'

'Bookings online, please,' said Roman. 'We will be having a pasta special.'

'Can't we, er, check out the facilities now?' asked Gadget Man, trying to put his contraption behind his back. 'My wife has...allergies.' He glanced at a tall woman next to him who nodded vigorously and muttered, 'Yes, allergies, lots of them, so allergic.'

'I cater for all allergic moments,' said Roman stiffly, his moustaches twitching. 'My facilities are very good.'

'No doubt, no doubt.' The man chewed his lip. 'But, to make sure-'

'The restaurant is closed,' said Geoffrey in voice that echoed forty years of policing, 'until further notice.' He nodded at Roman and walked towards the group, ducking under the tape at the thickest section of the crowd, forcing them to scatter as he marched through.

'You have to give it to Geoffrey,' said Jasper. 'He knows how to handle any situation.'

'Yes.' Rosemary watched as Roman shut the restaurant door firmly and the crowd started a dejected walk back to their cars. 'Hang on a moment.'

Gadget Man led the retreat. Rosemary walked across his path, making him stop. 'Sorry to intrude,' she said. 'I was wondering how Bunnie was after the car incident?'

He blinked at her with slightly red weepy eyes as if he didn't ever get much sleep. 'She's disappointed, she says, but she believes it will happen soon.'

'Oi,' said the tall woman behind him, rubbing her hands on her brown velour tracksuit pants. 'She's not asking that.'

The man turned to look at the scowling woman and his eyes went wide. 'Oh. I mean, she's fine, by all accounts. A little shaken, apparently.'

'I'm glad to hear she's okay.'

'She's fine, he said.' Tracksuit Woman pushed her way forward to face Rosemary. 'She's well looked after by her *friends*.' She rolled her eyes, stopping as Rosemary stared at her.

'Right.' Rosemary studied the woman. 'Is that peridot?'

Tracksuit Woman clutched the chunky necklace sitting low on her chest. 'Yes. So?'

'It must be heavy to wear.'

'It's part of our equipment. We all wear them.' She took the Gadget Man's arm to show Rosemary a black cord threaded through a roughcut green stone around his wrist. 'The sensible among us, anyway.' She strengthened her grip and tugged him away. 'Let's go. Nothing to pick up out here.' She pushed past Rosemary, dragging the man with her.

'How did that go?' asked Jasper, coming to stand next to her to watch the rest of the crowd return to their cars.

'Defensively.' Rosemary shrugged. 'I was only asking after Bunnie's health. Seems I got more information than I needed.'

'Oh?'

'Nothing I can make sense of.'

Jasper nodded. 'You know who they remind me of? A group of grim explorers.'

'Explorers.'

'Yeah, the sort of people that are dead set on exploring unknown territory despite the odds. It's sort of like they've got no choice.'

'Driven.'

'That's the word. They're driven, but not in a good way. They're quite serious. And what's with that box thing?'

'We need to do some exploring ourselves.'

Jasper held up his phone. 'Lucky I took photos then.'

Rosemary smiled. 'You're so much more than your good looks.'

Jasper's face, normally warm, went scarlet so quickly Rosemary grabbed his arm.

'Are you alright?'

'Yep, yep.' Jasper put a hand on his cheek as if trying to cool himself down. 'You said I had *good looks*.'

'You do. Is that news to you?'

'Well...' The scarlet rose to chilli-red. 'It's not something I think about unless *you* say something and then, well, you know.'

Rosemary shook her head. 'No, I don't but then maybe it's better that way. Right. Show me the photos you took.'

Jasper breathed out heavily, pulled his phone from his pocket, and flicked to his photo library. 'I think this is the best one.' He held it out so they could both see.

The photo was taken from overhead so Jasper must have held the phone up as high as he could. It showed the top of what the man had been holding. It had a half-moon shaped gauge with a fine needle pointing upwards. The details of the gauge were blurred, but it was coloured red, yellow and green.

Jasper touched the screen lightly to make the picture larger. 'Do you know what this reminds me of? The fire warning signs on the side of the road.'

Rosemary nodded, thinking of the electronic signs that indicated low to extreme wildfire danger using a colour coding like the gauges. 'Yes. It's a common way of reporting something that could move from not much to a lot.'

'So, what are they measuring?' Jasper glanced at the sky. 'The likelihood of danger? But what sort of danger?'

'No idea.' She moved the picture around the screen but nothing else gave any hints of the gadget's use. 'This is a similar thing to what I saw on Saturday night. The man carrying it said, "It doesn't lie".'

'What did he mean?'

'He said that there was nothing there. Whatever this thing is meant to do, it didn't pick up anything on Saturday night.'

Jasper peered at the photo again. 'Doesn't look as if it picked up much today, either. I took a couple of photos. The needle points to the green section in one and then only a few seconds later it's in the yellow.'

'You're right, Jasper.'

'Yes, you can see-'

'Not about the dial. About the fact we need to explore

further. Can you try matching that image to ones on the internet?'

'Can do, although I'll wait until I'm on my computer as it's easier to search.'

Rosemary nodded. 'Right. We'd better get back to our shops. Looks like people are hankering after your romantasies.' She pointed across the road to where several people from the tourist bus pushed their way inside The Read Mulbury.

'Horror.'

'Pardon?'

Jasper shrugged, putting his phone away and heading towards the shop. 'My current display is horror. I sold right out of romantasies.'

'Who would have thought,' said Rosemary dryly, but Jasper was already out of earshot.

A group of chatty ladies opened the door to The Preserved Mulbury, making the bell jangle furiously, so Rosemary started toward it. As she stepped onto Gold-market Road, a low coupe whipped around the corner. She jumped back, almost tripping on the kerb, and glared at the driver. He pulled over sharply and leaned out to watch her continue across the road. 'Apologies,' he called. 'Rosemary.'

She stopped in the middle of the road to look back. The man had short, tawny hair with a stylish wave unknown to her. His arm dangled from the car, its wrist heavy with an expensive watch. 'How do you know my name?'

'It was a guess, really.' He waved his hand lazily at her. 'Probably your plait.'

Rosemary caught her braid in one hand, feeling the tight twists of her brown hair. The silver streak running through it was the unique marker. 'Who have you been talking to?'

The man started his car again and pulled out onto the road, laughing as he did and shaking his arm toward Robert Sparkling's garage. 'Who else would I talk to about this little hamlet?'

Rosemary walked off the road, watching as the car hurtled into the mechanic's driveway. She didn't need to remember the photo on Robert's desk to realise she'd been speaking to Robert's brother.

NINE

Rosemary didn't see Robert Sparkling until Wednesday. He walked past The Preserved Mulbury toward Mulbury Feeds as she was serving a group of tourists, his fast pace catching her eye. As she discussed the flavours of her pickled cucumbers, she saw him glance her way but too quickly to establish eye contact. By the time the customers bought several jars of cucumbers along with more of quince jelly, Robert had disappeared. She followed the throng out the door and looked around for him. The doors of the animal produce shed were open but the yard was empty. Flicking her door sign to *Back in 5 Pickly Minutes*, she crossed the road to look.

The shed was full of hay and feed pellets but empty of humans. Rosemary walked to the office but only found Milly's little dog asleep on a bed made from straw-filled chaff bags behind the counter. A soft whisper of voices drifted her way from the room behind Rufus, and she went to its entrance. 'Hello?'

'Rosemary, come and see!'

How Heather Hubbard always knew who was speaking

from a single word was only one of the young woman's special skills. Another was her taxidermy ability. Rosemary went through the area where the women kept their accounts and then to the room behind. Heather stood at a vast table covered with strange implements and wires, most of her hidden by an enormous ibis mounted on a wooden platform. Its glassy eyes followed Rosemary as she went around to join Heather. 'That is a big bird.'

'Poor bird.' Heather smoothed a wing feather. 'A big bird among little wrens.'

'Where did you find it?'

Heather tipped her head. 'On the edge of Mulbury, in the paddocks they want to dig up. It hit a big sign.'

'Instant death.'

'Yes.' Heather touched Rosemary's sleeve. 'It's for Holly's birthday.'

Rosemary stared at the ibis, wondering how the large bird would post. 'I won't tell her.'

'I know.'

'And I won't either, darling.'

Rosemary startled at the voice behind her. She turned to see Rakisha sitting cross-legged on another pile of feed bags that Rosemary assumed were the little dog's second bed. Her long spiralling curls dangled into her lap. 'Rakisha. Are you helping Heather?'

'Oh no, darling. Heather needs no help.'

'Then what are you doing?'

Rakisha ran a hand through her salt and pepper curls, snaring her bangles and spending a moment tugging her arm free before answering. 'I am thinking, Rosemary, darling. I'm taking a moment out.'

'Out of what? The café?'

'Out of *time*, Rosemary. Free of the pressures of interaction and brownie making. I am watching a master at work and thinking.'

Rosemary moved around the table so she could see both women. Heather went back to making the last touches on the proudly erect ibis, while Rakisha fiddled with the ends of her scarf. 'Are you thinking of anything in particular, Rakisha?'

'I think of...' Rakisha closed her eyes '...past happenings, present moments, and future visions.'

'That's a lot to think about. You might be sitting there a while.'

Rakisha's eyes shot open. 'No, darling, you don't see, as you often don't. I think *simultaneously* of the many moments I have been through, am going through, and are yet to do.'

'You transcend, Rakisha,' said Heather, studying the ibis's eye carefully before using a scalpel to remove a speck of dirt.

Rakisha nodded vigorously, curls floating around her shoulders with the movement. 'Yes, Heather, darling. I am *transcendental.*'

Rosemary pressed her lips together to stop her saying anything, channelling Mrs Lionel. Rakisha plucked at a piece of straw protruding from the bag she was sitting on. From what Rosemary knew of transcending, Rakisha was not the picture of it. She looked more nervous than anything.

'Is something emerging from your transcendence that you want to share, Rakisha?' Rosemary asked.

Rakisha blinked rapidly. 'No, darling. I am not yet in that state.'

Rosemary crouched to the same level. 'When you reach it, we'll be here,' she said quietly.

Rakisha leaned forward and paused. The quiet of the taxidermy room broke with the footsteps of a customer coming to the counter and ringing the little bell the sisters kept there. Heather put the scalpel down carefully and walked out to serve. Rakisha straightened. 'Thank you, darling. But not yet.'

Rosemary stood, smiled briefly at the cross-legged woman, and joined Heather. The customer had wandered off to the worming tablets. 'Is Robert here, Heather?'

'Mr Sparkle?' Heather used both hands to lift the mass of golden curls from her neck before letting them drop. 'He's with Hannah at home.' She nodded to the back of the shed. 'Business talk.' She shrugged, as if business was the last thing on her mind although Rosemary wasn't fooled. Heather had the sound work ethic of the rest of her siblings even if she chose not to be bothered by the day-to-day running of a large animal feed store.

'Thanks. I haven't seen him since his father died.'

Heather's serene features twisted. 'He is worried.'

'Worried. Why?'

'It was better when his father was alive.'

The customer came back to the counter clutching packets of tablets and Heather turned to him. Rosemary left her to it, walking out of the enclosed area, through the shed and outside. The sisters lived in the original miner's cottage at the back of the property, a small but cosy arrangement. Through a front window, Rosemary could see Hannah and Robert sitting at a table. She knocked on the door.

'Come in if I know you,' called Hannah, so Rosemary did. 'Oh, hiya.' Hannah half stood. 'Is Mrs Lionel alright?'

Rosemary waved the young woman back into her seat. 'Why is it when I visit, someone invariably asks me about Mrs Lionel's health?'

'Well, she's *old*, Rosemary,' said Hannah, rolling her eyes.

'And healthier than most of the town's residents.'

'Yeah, true. But, you know, there'll come a day...' Hannah looked momentarily stricken.

'Not yet,' said Rosemary firmly. 'Not for a long time. You don't need to worry, Hannah.'

Hannah gave a curt nod, looking relieved. 'Okay.' She jerked around to Robert who sat with an ankle resting on his other knee, looking quietly amused. 'Oh, jeepers, Robert. I'm sorry. That was really thoughtless, what with your dad...' Hannah ran a hand through her spiky hair. 'I'm an idiot.'

'No, you're not,' said Rosemary, pulling out a chair and sitting down. 'That was an idiotic thing to say but you're quite bright.'

Hannah stared at Rosemary before bursting out in laughter. 'Thanks, Rosemary, I think?'

Rosemary frowned and turned to Robert. 'How was the funeral?'

Robert uncrossed his leg and put his elbows on the table. 'It was strange, to tell the truth. On the good side, my father had a massive stroke and they reckon he was gone just like that.' He snapped his fingers. 'As he was a man of law and order, the funeral arrangements had been long made. We just followed his instructions. As we did in life, we did in death.' He sighed.

Rosemary waited but Robert appeared finished. 'On the bad side?'

'On the bad side...' His head drooped. 'That's another thing altogether.'

Silence deepened in the little room. Hannah looked from one to the other before finally pushing her chair back and standing. 'Thanks for the catch up, Robert. You asked if we were going alright and we are, especially with Milly's help in the garden centre.' She tapped one finger on her lip. 'Do you think we should install a coffee machine? Maybe we could offer coffee and cake? Honey wouldn't mind making us some, would she, Rosemary?'

'She wouldn't mind.'

'There you go.' Hannah pulled her jacket from the back of the chair. 'I'm full of bright ideas because I am very bright! I'm off. Heather's going to Patricia's now. You two stay as long as you want.' She spun out the door, shutting it behind her with a bang.

Robert's head stayed down. Rosemary stretched her hand out on the table. 'I notice your brother's in town.'

Robert nodded slowly.

'Are you having a bit of family time with him?'

He raised his head. 'He's not here because I asked him.'

'Right. He's here...?'

'He invited himself.'

'Right.'

Robert sighed again heavily and leaned back in his chair. It was unusual to see him so downcast so Rosemary kept still. 'He's my father's executor.'

'Right. And does your brother have a name?'

'William. He was named after my father.'

'Nice. Who were you named after?'

'My mother's father.' A wisp of a smile ran across Robert's face. 'A lovely man. I'd rather his name than my unemotional father.'

'Unemotional.'

'Aemotional, actually. As in devoid of emotion. Brilliant businessman, though, if wealth is an indication of brilliance.'

Rosemary shrugged. 'There are other ways to be brilliant.'

'Don't I know it.' He sighed again.

'You sound like a steam train letting off its brakes.'

He laughed. 'Do I? Sorry.' He shook himself. 'Well, I'm in a right scrape, as my mother would have said.'

'In what way?'

'According to my father's will, I find myself between a rock and a hard place.'

'In what way?'

Robert pushed his chair back but didn't stand. Instead, he put his hands on his knees and bent forward.

'Are you in pain?'

'Metaphorically, yes.' He straightened stiffly. 'This pickle has landed other people into it.'

'Who?'

He waved his hand around, indicating the house.

'The Hubbard sisters? Why?'

Robert grimaced. 'I know you think I'm wealthy.'

'You have money, if that's what you mean.'

'Well, yes, I *did* have money. I bought the garage and Ravenshome with my money.'

'But you own Mulbury Feeds as well.'

'I do, I do.' Robert squirmed. 'But only because I borrowed from my father.'

'Right. Was that wise?'

'I thought it was at the time. I've got investments and a decent share portfolio.' He waved his hand around again.

'Good for you.'

'Oh.' He stared at her. 'I don't mean that in any way-'

'Stop.' Rosemary put her hands in her lap. 'I know. You are of the fortunate few who knows their future is secure. Although there's a problem, isn't there?'

'More than one.' Robert lowered his voice. 'My invest-ments can't be touched yet, not in a way that would be useful. I tied them up firmly, thinking I had enough for my life at the moment. I did all that before I bought Mulbury Feeds.'

'By borrowing money.'

'My father agreed. He always liked real estate. I was to pay it off when my investments came due in two years. Or, I thought, if he was to die, there'd be inheritance to take care of it.'

'But now?'

'Now?' He laughed but there was no mirth in it. 'Now I find out the conditions of his will.'

Rosemary smoothed her braid. 'You don't have an inheritance.'

'Oh, I do.'

'Lucky you.'

'Not really.' Robert rubbed trembling hands over his face. 'There are conditions, Rosemary. I should have known he'd do this...' He let his hands drop.

'What are the conditions?'

He cleared his throat and sat up. 'In order to keep Mulbury Feeds, I need to go back to the city and work for a year in the current business my father ran. Only then will I inherit enough to pay the estate back.'

Rosemary felt a tug in her stomach. 'Is that so bad? It's only one year.'

'You don't know what that business is.'

'So, tell me.'

Robert took a deep breath in and let it out noisily. 'My father owned D-day Development. It means I would be responsible for the destruction of Mulbury.'

TEN

The despair on Robert's face as he left Mulbury Feeds to go home haunted Rosemary all night. She woke early Thursday and lay in bed listening to the morning sounds of wakening magpies and the soft whispers of Mrs Lionel's radio on next door. Sunny curled in a tight ball at her knees, her tail around her face. She didn't open her eyes as Rosemary patted her. 'How about you stay in the warm until I get your breakfast?'

The ginger tabby didn't move. Her stillness said it all.

Rosemary chuckled as she slid awkwardly out around the cat and donned a thick dressing gown. The autumn days were beautiful with sweet temperatures but the mornings needed to be wrapped up against their chill. She moved to the kitchen, yawning widely, and made tea, thinking on Robert's dilemma. He'd bought Mulbury Feeds so the Hubbard sisters could keep working the business as if it was still their own. They didn't have the money to keep it afloat then so it was hardly likely they could buy it back from Robert now, especially with the eldest sister, Holly, living thousands of kilometres away.

And there was Milly's wage to consider, an added cost they hadn't had before even if Heather was countering that with her earnings from Patricia's. It was a grim situation.

A noise at the shop door made her pad through to investigate. The shop was dark so it wasn't until she reefed the blinds up that she saw the paper on the floor. Through the window, she spotted Roman in a pair of shorts and trainers pushing something under Mrs Lionel's entrance before jogging away over the Square to Franco's. He bent to deliver something there, earning a wave from the busy baker inside, and moved on to Mullings of Mulbury.

Rosemary picked up the paper. It was thick parchment, and covered in what she recognised as Jules' elegant handwriting. *"Memorial Dinner Saturday Night"*, it read. *"The Leftover Restaurant invites you to a remembrance evening for those whose lives have been unexpectedly taken in our beautiful establishment."* There was an RSVP date with the restaurant's phone number included. She went back to the kitchen and propped the invitation against a bowl of apples.

She'd barely finished breakfast before someone rapped at the door. Through the glass, Rosemary saw Honey holding a beanie-capped Tallulah who clutched at her mother's jacket, and a tail-wagging Cuddles. 'It's a bit early for visiting,' said Rosemary as she opened the door.

'My sense of time has shifted since this little one came along.' Honey kissed the baby's cheek. 'She likes the dawn almost as much as you.'

'Is she sleeping okay?'

'I think her teeth are worrying her.' Honey wiped away a bit of baby drool as Tallulah bit down on the jacket. 'She's a bit grumbly.'

'I'll hold her while you get yourself a tea.'

'Thanks, Mum.' Honey lifted Tallulah over. 'I'm dying for a cup.'

Rosemary settled the baby in her arms as Honey went for the kettle and the dog plonked onto the lounge rug. Tallulah smelled of sugar and roses, partly because she spent so much time next to her mother as she made exquisite cupcakes. The baby grabbed at Rosemary's braid, stuffing the end in her mouth before pulling it away in disgust. Rosemary chuckled and took the little hand in hers. 'Avoid eating that, little one' she said, earning a smile from her granddaughter.

'So, you got one as well?'

Rosemary positioned the baby on her other hip. 'What did I get?'

'This invitation.' Honey pointed her mug at the parchment.

'Yes. Roman delivered it.'

'I didn't see him. It was under the tearoom door.' Honey went to the fridge and rummaged around for bread. 'Will you go?'

'Yes. Roman and Jules will put much effort into it.'

'I wonder who else they invited?'

'Mrs Lionel, Franco and Kelly.'

'Is that all?'

Rosemary shrugged. 'That was all I could see.'

Honey put a slice of bread into the toaster. 'I have this feeling they won't just invite us.'

'You think he'll extend the invitation to Bunnie?'

'Well, that would be kind. And the other man's family as well. I mean, the funerals haven't happened yet so they haven't had a chance to do whatever funerals are meant to achieve.'

'Funerals are an important ritual.' Rosemary put

Tallulah on her tummy on the floor in front of a set of wooden blocks where she swatted happily at them. 'The coroner hasn't finished with the bodies yet so any funeral arrangements will be on hold.'

'All the more reason why the dinner is for them.' Honey buttered her toast. 'And I suspect Roman would like the restaurant to be considered something other than a place of death.'

'The dinner isn't until Saturday. He opens again tonight.'

'Oh, right, I hadn't realised. I wonder if he has any bookings?'

'Time will tell.'

'Yep.' Honey pushed the last of her toast into her mouth and chewed noisily.

'Hungry?'

The young woman nodded. 'Always.'

Rosemary glanced at the content baby on the floor and then back to her daughter. Honey had always been slim but she was, by any standards, getting thinner. Her hair, though, was its usual glossy shoe polish brown and her cheeks healthily ruddy. 'Are you managing, Honey? Tearoom, baby, making cakes...'

Honey yawned widely, laughing as she finished. 'Yeah, I'm fine, Mum. I'm not saying it isn't busy, but it's okay. I am perpetually hungry but I think a bit of that is the breast-feeding and I guess that won't last forever.'

'I need to make you more dinners.'

'No need. Ronnie's quite a good cook and he likes making huge pots of soups and stews.' Honey finished her tea in one swallow and upended her mug in the dishwasher. 'You know what I wouldn't mind, though, are some healthy snacks. I've got fruit and cheese, but I'm surrounded by cakes. It's too easy to eat a cupcake that hasn't turned out perfectly so I can't sell it.' She picked Tallulah from the floor, plucking a block from her hand to Tallulah's protests. 'You know, Mum, I can inhale a cupcake and it doesn't feel like I've eaten anything but air so I usually eat two. Or three.' She shrugged, kissing Tallulah repeatedly on the forehead until the baby smiled. 'Could you do that?'

'Inhale cupcakes?'

Honey grinned. 'The snacks.'

'I'll see what I can do.'

'That would be great, thanks.' Honey shifted Tallulah around. 'Okay, I'd better go. Thanks for the second breakfast.'

'Anytime.'

Honey clicked her tongue for Cuddles who lay wagging his tail at a distant Sunny, and walked toward the door. 'And I'll find out more.'

'About what?'

'About whom Roman and Jules have asked for dinner.' The bell jangled noisily as she pulled the door open. 'Jules is coming in to pick up apple pies. I thought they were for another day but maybe she'll want them for tonight.' Honey frowned as the door slowly closed, and called in through the gap, 'I hope she gets customers!'

IF THERE WAS any doubt about the number of customers wanting to dine in a place where two people had mysteriously died, it had gone by lunchtime. Cars and people movers arrived by late morning, and the people exiting were not dressed like normal tourists. Instead of straw hats, flowing dresses and sensible shoes, most of the people pouring from their vehicles were dressed darkly, as if they were cat burglars. Many of them wore matching T-shirts, so that it was easy to define groups. It was clear to Rosemary, as she watched from her nearly empty shop, that the groups didn't mix easily. They stood apart, members glancing over their shoulders at the others. Lunchtime came and went but apart from a designated coffee runner, no one broke rank to partake of Franco's delicious pies, Kelly's mundane slices or Rakisha's doubtful brownies.

Mrs Lionel visited for a quick afternoon tea. 'I see I was correct,' she said, as she settled at Rosemary's dining table.

Rosemary put a pot of tea and two cups on the table. 'Correct about what?'

'That people would be interested in dining in a death-ridden restaurant.'

Rosemary offered her friend milk from a white jug. 'It's morbid.'

Mrs Lionel indicated a small amount of milk for her cup. 'It's human nature. We are attracted to the inexplicable, the hint of drama.'

'Right.'

'Time will take the drama away eventually.'

'I hope time will leave us with our usual number of tourists. All those cars out there are blocking parking for people who want to explore Mulbury.'

'Yes, I've seen some drive off because they couldn't find anywhere to park.' Mrs Lionel sipped her tea and smiled. 'Lovely, dear.'

'A new blend. It has a little smokiness to it.'

'Delicious.' Mrs Lionel drained her cup. 'I'd best be going. Another hour and we'll be closed. It's getting dark so early, isn't it?'

'Yes. Winter won't be far off.' Rosemary pushed her chair back and stood up. 'Listen. Can you hear that?'

A mumble of voices came from outside, rising in volume. Rosemary and Mrs Lionel made their way into the shop and out the jangling door to the pavement as the voices lifted to the level of a shouting football crowd. 'What on earth?' said Mrs Lionel.

Goldmarket Square was a mass of darkly dressed people. The groups were no longer keeping separate, their similarly shaded black, brown, navy blue and maroon shirts shoulder to shoulder. They were facing something at the back of the Square. Rosemary stood up on her toes to see. 'It's Roman.'

Mrs Lionel strained to see. 'What's Roman?'

'They're looking at Roman. He's waving a piece of paper.'

'Why?'

Rosemary tried to make out what Roman's arm gestures were telling her. 'I think he's showing them the layout of the restaurant. How many tables does he usually have?'

'About ten is all they can manage.'

Rosemary watched as Roman held up both hands, fingers spread, and then closed one hand completely and tucked his other thumb into his palm. 'So, about 40 people?'

'That would be right.'

Rosemary stood back. 'How many people do you think are in front of us?'

'140?'

'I think so, too. There's one hundred people who want to dine in The Leftover Restaurant tonight and won't get in.'

'Good heavens. I hope his online booking system doesn't crash.'

'I think he'll be more worried about gate crashers than system crashers.'

'Can we do anything to help?'

'I'll offer to help with waitressing.'

'Good idea. I'll help with the dishes.'

'Can you help with my dishes, too?'

Rosemary turned to the new voice. 'Jasper, do your own dishes.'

He grinned and put his hands in his front jeans pockets. 'I know. Just thought I'd try. What's going on?'

'We think they want to dine at The Leftover Restaurant.'

Jasper nodded, frowning. 'Well, Roman is a great chef but even for his reputation this is sensational.'

'We think he might need help tonight to control events.'

'Okay. I'll be in on that. Do we need to let him know?'

'Let's just turn up after we close.'

Mrs Lionel pulled her cardigan closer. 'It may need more than us. How about we ask Gerry and Patti to come along as well?'

'Right. It's a plan.' Rosemary turned back to her shop. 'And we'd better tell Honey and Ronnie.'

'They'll be too busy to help, dear. And they have little Tallulah.'

Rosemary shook her head. 'I wasn't thinking about them helping in that way.' She indicated the crowd. 'I suspect Jules will need a lot more apple pies.'

ELEVEN

Right on five o'clock, Rosemary shut the door to The Preserved Mulbury, leaving Sunny watching from the distant living area, and greeted Mrs Lionel on the pavement. 'Better lock your door now,' Rosemary said. 'We have a lot of strangers in town.'

'Yes, dear, I've done it already.' Mrs Lionel crouched a little to look in through the glass.

'What's the matter?'

Mrs Lionel straightened stiffly. 'It's Percy. He's unsettled. It was like he didn't want me to go out.'

'Right.'

Mrs Lionel gave her friend a hard look. 'Don't say anything, Rosemary Exeter. He may be otherworldly but he looks out for me.'

'I didn't say anything.'

'You often don't have to.' Mrs Lionel gave a swift grin. 'It's in the bristling of your braid.'

Rosemary contemplated that as they crossed the road. Only Mrs Lionel had ever seen Percy but not for one minute did Rosemary think Mrs Lionel was making him up.

She could see him, he was of immense comfort, and that was fine. That Percy was agitated tonight was just another unusual event in a day of strange happenings.

They reached the edge of the crowd and pushed their way through. It had thinned a little as many realised they wouldn't all be able to dine at The Leftover Restaurant that night. Still, about half were left. They stood in a self-imposed set of semicircles around the entrance of the old bank building. 'Excuse me,' said Rosemary, elbowing carefully through the lines. 'Let us through, please.'

Although some looked at her with no intention of getting out of the way, they melted back to let Mrs Lionel pass. She went by Rosemary and created a clear path to the restaurant's front door where she used the heavy brass knocker to make their presence known.

'We're not open yet,' called Jules from the depths of the building.

'That's good,' said Rosemary. 'We've come to help you get open.'

Light footsteps hurried to the door and Jules opened it, beaming. 'Aren't you lovely? Gerry and Patti are here peeling potatoes and Jasper is helping me with the tables.' She glanced back at the interior. 'We've managed to create another two four seaters but even so we've had to turn dozens of people away.'

'They remain hopeful out there, dear,' said Mrs Lionel as she stepped inside.

'We're here to help with crowd control.' Rosemary inhaled the aroma of frying onions. 'That will make it harder.'

'What will?' asked Jules, eyes wide.

'Roman's delicious food.' Rosemary pointed her thumb over her shoulder. 'They think they're coming as voyeurs but once they're in, they'll realise how wonderful the chef is.'

'Why, Rosemary, what a sweet thing to say!' Jules smiled and moved a strand of her bangs away with a carefully manicured nail. 'Come in now and have a bite to eat before those doors open and we get too busy.'

Mrs Lionel followed Jules into the back of the vast room which once had been inhabited by tellers behind solid wooden desks. A few of the original features remained but the area was now more sophisticated dining than stamped bank cheques. Rosemary stopped at a table where Jasper was polishing a heavy set of cutlery. 'You got here quickly.'

'I took Snowy out early and then locked up.' Jasper shrugged. 'I'd sold out of paranormality.'

'Paranormality.'

'Yes.' Jasper indicated outside. 'Lots of them are avid readers of paranormal and supernatural fiction and non-fiction. I don't have a single book about ghouls left.'

Rosemary frowned. 'They don't look like a crowd of readers.'

'Oh?' Jasper paused, a knife in one hand. 'Do you mean they don't wear glasses and look pale from being inside all the time?'

'Don't stereotype people, Jasper.'

'You started it.'

Rosemary pointed at Jasper's back pocket where a folded paperback protruded. 'I mean, they must have stashed their books away as I couldn't see any in their possession. Not like some readers I know.'

Jasper felt for the book and patted it. 'Well, you never know when you're going to get a chance to read a few paragraphs. I like to be prepared.'

'Talking of preparation, did you ever try to find out

what the instruments were the man was holding the other day?'

'The ones with the dials? I put the image into the search engine and it came up with several options, all to do with measuring air waves. It was confusing.'

'Jasper, Rosemary,' called Jules from the kitchen. 'Come and join us.'

Rosemary followed Jasper, passing through the middle of the room and the spot where Bob Brownlee had lain entombed in the case. There was no sign of any misadventure, not that she expected there to be, but if that's what the crowd were wanting, there would be disappointment. She glanced back at the door of the room where the second man had died, but all seemed quite normal.

'Jasper,' said Roman as they came into the kitchen. 'Rosemary. You are the best of friends to us.' He pushed his toque back a little and beamed. 'You will sample some of my spinach orecchiette.'

'With pleasure, Roman,' said Jasper, accepting a plate of creamy pasta. 'But don't let us take all your food. You have a full house tonight.'

Roman tsked as he handed a plate out to Rosemary. 'It is no matter. I have kilos of pasta.'

'Roman's been making it all day,' said Patti, putting her clean plate on the table and rocking a little, making her full-skirted dress swing. 'We're helping with the vegetables.' She picked up a peeler and turned back to her task.

'Splendid, Roman,' said Gerry with a wistful look at the rest of the orecchiette. 'Well, if there's any leftovers from The Leftover Restaurant tonight, you know where to put them.' He patted his rounded belly.

'I doubt there will be much left over, dear.' Mrs Lionel

gathered empty plates and took them to the sink. 'When do the doors open, Jules?'

Jules glanced at her watch. 'Twenty-five minutes, Mrs Lionel.'

'Is everything on track, Roman?'

Roman nodded, his attention once more on the chopping board in front of him. 'I shall be ready.'

'We'll finish the tables,' said Jules. 'I'll put more glasses out.'

Rosemary and Jasper helped Jules in the dining area while the others continued in the kitchen. There was one window at the front of the room that overlooked the buildings edging the Square. The crowd outside gradually arranged themselves in a long line and she could see jostling and cross expressions as some tried to push into it. By the time Jules opened the restaurant door at quarter to six, the crowd was arguing noisily. It fell silent as Jules held up a list.

'Thank you for your interest in dining at The Leftover Restaurant,' she said pleasantly. 'Unfortunately, we were unable to cater for all requested seats. I have the bookings for tonight here and no known cancellations. Perhaps if I called your name and party numbers you could come forward and be seated?'

Maybe it was the sight of Jules's simple linen elegance or the sound of her warm but firm voice, but the crowd seemed happy to respond to the roll call that, to Rosemary, felt like she was back in primary school. Diners moved inside as Jules called their booking and Jasper took them to the relevant table. They sat obediently and didn't talk. The room filled quickly but when Jules finally shut the door to the remainder of the restless crowd, quiet prevailed. Jules looked momentarily surprised but moved forward to the first table and started talking softly to her guests while placing napkins on their laps. Jasper watched for a moment and did the same from the back of the room.

Rosemary pressed herself into the wall beside the storage room. From there, she had a view of everyone. As Jules and Jasper moved away from each table, she saw how at least one member from every one bent down to their bags set on the floor to pull something from them to lean half-hidden on the table's edge. By the time Jules and Jasper had seen everyone, blinking lights emanated from gadgets all over the room. And still no one said anything, although several of them jittered their feet on the floor in an uneasy rhythm.

Jules glanced across the room to Rosemary and gave a little shrug. Rosemary shook her head slightly. A silent ten minutes went by, and Gerry emerged, a crisp black apron around his middle and a waiter's order pad clutched in one hand. He waited for Jules's signal before going to the first table to ask for orders.

By the slightly puzzled looks on the faces of the diners, it was clear ordering food was not the first thing on their minds. They snatched up menus as Gerry, then Patti in a bright floral apron, went to each table with their pads. From what Rosemary could hear, most ordered the first item they saw. 'Roman's pasta will disappear tonight,' she said quietly to Jasper as he joined her against the wall.

He nodded, then shrugged a shoulder toward the nearest table. 'What on earth are those things?'

Rosemary stepped across to get a better view of a rectangular object on the table closest to her. 'They seem to be taking readings of some kind.'

'They look like the gadgets I was looking up. Geiger counters and the like.'

'Could be.' Rosemary stared harder. 'Maybe that's why they aren't reading much. I doubt there's any radioactive material to cause alarm in this building.'

'If not that, what? Oxygen levels? Carbon dioxide?'

Rosemary watched as a man shook his gadget and huffed as the dial crept up then fell. She recognised him as the one who'd spoken to Geoffrey. 'Whatever they're measuring, they can't be very accurate. Looks like all it takes is a decent movement and the dial shifts.'

Jasper was quiet for a moment. 'Rosemary,' he said in a low voice. 'Have you ever read any of *Spectre Season?*'

'That was the book series you mentioned the other day, wasn't it?'

'Yes. It's fiction.'

'First time I heard of it was when you talked about it.'

'Okay.' Jasper put his hand over his mouth and spoke behind it. 'It was very popular when the first books came out about ten years ago. They were going to make the series into a TV show but it didn't go ahead.'

'Right.' Rosemary tipped her head towards Jasper's. 'You're going to tell me why this is relevant as we stand here in a silent restaurant where no one is interested in eating.'

'Well, yes. I think it's very relevant.' Jasper inched closer to her. 'The first book in *Spectre Season* is about a group of scientists who discover an inexplicable level of electromagnetic activity in an old house. They stay overnight and find the house full of...' he lowered his voice further '...ghosts.'

'Ghosts.'

'Shhhh.' Jasper glanced at the room but no one had heard. 'The Spectreologists from the book used electromagnetic field detectors.' He nodded at the closest gadget. 'EMF detectors.'

Rosemary frowned. The blinking lights studded the

restaurant as if a cluster of stars had fallen inside. Most of the diners were gazing at the gadgets intently, which would have been comedic if it wasn't so strange, as some had to lean almost sideways to see their friend's device. 'Are you telling me,' she said in a barely audible voice, 'that I'm looking at a group of ghosthunters?'

'I don't think they'd use that word.'

'Spectreologists, then.'

'From all those books going out the door today, I'd use the term *paranormal investigators*.'

'BTPI.'

'What?'

'It's what some of them had on their shirts. BT Paranormal Investigators.'

'Big Town Paranormal Investigators.'

Rosemary straightened and eyeballed the room. Jules and Gerry were now serving steaming plates of pasta. As they placed them in front of the diners, the fragrance got the better of them and, one by one, they shifted their gaze from dials to their meals. The devices were slipped into laps where their blinking lights flashed under tables. 'They're looking for Bob Brownlee and Warwick Jones as ghosts.'

'That's my conclusion, too.'

'They don't seem to be having much luck.'

'Look.' Jasper pointed discreetly to a table on their left. 'They're trying a different approach.'

A woman pulled a slim rod from her pocket and placed it next to her fork. As if on cue, others around the room did the same. 'Thermometers.'

'To measure changes in air temperature which change abruptly with paranormal activity.' Rosemary glanced at Jasper. He shrugged. 'I've read all the *Spectre* books.'

'They've put the thermometers next to their plates. Of course they'll-'

A shriek shattered the quiet clinking of cutlery. The woman stood, her chair scraping noisily. 'Yes!' she said, holding her thermometer up. 'I have evidence!' She pointed to a spot on the ceiling. 'They're here! Bob and Warwick are here!'

TWELVE

Rosemary grimaced at the sudden noise of all guests talking at once. Half of them stood, waving their EMF detectors and kitchen thermometers. Some were shouting, 'Yes! Thermal changes!' while others said, 'Yes! EMF ratings!' The majority clasped each other, their free hands gripping the stones around their necks or wrists, and one or two sprinkled salt on the table.

Jules and Gerry emerged from the kitchen, their arms full of more plates of pasta. They stopped suddenly, Gerry doing a shuffle dance to keep the food from falling. Jules looked toward Rosemary but she could only shrug. Jules continued forward, putting plates on tables and rearranging napkins as people sat down again, her face a pleasant mask of professionalism as if excited paranormal investigators were a part of her every day.

As the tables filled with food, the noise dimmed a little. Although the expectant faces of the diners didn't change, the aroma of Roman's cooking was—as Rosemary had anticipated—too much for people to resist. They ate with gusto, all the while keeping an eye on the room as if Bob and Warwick were late guests to a special party.

'What do you think of that?' whispered Jasper as things settled.

'You don't want to know what I think of that.'

He was so close to her, their arms rubbed together as he spoke. 'I don't think you believe in ghosts.'

Rosemary thought immediately of Mrs Lionel. 'I haven't had an experience I could claim to be an encounter with someone, or something, appearing as though alive.'

Jasper was quiet for a moment. 'So...you don't believe in ghosts.'

She nudged him. 'I mean I've never seen one.'

'Oh. Okay.'

She studied him curiously. 'Have you?'

'No.' Disappointment crossed his face. 'When I found that poor woman's bones in my backyard, I thought I might have some sort of supernatural experience, but...'

'All you got was the forensic team digging up your yard.'

He laughed shortly. 'Pretty much.' He nodded towards the woman with the thermometer who was polishing her pasta bowl with a piece of focaccia. 'She seemed to detect something.'

'She had her thermometer next to her plate. I imagine Roman warmed the plates before filling them. Naturally, the thermometer reading went up.'

'But those EMF detectors are recording something as well.'

'Yes.'

'Ghostly activity?'

'You'd be surprised at the amount of electromagnetic activity we have around us every day. Many household items emit energy: toasters, microwaves, lamps.' She lifted her chin to the nearest table. 'Mobile phones and smart watches, for example. I can't imagine the devices in here are calibrated well. Those needles and dials look like blunt instruments. Look. They're all detecting different levels.'

Jasper spent a moment studying the nearest tables. The blinking lights occasionally changed colour, causing a flutter at the table concerned, but not enough to make people stand again. Or shriek. In fact, by the time Jules and Gerry brought out the apple pies people had ordered, quiet had once again descended over the restaurant, and the jittery legs were back.

Jules walked across the room, checking occasionally with her guests to see if they needed something else, and came to stand next to Rosemary and Jasper. 'Do you know what's going on?' she whispered.

'They're trying to detect ghosts,' said Jasper quietly. 'The devices are picking up abnormal activity.'

'*Normal* activity,' said Rosemary. 'There's nothing here out of the ordinary.'

'I've never had guests be so quiet.' Jules folded her hands together. 'It's quite eerie.'

'There's no doubt they're enjoying your food.'

'But it's not the atmosphere of a restaurant. It's more like a conference dinner with an important guest speaker who hasn't emerged yet.'

Jasper shifted closer to Jules. 'Is there any news on either of the gentlemen who...' He waved his hand around.

'No.' Jules nodded toward the storage room door behind them. 'The only things we had in that room were chairs. It's a mystery.' She passed a hand over her face. 'My concern is how he got into the building and what he was doing here.'

Rosemary looked around the room where most of the

diners had finished their meals and were studying their devices. 'Do you lock up after yourself?'

'Not always, but we had because the police had just concluded their investigation into Mr Brownlee. I'm so sure the outside door was locked.'

Jasper crossed his arms. 'He was here to try and locate Bob Brownlee as a ghost, don't you think?'

'That appears to be likely now that I see what's in front of me.' Jules sighed, stroked a stray hair from her face, and indicated the kitchen. 'I'd better go back.' She headed off, pausing at a table now and then to ask after the guests who stared sullenly at her.

'I'm not sure these people got what they came for,' said Jasper as the guests started packing up their detectors.

'It depends on their intentions. They may have wanted to see what levels of evidence were here.' Rosemary watched as the nearby lady placed her thermometer into her handbag with a grim expression on her face. 'They are very disappointed.'

'Do you think?' Jasper shook his head. 'They look more nervous to me.'

Rosemary kept her eyes on the diners. One by one they stood, stashed their devices away, and started for the exit. Jules hurried to the door and reminded them of their bills by holding the electronic payment system out as they left, causing increased beeping from the stowed gadgets and temporary looks of shock on their owners faces until they realised what was happening. The final woman to leave put her hand on Jules' arm as she exited. 'Be aware,' she said, waving at the near-empty dining room. 'You may witness activity yet.'

'Thank you,' said Jules politely. 'I will remain aware.'

With the many people helping, it wasn't long before the

restaurant was packed up, dishes done and tables wiped. When Rosemary put her sodden tea towel into a laundry bag, she realised she'd missed something. 'Where was Robert?' she asked Jasper. 'I thought you'd invited him along.'

Jasper paused in the middle of taking off his apron. 'I did. He said he'd be here.' He fished out his phone from his pocket. 'No message. He must have been caught up.'

'With William, perhaps.'

'Who's William?'

'Ah.' Gerry lifted his hand in apology. 'Sorry, not eavesdropping, but I heard the name.' He put a hand on Jasper's shoulder. 'William is Robert's brother.'

Jasper's eyebrows went up. 'I didn't know he had a brother.'

'I don't think anyone did.' Gerry let his hand drop. 'I can see why. He's nothing like Robert and the two of them have a very polite relationship.'

'Who does, sweetie?' Patti primped her hair to make it sit on her shoulders in a gentle roll.

'Robert and William.'

'Oh.' The usually sweet expression on Patti's face morphed into sadness. 'I wouldn't have described it as polite. More...cold.'

Jasper finished taking his apron off and threw it into the hamper. 'Robert doesn't like his brother?'

'He hasn't said anything.' Gerry rubbed the top of his bald pate. 'William is staying in Ravenshome so we get to see how the brothers interact.'

'They don't,' said Patti.

'They don't what?' asked Rosemary.

'Interact, sweetie.' Patti put on a blank face and marched up and down on the spot for a few moments.

'They walk past each other as if each is invisible. Robert was going up the stairs this morning and William was coming down. They were completely oblivious to each other.' She shuddered. 'It's very awkward, isn't it, Gerry?'

'My word it is.' Gerry looked troubled. 'I mean, I love my brothers with all my heart and don't see them enough, so it's terrible to witness siblings with such...'

'Emotionlessness?' suggested Jasper.

'Animosity, I was going to say.' Gerry sighed. 'But that would mean I've seen them speak. Or react to each other. I haven't seen either action.'

Rosemary checked the kitchen but except for Mrs Lionel polishing a last saucepan, every task was finished. 'I don't see how that should affect Robert coming to help here tonight.'

'I guess it wouldn't directly.' Gerry grimaced. 'Perhaps William's presence alone is making Robert behave differently.'

'Why is he here?' asked Jasper. 'I mean, apart from the fact he's Robert's brother and their father has just died?' He looked at Rosemary. 'You know, don't you?'

'Yes.'

'You can't say?'

'It's not my business to say anything.'

Gerry, Patti and Jasper went still, staring at Rosemary as if hard gazes alone would make her speak. 'Is it bad?' asked Patti eventually. 'Robert's normally such a relaxed type of person but with his own brother it's as if he's frozen.'

'Yes.'

'Yes, what, Rosemary?' Gerry plucked absent-mindedly at a loose thread on his shirt. 'Is he frozen or is it bad?'

Rosemary hesitated but the anguished look on her friends' faces couldn't be ignored. 'It's bad.'

'Oh!' Patti put both her hands to her mouth. 'Poor Robert!'

Jules walked into the kitchen from the dining area in time to see Patti's reaction. 'What's happened? Is Robert okay?'

'Something bad is happening, Jules.' Patti waggled a finger at Rosemary. 'But it's a secret.'

'A secret Rosemary knows but isn't telling.' Jules pursed her lips thoughtfully. 'I guess that's how it is, then, until Robert tells us more.'

'Roberto?' Roman and Mrs Lionel joined the group, a tea towel draped over Roman's shoulder and his chef's coat lightly sprinkled with sudsy water. 'Is he not okay?'

'He was meant to be here tonight but he didn't come along.' Gerry stifled a yawn and patted his pocket, making his keys clink. 'I guess it's time for us to leave. Unless there's anything else for us to do, Roman?'

The big man shook his head. 'No, my friend. It is all honky donky, thanks to your good work.'

'Honky dory,' corrected Jules automatically. 'Thank you, everyone. It was an odd night, and we're grateful you could help us out.'

'Was there any conclusion to the night, do you think?' asked Mrs Lionel. 'The diners were after something, weren't they? Other than your delicious food, Roman.'

'By their disappointed faces, I don't think they got what they came for,' said Rosemary.

'But what was it they wanted with their flashing devices and funny silences?' said Gerry.

'Ghosts.' Jasper pointed out the doorway. 'We think they were paranormal investigators looking for any traces of Mr Brownlee and Warwick.'

'And you think they didn't find anything?'

'They didn't find enough or Roman and Jules would have had a riot on their hands rather than a pile of dirty dishes.'

'So, there are no ghosts in The Leftover Restaurant.' Roman nodded thoughtfully. 'I could have told them that. I am here every day and no apparitions have ever appeared, before or since the untimely death of those unfortunate gentlemen. They must be content.'

'What do you mean, old fellow?' asked Gerry, frowning.

Roman shrugged. 'Ghosts are the remnants of people's spirits, no? That's what I've always thought. Ghosts are left behind when someone has unfinished business or they were taken suddenly. Perhaps the two deceased gentlemen were happy with their lives and ready to go.'

'But one was stuffed in a mannikin's case!'

Roman put his hands up. 'I am only surmising, my friend. In any case, that mystery is not as obviously solvable as the mystery of Robert's brother's appearance.'

Rosemary stiffened. 'You know why William is here.'

'Oh yes.' Roman smoothed his moustaches with two spread fingers. 'Robert came to me to see how much I thought it was worth.' His mouth drooped. 'It appears he has to sell.'

'Sell?' Jasper looked at Rosemary, confused. 'He has to sell the garage?'

'It won't be worth enough for his current problem.' Rosemary crossed her arms. 'It's Mulbury Feeds he was asking you about, Roman.'

Roman shook his head. 'No, Rosemary, it was not.' He glanced at Patti and Gerry. 'I am so sorry. Alas, it's his dwelling. Robert must sell Ravenshome.'

The shock on Patti's face troubled Rosemary through the night and into the next morning. She woke on Friday and reached for Sunny at her feet but the ginger tabby wasn't there. Rosemary sat, rubbing her face. Her restless night wouldn't have suited a cat who liked peaceful sleeping and, sure enough, as Rosemary stumbled to the kitchen, Sunny was curled in a rug on the couch. 'Sorry, Sunny,' Rosemary said as she flicked on the electric kettle. 'But I thought Patti was going to collapse.'

Sunny stretched her forelegs out and turned so her head was hidden before going back to sleep. *Not my problem,* her attitude said.

Not really mine either, thought Rosemary as she made tea. But was that correct? If Robert sold Ravenshome, Patricia's would move back into the shop under the veranda where Honey and Ronnie had set up Honey B's Teas. Where would the tearoom go? Perhaps she could close The Preserved Mulbury and the tearoom take over the space, but where would she live? And if Mulbury Feeds was sold instead, Hannah and Heather and now Milly would be out of work. New owners may not be as generous as Robert, and the Hubbard sisters would have to move house as well. There were no empty shops in Mulbury anymore and, without their businesses, no one had money to stay. It would be, to quote Robert, the destruction of Mulbury.

'I take it back,' Rosemary said to the snoozing Sunny. 'This is very much my problem.'

Knowing she had a problem way beyond selling enough jam in a week but not having the power to do anything about it made Rosemary unintentionally curt with her customers. She had to grit her teeth when one man spent ten minutes deciding whether lemon or grapefruit marmalade was better on his wholemeal toast, and another wanted Aunt Lilibeth's recipe for green tomato pickles. She gave the first man a two for one deal just to get him out of the shop but didn't budge on the recipe. By the time that man had left, she'd convinced him to buy all three tomato pickles to try and differentiate the ingredients himself. Strangely enough, he was overjoyed at the thought.

At lunchtime, Mrs Lionel slipped in through the jangling doorway with a lunch basket. 'Having a bad day, Rosemary?'

Rosemary finished adjusting the remaining pickle jars and turned to her friend. 'Why do you say that?'

'Oh, just from the general clanking and thumping I hear through the wall. The more there is, the worse things are.'

'I don't clank and thump.'

Mrs Lionel used the basket to point at the display of salted olives on a stand of wooden boxes set in the middle of the room. 'That wasn't there yesterday. You clanked and thumped it into shape this morning.'

Rosemary studied the big jars on their rustic platoons. 'The shop needed something less fussy so I created that.'

'It's very nice and I'm sure setting it up helped with your mood.' Mrs Lionel raised the basket. 'Tomato soup and cheese scones. Come and eat.'

The light meal was delicious and Rosemary felt soothed by Mrs Lionel's thoughtfulness. They chatted for a while about their autumnal gardens, Rosemary noting the roughness of her friend's hands from constant pruning. 'You need some of your own hand cream,' she said, catching one of Mrs Lionel's hands in hers and rubbing a thumb along a deep crack in the skin.

'Yes, I do. I have a particularly good one with shea butter.' The older woman lifted her hands to study them better. 'Goodness, sometimes I feel like my skin doesn't belong to me. It looks so aged.'

'It's only as old as you are.'

Mrs Lionel lowered her hands. 'Yes, thanks for that reminder.' She sipped a little tea. 'Tell me, Rosemary. Last night. We have trouble brewing, don't we?'

'Are you talking about the influx of ghosthunters or Robert's pressing issue?'

'Both, really.'

'Both.'

'Well, yes.' Mrs Lionel wrapped her hands around her cup. 'I'm very concerned about Robert. He's been so generous with his support of Mulbury, particularly with the girls. I can see him selling his house to solve whatever his problem is with his father's will rather than sacrificing the animal produce store.'

'Although that leaves Patti and Gerry in a pickle.'

'I understand.'

'There is another way for him to go. If he returns to the city to work in his father's business, he gets to keep the lot.'

'But he won't be in Mulbury anymore.'

'No.' Rosemary quashed the urge to tell Mrs Lionel about D-Day Development.

Mrs Lionel sat quietly. 'There's another thing,' she said eventually.

'Another thing?'

'Yes. You must promise not to laugh.'

'I would never laugh at you.'

Mrs Lionel smiled. 'No, you wouldn't. Thank you. Although I'm still worried this might sound laughable.'

'Try me.'

Mrs Lionel took a deep breath in and let it out loudly. 'Well, it's Percy.'

'What about Percy?' Rosemary sat up. 'Has he gone?'

'No, no, he's still there. You see, he's my companion. Mine.'

'Yes, I know. He stayed on after his death as a last link to Mr Lionel.'

'That's right. Percy was still a puppy when Mr Lionel died, and he developed into a good friend through very lonely times.'

'You've told me how important he is.'

Mrs Lionel pushed her soup bowl away and put her hands palm down on the table. 'He is. Very important. And only you know about him. You accept him. Well, you accept that only I can see him.'

'Yes. What are you saying?'

Mrs Lionel rubbed the table, her hands squeaking a little on its smooth surface. 'We have all these ghosthunters hanging around with their little machines.' Her hands stilled. 'What if they detect Percy?'

'They...' Rosemary stopped.

'They won't because there's no such things as ghosts?'

'I wasn't going to say that.'

'Perhaps not.' Mrs Lionel put her hands in her lap. 'You can see the issue, though. If those gadgets of theirs work in any way they say they do, then the perfect place to test them is my shop.'

'There's no reason for them to be using any paraphernalia in your shop.'

'I suppose not.'

Mrs Lionel looked so glum Rosemary reached across the table for her friend's hand. Mrs Lionel gave one to her reluctantly. 'I wouldn't worry. They'll concentrate on The Leftover Restaurant.'

'Yes, I guess you're right.' Mrs Lionel shook her head, slid her hand free, and stood. 'Anyway, you've settled down and we both feel better for having lunch so I suppose it's time to go back to work.'

Rosemary collected their plates and took them to the sink as Mrs Lionel repacked the lunch basket with her containers. As they walked to the shop door together, she turned to Rosemary. 'What do you suppose they do, these people, if they detect any ghosts?'

'I'm not sure. Try to talk to them?'

'Roman thinks ghosts are lost souls who have incomplete tasks.'

'That's what he said.'

'Perhaps the ghost hunters help the ghosts complete them. Maybe we aren't giving them the credit they're due?'

Rosemary shrugged. 'Perhaps. Although it didn't look like the mob last night had any intention but *detection*, and even then, they seemed worried about that.'

Mrs Lionel laughed, making Rosemary relax. She held the door open for her friend and waited until the croaking frog indicated Mrs Lionel had gone back inside The Green Mulbury. It was hard to see her friend worried, particularly about something so close to her heart. They just had to hope the paranormal investigators never needed any handmade biodegradable green products.

Rosemary had locked up for the evening when there was a rap on the door. She peered through the blind before opening up again. 'Honey. Ronnie. Everything alright?'

Honey shook her head. 'No. Yes. We don't know so we're here.' She stepped in and went straight for the kitchen. Ronnie followed, Tallulah in his arms and Cuddles the Golden Retriever by his side.

'She needs to talk to you.' Ronnie tilted his head toward his wife. 'Sorry to barge in like this.'

Rosemary shut the door and waved a hand towards her living quarters. 'You can barge in any time you like. What's going on?'

Ronnie followed Cuddles as the dog made a beeline for Rosemary's couch. 'We heard something disturbing today.'

'So, we've come to confirm it with you,' said Honey, her head in Rosemary's fridge.

'If you're looking for something to eat, there's leftover quiche in there.'

'Great, thanks.' Honey lifted the dish out. 'Ronnie?'

'If that's okay, I'd love some.'

Rosemary took Tallulah from Ronnie so he could take a plate of quiche. The little girl chuckled at Cuddles who was wagging a furry tail at Sunny. The cat sat primly at her end of the couch, refusing to acknowledge the dog despite a very large nose about an inch from her head. Rosemary shucked the baby around and sat at the dining table where Tallulah reached for a rattle. 'What's disturbing, then?' Rosemary asked as she gave the baby the toy.

Honey sat down and took a mouthful of pie. 'Well, Jules came in to thank us for the apple pies and she said that

Roman had been talking to Robert and that Robert had been talking to you and then Roman was talking with Jasper, Gerry, Patti and Mrs Lionel last night about Robert and his brother William. Is that right?'

'Yes.'

'And what you were talking about was that Robert is in financial difficulties he has to fix in order to accept the terms of his father's will and to rectify the situation he will have to sell his Mulbury properties.'

'Almost correct. He has a loan to pay for his affairs to be in order.'

'Which means he'll need to sell something.' Honey finished the quiche and put her fork down noisily. 'Mum, we've just opened the business! We can't move anyway. We don't have the money!'

'First of all,' said Rosemary, jiggling Tallulah on her knee, 'nothing's happened yet. We don't know what Robert will do. I don't think *he* knows what he'll do.'

'He'll be so worried,' said Ronnie.

'And secondly?' Honey cut herself another slice of pie. 'What else?'

'Secondly, if you had to move, the tearoom could come in here and we'd share the business premises. Cupcakes and jam would sell quite well together.'

Honey's fork hovered in mid-air. 'Oh, Mum, that's so nice of you! But...' She waved the fork around the room. 'We couldn't live here as well. We wouldn't all fit.'

'Let's work that out when or if we need to.'

Honey sat back, shaking her head. 'Thanks, Mum, but I'm not sure it would work out at all. Do you think there's anything we can do to help Robert?'

'I don't know. I'm guessing not. He has to work it out for himself.'

'Yeah.' Honey sighed. She looked down at her plate as if noticing it for the first time. 'Oh, I'm so sorry, Mum. We've probably eaten your dinner. I just seem to suck food up like a vacuum without stopping to think.'

'I've got fish for my dinner.'

'Lucky then.' Honey watched Tallulah play.

'Do you want to stay?'

'Thanks, but no,' said Ronnie. 'I've got a beef casserole in the slow cooker. Although your quiche, Rosemary, was a fantastic lunch.' He leaned over to stroke Tallulah's cheek. 'We've got Uncle Geoffrey visiting tomorrow.'

'He's got the day off,' added Honey. 'He wants to see Tallulah for a bit longer than he did the other day. And I think he's up to something else as well.'

'Right.'

Honey grinned at her mother. 'Nothing to do with any current investigation, more to do with life plans.' She stood and clicked her fingers at the dog. 'Come on, Cuddles. Ronnie, we've disturbed Mum enough. I guess we'll have to wait some more to see what happens next.'

Ronnie pushed back his chair and took Tallulah from Rosemary. 'Thanks for the reassurance, Rosemary.'

'I gave none.'

'Still.' He stood, settling Tallulah in front of him as she grabbed at his ears. 'We needed to get your view.' He lowered his voice as Honey cleared the table. 'She needed to get your view.'

'All good.' Rosemary led them to the door and waved as they wandered along the pavement to the tearoom. Honey lifted her hand one last time as they went inside, and Rosemary turned to go back in.

Someone blocked her path. The someone had long grey

curls dangling over her shoulders and layers of faded clothing that draped to the ground.

'Rakisha, are you alright?'

The woman stepped close to Rosemary, a strong smell of lavender and sandalwood dominated the air. 'Rosemary,' she whispered. 'No, I'm not.' Rakisha came closer still. 'And tomorrow will be worse.'

FOURTEEN

Rosemary eyed the woman. Rakisha's usually open face was creased in worry, with her eyes barely visible through a veil of hair. Never the neatest person, nonetheless Rakisha looked like she'd dressed in the dark, possibly pulling a velvet cloak over the top of an embroidered cotton nightie while adding some scarves for warmth. It was always difficult to differentiate the woman's day from night clothes, but the lambswool slippers she was wearing was of particular concern to Rosemary. 'Something's upsetting you, Rakisha.'

'Oh.' Rakisha wrung her hands. 'My chakra is wobbly today, darling.'

'Have you eaten anything?'

'Many things in my time, darling.'

Rosemary stifled a sigh. 'I meant, have you eaten anything *today*?'

'Today?' Rakisha frowned and tipped her head in thought. 'I don't know, darling. I've been so...' She shook herself, reminding Rosemary of the way dogs do when they're wet.

'Would you like to join me later for dinner?' Rosemary dismissed the fish option. 'I can make a vegetable curry.'

'A curry?' Rakisha's eyes widened. 'Oh, darling, that sounds marvellous but I have Milly, you see. Milly needs dinner after her hard day's work with the potting mix.'

'I'll make enough for Milly as well. You go and find her before she heads home.'

'Yes, yes, darling, I will.' Rakisha rocked backwards and forwards until Rosemary put gentle hands on her shoulders to steer her around. 'Thank you, darling, I'll tell Milly.'

Rosemary watched as Rakisha set off in a crooked line towards Mulbury Feeds, resisting the urge to run after the woman as she crossed the road without checking for cars. Rakisha made it to the other side without injury, and Rosemary had her hand on the door handle to go inside to hunt down vegan suitable ingredients when a bellow from Mulbury Feeds stopped her. In the distance, she saw four people come out of the big shed just as Rakisha arrived. The yell came again, and Rosemary saw Hannah Hubbard put her hands on her head and walk around in a tight circle.

The vegetable curry fell in immediacy. Rosemary hurried down the path, across the road, and joined the group. Hannah was now crouched on the ground, giving out strangled moans, while Heather stood stiffly next to Milly, a look of terror on the young woman's face. Rakisha stood back as Rosemary arrived, clearing the view to Robert squatting next to Hannah.

'What on earth is going on?' Rosemary asked.

Robert's face twisted. 'Hannah heard about my dilemma.' He glanced at Rosemary. 'Apparently everyone knows.' He reached his hand out to the young woman but didn't touch her. 'It's okay, Hannah. I won't have to sell Mulbury Feeds. I promise.'

'Don't say that.' Hannah lifted her head and stared angrily at him. 'Don't make promises you can't keep. Dad did enough of that when he was here. I expect you to be honest.' She stood. 'No. I expect you to treat us as business associates and tell us when things happen. I don't want to find out second hand through kindly people like Gerry and Patti. Got it?'

Robert heaved himself up. 'I'm so sorry, Hannah, really, I am. I didn't expect the news to spread quite so quickly.' He shot a look at Rosemary who held up her hands. 'I should have known it would once I confided in people.'

'Yes, you should have.' Hannah wiped at her face, spotted Heather's distress, and ran to her sister. 'We're strong enough to handle anything, aren't we, Heather? But not surprises. They're hard.' She rubbed Heather's back and the younger sister nodded.

'Okay, I'm sorry, I didn't think. I was trying to...' Robert flung his hands up.

'I know what you were trying to do.' Hannah's voice softened. 'Thanks, but don't do it again.' She looked around at the little crowd. 'Sorry to make a scene.'

'It wasn't a scene, Hannah,' said Milly, pulling off her gardening gloves and slipping them into her apron pocket. 'You were shocked. We were all shocked.'

'Selling Mulbury Feeds is very low down on the list of things I'm going to try first to resolve the situation,' said Robert, rubbing a hand down his face. 'I'll work it out.'

'Well, don't do it by yourself.' Hannah put her hands on her hips. 'The whole town knows you've got financial troubles. Let *us* help you work it out. Lots of heads must be better than one.'

'I don't know...'

'Robert, Robbie.' Heather stepped over to him and rested her head briefly on his arm. 'Mr Sparkle. We'll help.'

Robert smiled, the tension in his face easing. 'Thanks, Heather. It's kind of you.'

'It's not just kind.' Hannah slapped at the knees of her jeans, brushing dirt from them. 'This is our livelihood. We've a vested interest in keeping you afloat, Robert Sparkling.'

'Yes, well, I suppose you have.' Robert laughed shortly. 'Can you give me a bit more time, though? I have my brother staying with me, another thing everyone seems to know. I need to talk further with him. He is my father's executor.'

'So, he's the one that will push for the will to be followed to the letter?' Hannah studied the ground for a moment. 'What about if he meets us? Maybe seeing what we do and how important it is to us will help him see things differently?'

'He would never go against our father's wishes.'

'Maybe not. Worth a try, though?'

Robert shook his head. 'I guess so but be prepared. We are very dissimilar.'

'Right then.' Hannah tapped her right foot. 'When will you bring him to visit?'

'Which *him* are you talking about?'

The small crowd spun around. William Sparkling stood in the dirt, a faint covering of dust on his polished leather shoes. He had one hand in his trouser pocket, the other dangling casually by his side. Sunglasses hid his eyes but Rosemary saw the tightness around his jaw.

'You, actually.' Hannah rubbed her head, making her hair spike. 'We want to show you Mulbury Feeds.'

'Why?' William leaned over to look past people into the shed. 'I don't have any cows.'

'We don't just cater for cows,' said Hannah, scowling. 'Come and look.'

There was a moment when Rosemary thought William would refuse, but he followed Hannah inside the shed, walking casually with his hand still in his pocket. Robert looked at Rosemary, closing his eyes briefly to shake his head, then went in behind them. The rest of them trailed behind, Rosemary coming along last.

The shed was cooler than outside. It was full of earthy odours from the sun-dried hay and displays of potting mix. They were comforting smells to Rosemary, reflective of animals and gardens, but she saw William's shoulders stiffen. As Hannah pointed out the range of products as they passed, his steps became shorter and his head tipped back as if repelling smells.

Hannah stopped at the entrance to the partitioned area where the more delicate items were sold. 'You can see how we've expanded the business. It supports us well.' She cast a wide-eyed look at Robert.

'Yes,' he said, stepping towards his brother. 'Mulbury Feeds is a viable, should I say profitable, business, thanks to the work of the Hubbard sisters and Milly, of course.'

Milly shook her head and pointed at Hannah.

William didn't react. He stared into the shop. 'Is that a stuffed bird?'

'Rescued,' said Heather, smiling at the raven on the counter. 'Poor thing.'

'You stuff birds?' One corner of William's mouth lifted.

'Restore,' said Heather, more loudly. 'Rescue.' She clutched at the hem of her shirt.

'Heather is very talented,' said Robert.

Again, his brother appeared not to hear. He looked through the open back shed door. 'Is that a house?'

'Home,' said Heather quietly. 'Our home.' The bottom of her shirt creased in her hand.

'That's where we've always lived,' said Hannah, scowling at William. 'It is very definitely our home.'

William turned to look at her, then Heather, and back to Hannah. 'I understand your sister got out?'

'What? Holly? She went with Toffee-'

'She got out.' William nodded. 'As you two should do, given the opportunity. Especially for an artist like you.' He nodded at Heather, indicating the satin jacket she was wearing. 'You are a gifted seamstress.'

Heather smiled at him. 'I don't need to leave to be artistic, Mr Sparkle Two. Mulbury is my home and my muse.'

William stared at her for a moment, something unreadable crossing his face like a spasm, before he swivelled around, his shoe crushing a few blades of lucerne lying on the floor. 'Thanks for the tour.' He raised his free hand and walked with long strides down the length of the shed.

There was silence until Hannah clapped her hands, breaking the uneasiness. 'Right, well, we're locking up for the night. Come on, Heather.' She strode off but stopped when her sister didn't follow. 'What is it?'

Heather curled a length of hair around her finger. 'That Mr Sparkle.' She nodded in the direction of William's exit. 'He doesn't understand home.'

'Yeah, well, lucky we do.' Hannah reached for Heather's hand to tug her gently away. 'Come on. There's work to do.'

As Rakisha filled Milly in on dinner plans, Rosemary went to where Robert was still standing. His gaze didn't leave the container of garden soil in front of him. 'Thinking about growing vegetables?'

'Sorry?'

Rosemary pointed at the soil. 'You'll need to add a bit more organic matter.'

He frowned and twigged to what she was saying. 'Oh. Sorry. Miles away.'

'What's next, Robert Sparkling?'

'What do you mean?'

'How are you going to win over your brother?'

He went back to staring at the soil. 'You don't win over William, Rosemary. I'll have to work out another way to solve this.' He thrust his hands into his pockets. 'Roman has invited him to the memorial dinner he's hosting.'

'Right.'

'I wish he hadn't. I prefer the family dynamics stay within the family I have left.'

'What is he doing here, Robert? He doesn't have to visit Mulbury to execute the will.'

'Ah.' Robert rocked back on his heels. 'That's the issue, isn't it? We hadn't spoken for five years before our father's funeral and suddenly he invites himself to Mulbury. The business occupies his life and his after-hours time is full of beery parties with fellow entrepreneurs. His time out is usually to do some high-risk adventure holiday with the same people. Running with the bulls. Visiting Chernobyl. Caving. All with expensive guides.' He sighed, 'But it isn't enough. The game we've played all our lives is *I want what he's having*. That's how he thinks.' He grimaced. 'I must have given him the impression I very much like living here and he wanted to find out why. And it's to do with...well, other things.'

Rosemary nodded slowly. The strain in Robert's voice

was hard to hear. She was much more used to his casual contentment with life, and his generous support to anyone who needed it. 'This is more than normal sibling rivalry.'

'Oh, there's nothing normal about our relationship.'

'How did it happen, Robert? What caused this rift?'

Robert looked up at the ceiling as if checking for cobwebs and Rosemary scolded herself.

'My apologies. It's none of my business.'

He turned to her and shrugged. 'I'm not sure there was one specific thing, Rosemary. A cumulation of childhood incidents, including stupid competition for our father's favour. Maybe one day I'll tell you the horrible stories.'

'You don't have to.'

'I know.' His gaze went over her shoulder to the road going up the hill. 'But of all the people I've met over the last decade or so, you are the one I think would listen without judgement.'

'Right. When you're ready then.'

'Oh, darling, I'm ready now.' Rakisha stumbled in behind Rosemary, clutching her arm as she nearly fell. 'Milly is coming along. So kind of you to invite us.'

Rosemary steadied the woman, feeling through the layers of clothing an arm sharp with boniness. 'It's no problem.'

'It is kind of you,' Milly said, coming up alongside Rakisha. 'Is it alright if I bring Rufus? He's usually very placid.'

'He's very welcome. Sunny will let him know if he's not placid enough.'

Milly laughed, stooping to pick up the tiny dog at her feet. Rosemary reached out a hand for him to sniff and he gave it a thorough going over before extending a pale pink tongue to lick her fingers. She smiled at the terrier's enthusiasm. 'Looks like we're friends.'

The three women left Hannah to close and went back to The Preserved Mulbury where Milly chatted brightly of the work she'd done that day—lots of potting on—while Rakisha helped Rosemary prepare the vegetables for the curry. Despite a bit of flapping around and the occasional dropping of utensils, Rakisha was surprisingly adept at cubing carrots and sweet potato, so much so that Rosemary couldn't help saying, 'You've done this before, Rakisha.'

'Oh, yes, darling.' Rakisha tipped the vegetables into a bowl and reached for a stem of bok choi. 'When I was in the commune, one of my jobs was vegetable preparation. I did it for years.'

Rosemary continued stirring the pan, suddenly aware of the little she knew about Rakisha despite being neighbours for more than five years. 'You were in a commune, Rakisha?'

'I know, darling, I'm sure you can't imagine me there.' Rakisha hoisted her arm up to make her sleeve fall away from her hand, multiple bangles rattling along with it. 'We had such a lovely time until...'

'Until?'

'Oh, darling, until we didn't, if you know what I mean.' She fell silent, deftly chopping the rest of the green vegetables.

Rosemary waited, stirring quietly. 'I don't know what you mean.'

'You see...' Rakisha rested the knife on the board and looked across as where Milly sat on the couch with Rufus. 'We had a comfortable, hard-working lifestyle with every day filled with the bounties of Mother Earth and nature's gifts as we reaped what we sowed according to the cycles of the moon.'

Rosemary had a vision of twenty people dressed like Rakisha dancing in the moonlight. She shook her head to free it. 'Sounds idyllic.'

'Yes, doesn't it? Falling into our beds every night, exhausted but content. Singing around fires, weaving our fabrics... idyllic, darling, yes.' She paused. 'But, darling, times change. It only takes one person to throw a stone into a puddle to make ripples.' She wiped her face free of flyaway curls and started slicing tomatoes with her head down, making the last words hard to hear. 'One person, another way of looking...'

'What happened to the commune, Rakisha? In the end?'

'It finished, darling, as do all things in time.'

'Because of one person?'

'One person with an obsession can do a lot of damage, darling.' Rakisha sighed and went back to her tomatoes.

Rosemary put the rest of the vegetables in the curry and stirred in silence. One person had interrupted Rakisha's world just as one person seemed intent on ruining Robert's. One person was enough.

FIFTEEN

Saturday started with a bang, literally. Two visitors in a white sedan collected another couple in a red sports car right outside The Preserved Mulbury, resulting in many loud exchanges of insults and a nasty scratch down the side of the sports car. Rosemary watched the action through her front window with Sunny in her arms, ready to head out to help reconcile the situation. She wasn't needed, however, as a burly man walked over to the arguing drivers and had it all sorted within moments. The visitors exchanged information and went on their way. 'Geoffrey did that quickly,' said Rosemary to the cat. 'Lucky he was around.'

Sunny waved her tail as Rosemary put her down as if in agreement.

Geoffrey's visit to see Tallulah had gone completely out of Rosemary's mind. She opened the door of the shop and stepped out to greet him.

'Rosemary,' the detective said. 'Good to see you. How is Mrs Lionel?'

'She's very well.'

'I'll drop in on her after I finish your daughter's excellent rhubarb and apple slice.'

'A bit early for cake.'

'Well.' Geoffrey shook his head ruefully. 'The older I get, the less I care about what I should be doing and the more I think about what I'd like to do.'

Rosemary couldn't argue with that. It was what she was feeling more and more as well, but to hear it from a senior police officer who spent his days chasing law and order could mean only one thing. 'You are about to retire.'

Geoffrey straightened. 'What? How would you know that?'

'It's a topic you usually stay away from but here you are, in Mulbury, early on a Saturday, coming to visit a baby. I'd say you're getting into practice.'

The older man was still for a moment, staring at her with the hint of the command Rosemary suspected he used on the younger members of his unit. He relaxed suddenly. 'You are quite amazing, Rosemary.' He sighed heavily. 'Yes, I've given my superiors a date, and I can only imagine the gleeful rubbing of hands from those priming for my position. It's not for a couple of months.'

'Are you happy with your decision?'

He thought for a moment. 'Yes. In fact, the more I think of it, the happier I am.' He turned a steely gaze to Rosemary. 'I've been working six days a week for the last ten years. Even when I'm home, I take work with me. I've seen more dead bodies than I've had decent dinners in that time.' He put his hands behind his back and tilted his chin at the display of quinces in the window. 'Perhaps I'll have time to help out my friends in their business endeavours.'

'You will be very welcome. Mrs Lionel in particular

needs a hand now and then.' Rosemary paused. 'And Roman would like help in his restaurant.'

'Ah.' Geoffrey smiled broadly. 'I see your segue, Rosemary Exeter. You want to know what's happening with the investigation.'

'Of course.'

He laughed, a deep guffaw that rocked his shoulders. 'You know I can't share anything with you.'

'I understand.' Rosemary stepped closer. 'Perhaps you could confirm, or not, my suspicions.'

'Hmm.' The detective rocked on his heels. 'Try me.'

'Two bodies have been found in The Leftover Restaurant. Bob Brownlee was stuffed into the first aid CPR mannikin's case, which is noticeably suspicious and therefore remains a homicide enquiry.'

Geoffrey gave the smallest of nods.

'The other man, Warwick Jones, was unfortunately doing an investigation by himself and his death was untimely but not premeditated.'

'What makes you say that?'

'He had many things against him: age, size, evidence of chronic conditions. I'd say he was unlucky for his death not to occur in a better place. He had broken into the restaurant, however, so had he been caught alive, he may have been charged with that.'

Again, Geoffrey nodded.

'But the homicide investigation is focused on who, why and where Bob Brownlee met his end. I suspect you're waiting on the postmortem results as, to my untrained eye in the short time I saw the dead man, there was no obvious signs of how he died.'

Geoffrey narrowed his eyes at her. 'You aren't after my job, are you? Even before I retire.'

'No thanks. I'm quite happy making jam.'

'Hmm.' Geoffrey tugged at his sport coat. 'Talking about jam, I'd better go back to my cake before Honey thinks I don't want it. I might see you before I go when I drop in on Mrs Lionel.'

'See you later, perhaps.'

Rosemary watched as Geoffrey went back into Honey B's Teas, reluctant to go back inside away from the mild day with its crown of beautiful blue sky. She stood there so long, a door sighed behind her and Jasper stepped out of The Read Mulbury to join her. 'Lovely day,' he said, hooking a piece of hair behind his ear where it sprang out immediately.

'Your hair's not quite long enough yet to always stay put.'

'Getting there.'

'Yes.'

Jasper put his hands in the front pockets of his jeans. 'You were talking to Geoffrey.'

'Yes. He's retiring.'

'Is he?' Jasper shook his head. 'Never thought I'd see that day.' He swayed to and fro. 'And did he reveal much? About...' He pointed his head to the Square.

'No. As tight-lipped as ever. Although he did confirm they are investigating a murder in Bob Brownlee's case, not the other man's.'

'Oh, right.'

Rosemary was quiet for a moment. 'Jasper, didn't you organise the first aid training?'

'Yes. Looks like I'll have to organise another time so we can complete it.'

'Where is it based?'

'The training business? In Big Town.'

'Do you think they'll be open today?'

'Maybe. It's Saturday. I could ring them.'

'Ask whether we can visit to talk about an advanced course designed for business owners.'

'But we haven't done the basic course yet.'

'I know.'

Jasper studied her. 'You don't really care about an advanced course.'

'I care, of course.'

'Okay, you care, but that's not why you want to visit them today.'

She smiled. 'How well you know me.'

He shrugged, turning back to his shop. 'Sometimes you don't realise how obvious you are. I'll go and ring them.'

A busload of older people turned the corner into Goldmarket Road and Rosemary went into The Preserved Mulbury to prepare for the rush. She almost missed Jasper's text—*Meeting Bern at two o'clock*—in the franticness heralded by the bus as twenty women intent on marmalade crowded the shop. Somewhere in that time, though, she managed to ask Milly to look after the place for a couple of hours in return for several jars of pickles to liven up the tofu and bean dishes at Rakisha's, and Heather to manage the bookstore in return for any dead birds they might see on the journey to and from Big Town. At half past one, she met Jasper under the veranda in front of his shop.

'I get to ride in your new car,' said Jasper.

'It's just a car, Jasper,' she said as she opened the mauve vehicle.

Jasper slid into the passenger's seat. 'You and I both know that's not true.'

Rosemary froze momentarily before slipping behind the steering wheel. Jasper knew about Alasdair, everyone did, but she thought she'd kept anything to do with him well-hidden. 'What do you mean?'

'I mean, you wouldn't have this car if it wasn't for Ken.' He reddened slightly. 'It was nice of him to give you a discount.'

Rosemary started the car and pulled from the curb. 'He gave me a discount because of you.'

'What do you mean?'

She concentrated on turning onto the road to Big Town, wondering whether Jasper was testing her. The tango classes were an opportunity for Ken and Jasper to get to know each other more but it seemed it hadn't occurred to Jasper just why Ken wanted his company.

'Nothing.' She put her foot down as they went outside Mulbury's speed limits.

Jasper grunted but his attention was taken by the D-Day Development's billboard. 'I heard they're proposing a shopping mall. And a 24-hour petrol station! That would be hideous.'

Rosemary said nothing but an image of Robert's face loomed in her head.

Big Town had the half-deserted look of a medium-sized rural town on a Saturday afternoon. Except for the big supermarket and a handful of cafes, everything else was closed. Jasper directed her along the main road to a dark office building lit only by the light in one area showing the silhouette of a solitary man working at his desk. She pulled the car up alongside. 'This is where they are?'

'Apparently they share the area with other classes.'

Rosemary peered into the area. 'Looks empty. Not much happening now.'

'Finished for the day is my guess.' He unclicked his seat-belt. 'Coming?'

They got out and stood on the footpath. She recognised the building as also home to the rural insurance company she'd seen as she'd first driven her new car home. The door in front of them, though, was locked. 'Are you sure Bern's here?'

'Of course, I am.' A man walked up behind them, scowling. Rosemary remembered him immediately as the curt instructor from their incomplete basic first aid course. He tapped a large watch on his wrist. 'It's gone two o'clock. I've been looking for you.'

Jasper held out his hand in greeting but when Bern didn't take it, thrust it into his pocket. 'Thanks for seeing us. We didn't quite get our class finished last time.'

'No.' If Bern's scowl had been any deeper, he wouldn't have been able to see. 'Total waste of an afternoon, that one. And they took my mannikin's case and haven't given it back.'

'Oh, well, perhaps you have another one in there?' Jasper waved his hand at the building.

'You think I have mannikin cases coming out of my ears, do you?'

'Well, no...'

Rosemary cleared her throat and Bern's stare turned to her. 'Did you find the mannikin itself? The one that should have been in the case?'

'I didn't. The police did.'

'Where?'

'Among Silviana's things.'

'Silviana?'

'You know, the woman who does...' Bern waved his hand around '...yoga. Cecil was propped up in her mats, half-hidden by those cushiony things they have.' He rolled his eyes. 'The police joked he looked very *Zen*, whatever they meant by that. They tried to take him away, too, but in the end, they only dusted him for fingerprints. Nearly ruined, Cecil was. All that powdery stuff over his skin. Took me an age to clean.'

'Did they find any fingerprints?'

'No, of course not. I clean him after every use. It was a total waste of time. Someone had just heaved him out of the case to do...' He waved his arms in a large configuration that could have meant anything from practising CPR to death by dancing. 'Amazing he wasn't broken. He was very expensive, you know. High-fidelity model and all.' Bern flicked his gaze back and forth between them. 'You want to book another course?'

'We'd love to talk to you about a specific course for small business owners but feel we should run it on your premises considering what happened last time.' Rosemary tried a winning smile but Bern only blinked at her. 'We have some more elderly members of our community and need to check your facilities first.' She sent a silent message to Mrs Lionel to say she didn't mean her.

'Right. Come in then.' Bern unlocked the door. 'I haven't got all day.'

They followed him in and up a flight of stairs where he tried to unlock another door, cursing slightly under his breath as it stuck. Rosemary had a chance to look around the foyer, noticing its one clumpy monstera plant in the corner and a single chair next to a coffee table holding tractor magazines. Tractors? She looked into the adjacent office to see it was the home of rural insurance. In fact, the lone man at the desk was heading towards them, looking with concern at Bern's attempt to open the door.

'Everything alright, mate?'

Bern waved a key at the man as he approached. 'Ridiculous, Terrence. I've asked maintenance to look at this lock just as you've asked them to fix the light in your office. How many times do we need to ask?'

'As many as it takes.' The insurance man produced a set of keys from his pocket and handed them over. 'I don't think it's the lock, I think it's your key. Mine works okay. Try these.'

It took Rosemary a moment of staring at the men's actions to work it out. The keys, attached to a ring from which a dark stone dangled, were passed from one to the other. By the time she looked at the insurance man's face, it was clear he'd recognised her, as well. Terrence was the driver of Bunnie Brownlee's car on the night of the accident.

SIXTEEN

'Ah,' said Terrence, his expression wary. 'It's Rosemary, isn't it?'

'Yes.' Rosemary tried a smile. 'You are...?'

'Terrence.' The man hesitated before holding out his hand. 'Terrence Wright. I didn't get a chance to introduce myself last time we met.'

'You know each other?' Bern asked as he unlocked the door. 'Got insurance with him, have you, Roslyn?'

'We've met, although only in the dark.'

'Ah,' said Terrence again, his hand going to the heavy mop of hair on his head. 'That's right. It was dark.' He smoothed the thickness flatter with a practised hand. 'I should thank you for stopping that night because I don't think I did at the time.'

'No, you didn't. You had other things on your mind.'

'My word I did. I didn't expect a kangaroo to jump out like that.'

'Really? Don't you sell rural insurance? I thought you'd drive on country roads all the time.'

Terrence blinked a few times and looked at Jasper as if

he might save him. 'Well, yes, true, I do. Perhaps not in those circumstances. You know, at night, etcetera etcetera.'

Jasper nodded briefly. 'You have to be extra careful at night.'

Terrence smiled widely. 'Yes, yes, indeed. Got it, Bern?'

'Thanks.' Bern handed back the keys. 'Can you lock up after we leave, Terrence? You have a better key than mine. On Monday, I'll make an official complaint to maintenance about the effects a non-working lock will have on occupational health and safety of those with a deficit key.' He opened the door and beckoned Jasper in. 'It's not the first time they've breached the standards of this building, quite ridiculous how many times...' His voice faded as he went into the room, Jasper glancing back at Rosemary as he followed. She waved him on and held the door before turning back to Terrence. 'You work on Saturdays often?'

'I'm always here on a Saturday,' said Terrence. 'It's when I catch up on all the paperwork after spending most of the week on farms. It's quiet, particularly when Silviana finishes her classes at lunchtime.' He pointed to the room beyond the door. 'Yoga. Meditation. Lying around on mats. All that chanty, spiritual music and no wonder they look asleep. I get lots done when everyone leaves.' Terrence nodded at Bern who'd noticed Rosemary's absence and had stopped, tapping his foot on the ground. 'I'll leave you to it.'

'Thanks.'

Terrence nodded and hurried away.

'Coming, are you, Roseanne?' Bern called, his arms folded across his chest.

'Yes.' Rosemary went through the doorway, letting it shut behind her and getting a glimpse of Terrence back at his desk now staring out the window, the paperwork apparently forgotten for the moment.

'Right, then, must get on with it. Haven't got all day.'

Bern led Rosemary and Jasper into a large area which was set up for a meditation class but which, he explained, could easily hold up to thirty people for first aid training as lots of other groups used it. As Bern droned on about the importance of safe distancing and the washing of training bandages which added to the cost of any course, Rosemary studied the room. Big windows took in a view of roof tops and around its edges were three doors, all set with little glass windows. As Bern toured them around, she glanced in the first one which was obviously a chair storeroom. The second housed yoga mats and bolster cushions and it wasn't hard to imagine Cecil lying back amongst them. Through the third window, neat shelving held boxes of plastic bags, neck braces and books. 'Is this where you store your equipment?' she asked, not waiting for an answer as she pushed her way in.

'Well, yes, Rosalind.' Bern went in after her, scowling, leaving Jasper holding the door. 'I don't allow students in here, you know. Too many missing knee braces in the past, if you know what I mean.'

'Very understandable.' Rosemary went deeper into the room, ducking to peer under the last shelf. 'This is where Cecil lives.'

The resuscitation mannikin lay on his back on a collapsed trolley, dressed impeccably in a dark suit. His arms lay by his side, and he stared straight up with half-lidded plastic eyes. A modern style wig fashioned into respectable spikes finished the impression of a wealthy entrepreneur.

'Isn't he a beauty?' Bern knelt and touched the mannikin's arm reverently. 'Dressed him myself. Helps students to think of him as a businessman having a heart attack from all that stress.'

'A little stereotyped, isn't that notion?'

Bern shrugged and stood, the heavy scowl back on his face. 'Stereotypes can help with teaching, Rebecca. Don't you think, Jerry?'

Jasper nodded. 'I'm sure you'd know, Bern.' He indicated the room. 'Plenty of space in here, anyway.'

'Cecil usually takes up more room when he's in his case.' Bern tutted. 'If I ever get that case back after this unfortunate happening.'

'How do you think it happened?' Jasper pointed at Cecil. 'This unfortunate... happening?'

'They obviously dragged Cecil out of here and threw him into the next room.' Bern shook his head. 'If he'd landed on his face, it could have broken his airway and then what would we do? A resus mannikin without an airway? Useless!'

'I was thinking more of what you think about the murder itself.' Jasper's face warmed. 'I mean, how the murderers got the case in the first place to put Bob in.' He swung the door a little. 'This doesn't have a lock.'

'Yes, bad, isn't it? None of these storerooms have a lock. Another item I've asked the maintenance team about. It wouldn't be hard, eh, to put a lock on a door but they won't, they won't.' Bern threw his hands up. 'They say it's enough to have the front door and office area locked and that we can trust the other users of the big room.'

'Do you?' Rosemary pulled her gaze away from Cecil and his half-lidded stare.

'Do I what?'

'Trust the other users? The yoga instructor mainly, I'm guessing.'

'Silviana? She's not from around here but she's a harmless sort of hippie.' Bern looked to the ceiling as if having a hippie yoga instructor would be the living end. 'Other groups use the room for regular meetings or classes and Silviana's here nearly every day. The others get the key from me or Terrence or her. If you have a key you can get to any level of the building. They're master keys. Silly, isn't it? Giving tenants a master key! Ridiculous.'

'Did the police search in here?'

'Oh, yes. I couldn't get into the room for days, not even to get the van keys.' He pointed to a hook next to the door trim with a set of car keys on them. 'Then I had to clean up after they'd trashed the place. They found nothing of interest.' He shrugged and put out his hands to shoo them from the room. 'Now. We were talking about the suitability of the area for your first aid training.'

Rosemary let Jasper talk to Bern about their requirements while she trailed behind them, studying the big room for any other telltale signs a murder had taken place. Apart from the fact the room was equipped with sound proofing to subdue noise, it was just a large, empty area. Plenty of space to haul Bob Brownlee around with or without a mannikin case to stuff him in, with the likelihood of discovery very slim at a time as quiet as this one. She stopped suddenly. 'Bern.'

'Yes, Raylene?' Bern turned to her. 'Worried about the cost?'

'No. I'm more worried about your occupational health and safety.'

Bern glanced around the room as if it was full of hazards. 'What aspect of it?'

'Cecil is a full-sized, full-bodied mannikin. He must be

heavy, especially in his case. How do you lift him without hurting your back?'

Bern's face lit up. 'Thank you for asking! I take occupational health and safety very seriously, you know, Roslyn.'

'Indeed, I know you do.'

'I can answer your astute question.' Bern puffed his chest out, his eyes sparkling. 'When we raised money to buy Cecil, I put to our reference group we needed a trolley to move Cecil about. It added a bit to the overall cost, but it was necessary, you see, and we often hire the trolley out to others who need to move decent loads. Adds to our fundraising efforts.'

'Yes, I do see. Cecil weights quite a lot, I imagine.'

'He does! About the weight of a real man, and add the case to that, you have a very heavy object indeed. We needed a trolley that can go up and down so Cecil could be easily moved on to the floor and then back in his case with minimal effort.' Bern squatted suddenly and rose again. 'See? I can always keep my back straight while manipulating him.'

'Clever,' said Jasper.

'Necessary,' said Bern.

'And that's how you move him in and out of the van.'

'Yes.'

'So, the day you came to do the course with us, you came in early to pack?'

'No.' Bern shifted irritably. 'For Saturday afternoon courses, I have to wait for Silviana to finish her yoga-ing or whatever classes she has. She nearly has a pink fit if I come in early.' He jabbed a finger at Jasper. 'Never disturb a hippie playing sounds of nature.'

Jasper nodded thoughtfully. 'Thanks for the tip.'

'I make sure I leave everything clean and ready to be

packed in the van so I don't have to worry about the correct number of gloves for a session. I leave the van key in its place ready for me.' Bern stamped his foot. 'That Saturday, Silviana was running overtime, something about needing a longer shavassing.'

'Shavasana,' said Rosemary absently.

Bern frowned at her. 'I had to rush in, grab the keys, load my boxes and Cecil on the trolley, and head down to the van. It was a rush to get to your class in time.'

'When you packed the van, you didn't notice anything about the mannikin? It wasn't heavier than usual?'

Bern frowned. 'Cecil is as heavy as a real man. I didn't notice anything different.'

'Before our class, when had you last used Cecil for training?'

Bern's eyes narrowed. 'Are you sure you don't work for the police? This is what they asked me. I'll tell you what I told them. I had a class Tuesday morning at a school, brought the van back at lunchtime, and took everything back to the storeroom. I wiped Cecil down, restocked my equipment, and had my equipment ready for my next session which happened to be yours. I always leave everything ready for next time.'

Rosemary put a finger against her bottom lip and tapped in. 'When did you say you found Cecil?'

'I didn't, Rachael. The police did.' Bern's eyebrows went up and down a few times.

'Not Silviana?'

'She said he wasn't there Saturday morning.'

'What do you mean?'

Bern frowned. 'He wasn't there when she set up her class. She had to get her mats out and she swears he wasn't there.'

'Perhaps he was and she just didn't see Cecil amongst the cushions.'

'You could be right, Roberta. The police said he was right at the back but I wouldn't trust Silviana to see a banana peel on a pavement.' He huffed. 'She doesn't have her feet on the ground, that one.'

Jasper peered back in the yoga storeroom. 'And you didn't see Cecil when you came in to pack? There's glass in this door.'

Bern frowned so hard, his eyebrows hid his eyes. 'Listen here, Juniper. Like I told the police and they wouldn't believe me either, Cecil was not in view when I came in. I was busy packing but I am a *noticer*, young man. A *noticer*. I would have noticed an eighty-kilogram CPR mannikin lying among a bunch of flowery mats.'

Rosemary put her hand on Jasper's arm as he opened his mouth, no doubt to apologise, for his face had gone alarmingly red. 'We believe you, Bern. You are a noticer.'

'Thank you, Richelle. Much appreciated. Now.' He waved his hand to take in the room. 'Will we talk about costs?'

'I think not,' said Rosemary, looping her arm through Jasper's and starting slowly for the exit. 'The room is lovely and very adequate for our purposes. If you wouldn't mind emailing Jasper the information so our business committee can decide on what to do.'

Bern rubbed his hands together. 'Certainly, certainly. I will do that right away.'

'Thank you.' Rosemary let Jasper go. 'And now, we must be off. Things to do.'

'Yes, away you go.' Bern's attention was on something in the storeroom. 'I must count my gauze pads before I leave.'

'Goodbye,' said Jasper, but Bern had already disappeared into the back of the room.

They left him to it, pushing their way out the door and down the steps. Terrence was still at his desk, facing the screen in front of him, his large silhouette smooth against the light of the window.

'What do you think?' said Jasper, as Rosemary turned the car around to head home.

'I think, if we wanted, we could have a course in that building.'

'Huh?' said Jasper. 'Is that the real reason we went there today?'

'What do you think?'

Jasper was quiet for so long they'd almost reached the D-Day Development board before he spoke. 'I think,' he said quietly, 'that I have no idea what you think but that it's a step in the right direction. Yes?'

Rosemary glanced at Jasper, partly to not look at the billboard and partly to smile at him. 'Jasper, you are one hundred percent correct'.

SEVENTEEN

Despite now being able to imagine Bern the first aid instructor loading an already-packed Bob in the case onto the trolley and into the van bound for Mulbury, Rosemary couldn't quite reconcile how Bob was so neatly in the case. He was a blubbery sort of fellow and would have been quite difficult to arrange. She slowed down for the turn into Mulbury.

'You're thinking very loudly.'

'You can hear me thinking?' She glanced again at Jasper, who had twisted around to watch the tacky D-Day Development billboard as it melted into the distance. 'I can hear you doing the same.'

'That development scheme... it's too horrible to contemplate.'

Rosemary chewed her lip for a moment. 'It's a Sparkling company.'

Jasper switched his attention to her. 'What?'

'D-Day Development. It was owned by Robert's father.'

'*Was* owned? Robert's father is dead. Who owns it now?'

'It remains in the family.'

Jasper stared straight ahead as the car crawled past houses. 'What does that mean?'

'Just what it says.'

'Is that another reason why William is here?'

'Perhaps. It all has to do with their father's wishes.'

Jasper sighed, putting his arm along the windowsill as The Exceptional Tree came into view. 'Robert's situation is not quite as straight forward as it seems. This has more to it than simply selling one of his properties to support another.'

'Yes.'

'But you won't say what it is.'

Rosemary felt her cheeks warm. 'I've said too much already. I shouldn't have started the conversation that night in the restaurant. Robert told me in confidence.'

'It wasn't only you. Roman knew all about it.' Jasper rubbed his face as they pulled up in front of The Read Mulbury. 'It doesn't really matter. Robert should know we're only trying to help him figure a way out of the mess he's found himself in. I was wrong, you know.'

Rosemary turned off the ignition. 'Wrong about what?'

'I said Robert was lucky to be wealthy. Being rich has its own set of problems.'

'Yes.' Rosemary reached out to touch Jasper's arm. 'Problems I hope we can help with.'

'How?'

'I don't know yet. Something will come to me.'

'Okay, I trust you.' Jasper put his hand briefly on Rosemary's. 'I'd better go. I see Heather's got her hands full.'

Rosemary ducked to see out the passenger side window. The bookshop was brimming with people. 'What's happening in there?'

'I forgot to tell her about the sale I've got on. Two free books with every one purchased.'

'*Two* free books?'

'Yeah, I know. I was trying to get rid of old stock and multiple copies. Looks like I underestimated the appeal.'

Jasper pushed his way out of the car and ran into the bookshop while Rosemary took her time getting out. The Preserved Mulbury looked empty, as did The Green Mulbury next to it. Books were winning in the sales department that afternoon. Rosemary took the chance to thank Milly by loading her up with chutneys as she left before flicking the door sign to *Back in 5 pickly minutes* and heading to Honey B's Teas. Unlike the other shops, the tearoom closed at four o'clock, and she could see Ronnie sweeping the floor with Cuddles patting the broom with a paw. Honey and Tallulah were nowhere to be seen.

'Hi, Rosemary,' said Ronnie as she pushed open the door. 'What's up?'

'Just saying hello.'

'Okay.' Ronnie scrubbed at his head, making his wispy hair tangle. 'Honey's having a nap with Tallulah.'

'That's good. Is she alright?'

'Tallulah or Honey?' Ronnie chuckled. 'Actually, they're both the most beautiful things I've ever seen. And they're both alright.'

Rosemary tried not to shake her head at Ronnie's melted expression. 'Ronnie, are you doing any work at the moment for Geoffrey?'

Ronnie shook his head. 'No. I just can't fit in any more jobs. He wanted me to help with the restaurant murder, but I don't have time.'

'What did he want you to do?'

'Dig around for information about some people. He didn't say who.'

'Did he give you any clues?'

Ronnie frowned, concentrating. 'He said what he usually says: most murders are committed by someone known to the victim.'

'He wanted you to investigate those closest to Bob Brownlee.'

'Most likely. It would be a sensible place to start.'

Rosemary smiled at her son-in-law. 'You've changed, Ronnie.'

Ronnie's face mottled. 'Oh. I have? Is that good? What did I say?'

'You used the word *sensible*. I don't think you would have a few years' ago.'

'Wouldn't I have?' Ronnie's face now had the colour of a liquefied strawberry and vanilla ice cream. 'Gosh.'

Rosemary put up a hand. 'Anyway, will we see you tonight?'

'Actually, no. We told Roman we wouldn't be there. Tallulah's not sleeping so well because of her teeth. We're all a bit tired.'

'That's sensible.' Rosemary grinned as she backed out the door, leaving Ronnie patting at his hot face.

IN DEFERENCE to the memorial dinner, Rosemary dressed soberly before heading out the door at six thirty to collect Mrs Lionel. The older woman had thought the same and sported a navy dress with matching coat as she stepped out of The Green Mulbury to join Rosemary. 'You are reminiscent of Queen Elizabeth II,' Rosemary said.

Mrs Lionel tugged at the coat's lapel. 'Thank you. I just don't have a handbag to match.'

Rosemary smiled, linking arms with her friend as they walked across Goldmarket Road to The Leftover Restaurant. They were right on time but everyone else was early, for they opened the door of the old bank building to a hum of noise and people seated at a long table. Heather and Hannah faced each other across the table, Heather superb in one of her upcycled creations possibly crafted out of a beaded evening gown while Hannah had traded her worn oilskin jacket for a slightly less worn red leather one. Rakisha and Milly sat with Jasper in between them, while Robert had his back slightly turned away from a stylishly cut version of himself seated with Kelly. 'William's here,' said Rosemary quietly.

Mrs Lionel nodded. 'Yes, he looks so much like Robert, only...harsher.'

William noticed them enter and smiled at Rosemary but it was thin-lipped and didn't reach his eyes. 'I see what you mean,' she said softly.

On one side of the table, four people wearing maroon shirts, each adorned with an embroidered 'A-BTPI', huddled together talking. Bunnie Brownlee sat back in her chair, almost lost in the folds of the man and woman either side of her, with her hands, resplendent with two rings made from dark stones, resting on the edge of the table. Another man leaned in on the conversation, his broad torso squashing the woman on the left of Bunnie back in her chair. Rosemary walked over to sit next to him, recognising his sleek hair from earlier that afternoon. He didn't look up as she sat.

Jules came over to Mrs Lionel, holding the chair out at

the head of the table. 'For you,' she said as the older woman sat down. 'We saved it especially.'

'Thank you,' said Mrs Lionel, studying the table. 'Is there room for everyone?'

'Oh, yes.' Jules placed Mrs Lionel's napkin on her lap. 'Patti and Gerry had something else on so everyone who's coming is here. Roman will be in soon to announce dinner.'

In the ten or so minutes it took Roman to appear, Rosemary sat quietly to listen to the voices around her. Milly explained to Jasper what was meant by hot composting as Rakisha sat fidgeting with her bangles and looking as if she'd rather be on another planet than in the room. Across from Milly, the memorial guests from Big Town continued in hushed tones, although Rosemary caught the words 'tonight', 'happy', and 'electricity'. Kelly had William engaged with a long, boring story about something irrelevant as William's expressionless face told Rosemary. Robert succumbed to Heather plucking at his shirt and describing how it could be made more enchanting with an embroidered upcycle. Hannah talked earnestly to Mrs Lionel about the future of Mulbury Feeds, and Mrs Lionel caught Rosemary's eye with a look of alarm.

'Welcome, friends.'

Roman stood at the other end of the table dressed in black trousers and a pristine white coat. He held his toque in his hand and directed a sober look to the out-of-town guests.

'I thank you for attending our dinner tonight and welcome all to The Leftover Restaurant. I hope this small celebration of the lives of the two men who died here will be of some comfort to his friends and family.' Roman dipped his head, his moustaches wobbling.

'Thank you,' said the man hunched over Bunnie as he

sat back. 'Bunnie and our team are very grateful for this opportunity to consider Bob and say goodbye to Warwick.' He leaned back to see the table's occupants, startling a little at Rosemary. 'I'm Terrence. This is Alicia and Donald. And you know Bunnie.'

Roman introduced the rest of the table. Terrence nodded his head solemnly at each person but Bunnie didn't seem to hear. She swivelled around every few seconds, looking over one shoulder then the next.

'It is lovely to have you here, Terrence,' said Mrs Lionel as Roman finished. 'Would you mind telling me, dear, what your team represents?' She touched her lapel and indicated the writing on the maroon shirts.

Terrence mirrored her action, smoothing the letters. 'We are the A Team of the original Big Town Paranormal Investigators. A-BTPI.'

Mrs Lionel smiled. 'And what does that mean, dear?'

Terrence leaned forward, a sparkle in his eye. 'We examine evidence of the supernatural.'

'Oh, you're part of the larger group that gathered in the Square this week?'

'No!' Terrence raised his hand in admonishment as his shout died down. 'No, we're a functioning, lone team surrounded by idiots.'

William reached for his wine glass. 'You're ghosthunters.'

Terrence's lip curled. 'A crude interpretation of the valuable work we do. That's what the uninitiated say.'

William raised his glass. 'Or the sceptical. Or even those who trust in science.'

Terrence clasped his hands tightly on the table. 'Or those who fear trusting their own experiences. Would that be you?'

'No, mate.' William grinned. 'The only thing I'm scared of is litigation.'

Terrence scowled. 'The common view is wrong. Paranormal investigation is scientific. It brings science to the explanation of unexplained phenomena.'

Rosemary thought William would continue but he seemed to lose interest, instead draining his glass and keeping a cold eye on Terrence. No one asked any more questions and the A-BTPI team offered nothing more, so an uncomfortable silence covered the table until Roman cleared his throat. 'I will shortly be bringing you first course, a seasonal expose of roasted zucchini and tomato.'

'Yes!' Bunnie Brownlee leaned forward, elbows akimbo, pushing her companions out of the way. 'Zucchini is Bob's favourite vegetable!'

Roman stiffened, momentarily startled, then smiled magnanimously. 'Splendid. I will be but a moment.'

'Did Roman do that on purpose?' asked Hannah in Rosemary's ear. 'Is he going to cook everything the dead man liked because, let's face it, it's not going to matter.'

'I'm not sure it was deliberate.' Rosemary kept her eyes on Bunnie. 'This may be the theme of the night.'

As Bunnie exclaimed at all five courses Roman presented, Rosemary's guess was correct. 'Mushroom, Bob's favourite soup!' 'Chicken, Bob's favourite meat!' 'Toffee and date, Bob's favourite dessert!' 'Cheese, Bob's favourite-'

'Dairy food?' suggested Hannah under her breath.

'-dairy food!'

'Unbelievable,' said Hannah, taking a slab of blue to add to a cracker.

Rosemary watched Bunnie's agitation, and the way her hands shot out with each shout as if she was having a spasm. Her fingers were long and frail-looking, the look exaggerated by the heaviness of the rings with their chunky stones. Quiet conversation had permeated the meal, mainly from Mrs Lionel and Jules. Jasper managed a quick chat about book genres with Robert along the table but Robert kept asking the same question about the definition of Nordic noir, so Jasper stopped and tried to talk to Rakisha but she didn't respond to his cheery remark about the depth of the purple in one of her cheesecloth layers. Kelly blabbed on about something but as William didn't engage, she let the words fade away.

Heather's leaned over the table to Rosemary. 'I finished my ibis,' she said softly. 'Would you like to see my birds?'

'Yes,' said Rosemary just as quietly. 'Very much so.'

'Tomorrow? Ten o'clock?'

'Okay. I'll come down to you then.'

Heather shook her head. 'No, I'll come and get you.' She sat back and smiled, her hands stroking the linen table-cloth as if imagining it as a summer skirt.

The loudest actions at the table were Bunnie's exclamations. Perhaps everything Roman served *was* Bob's favourite, but it can't have been Bunnie's, as she barely touched a thing. She was too busy staring around, not at people, but at the walls and the doors and even, at one stage, the floor. The Mulburians politely ignored her odd behaviour. Most of them, anyway.

Rakisha's fidgeting reached an all-time rattle as the last of the cheese board disappeared. Jasper pushed his chair back in alarm as Rakisha jumped to her feet, her curls snagging on her plate, sending it crashing to the ground. 'Bunnie Lamont!' she shouted. 'Stop it, darling, just stop it!'

The room stilled. Bunnie's attention, which had been astray all night, suddenly fastened on Rakisha. The two women locked gazes, Rakisha's mouth trembling as she tried to form words while Bunnie's eyes widened. 'You,' she said finally. 'Raving Rakee.'

'You,' Rakisha said. 'Bunnie Boo.'

'Don't call me that.'

'Why not, darling?' Rakisha shook herself to fling her hair back. 'It suits you.'

Bunnie glared at Rakisha. Her eyes were deep set in her narrow face and surrounded by shadows from the low dining light and, Rosemary assumed, by fatigue. 'You tease me, like they always did.'

Rakisha's bangles clanked as she tugged furiously at her jacket. 'Not me, darling. I didn't tease.'

Bunnie shrugged, looking over Rakisha's shoulder. 'They teased. I was right, though. We had...' she lowered her voice to a hiss '...visitors.'

Rakisha closed her eyes briefly. 'We had visitors but not who you think. Our visitors, darling, were people coming to buy our produce or wanting connection to Mother Earth in all her natural beauty.'

'Hang on,' said William, smiling broadly. 'Were you both in a *commune*?'

'We preferred the term *community*, darling,' said Rakisha still staring at Bunnie. 'We were communitarians.'

William snorted. 'Right, *communitarians*.'

Mrs Lionel shifted in her seat. 'People living in communes in the 60s and 70s helped pave the way for eco-villages and the concept of simple living.'

William opened his mouth but stopped when he saw the warning look on Mrs Lionel's face. Instead, he reached for the wine bottle and topped his glass up. 'Okay then.'

'So, you both lived in the same commune?' Hannah asked. 'I bet that was fun.'

'It was...' Rakisha waved her arms around, bumping Jasper. 'It was...' She dropped her arms. 'And then it was gone.'

'And you came here to live,' said Mrs Lionel kindly. 'Mulbury gained a fine citizen.'

Rakisha blushed, blinking at Mrs Lionel with watery eyes. 'Thank you, darling. Mulbury embraced me with all its natural attributes and opportunities to share what I learned about the abundance of organic ingredients with my many happy customers!'

Rosemary covered her mouth with her napkin so Rakisha couldn't see her smile. Rakisha's customers often seemed more perplexed than happy, although Rosemary couldn't deny there were a certain number who returned for more brownies despite their rock-hard constitution. There was, she thought, no accounting for taste.

'What happened?' Hannah leaned her chin into her

hand and gazed across the table. 'Why did the commune close?'

Rakisha shook her head so it was Mrs Lionel who answered. 'All things have a time, Hannah. Nothing lasts forever.'

Hannah sat back, nodding. Eyes went to Bunnie and Rakisha again so it was only Rosemary who saw the tightening of Hannah's face and its paleness as she looked to Heather. The younger Hubbard sister, however, was humming to herself and smoothing the linen tablecloth.

Rosemary frowned but a squawk from the other end of the table made her swivel back to Bunnie Brownlee. The little woman was on her feet, pointing into the corner shadows of the dining room. 'Bob! Bob! I'm here!'

The scraping of chairs was loud as the guests turned to where Bunnie was indicating. Rosemary stretched up to see over Heather's head. There was something in the shadows, a blurred pale movement close to the ground.

Bunnie put both arms out. 'Bob, my love! Come to me! Be with me again!'

The blob paused and then ran out into the lit area.

'Rufus!' called Milly, bending down to sweep the little terrier into her arms. 'How did you get in here?'

Bunnie glanced at the dog before sticking her head out further to scan the shadows. 'Bob?'

'Unless Bob's a dog,' said Kelly, folding her arms across her chest, 'I don't think it's him.'

Bunnie scowled, peered once more at the wall, and sat heavily.

From his seat opposite Mrs Lionel, Roman twisted around to look towards the kitchen doorway. He got up and disappeared through it, returning a moment later, nodding.

'It is the back door. I now notice the latch is not catching. The little dog pushed, it opened.'

'That explains something,' said Rosemary, moving to face Terrence. 'Warwick Jones made his way into the restaurant, probably via that same faulty door. Sadly, he didn't make his way out again. He was a member of your team, wasn't he?'

Terrence looked grim. 'Warwick was a faithful A-BTPI.'

'But?'

'What do you mean, *but*?'

Rosemary tilted her head towards the window. 'I saw you and your *team* on Saturday night. Warwick was with you. He seemed reluctant.'

'Reluctant?'

'Whatever you were doing under the cover of darkness, he didn't want to be part of it.'

Terrence bit his lower lip, glancing at Alicia before he answered. 'He didn't understand.'

'Understand what?'

'The importance of what we were doing. The importance of teamwork. He thought he could do it himself.'

'Do what?'

Terrence shook his head. 'The work.'

William leaned forward over his empty plate. 'Just what is the work you want to do?'

It took a long time for Terrence to answer. He checked silently with his friends. They stared blankly back at him. Just as Rosemary thought he wouldn't answer, he said, 'We seek evidence of supernatural phenomenon.'

'Ah.' William laughed as he relaxed into the chair. 'You're ghosthunters but you've never seen a ghost, have you?'

'We have...'

'You have what?'

Terrence clicked his fingers and Donald reached under the table, pulling out a gadget from his backpack. 'We have readings on this and other devices.'

'EMF detectors and thermometers,' said Rosemary. 'Not the most accurate of instruments.'

'They're an indication.' Donald put the gadget back on the floor. 'They're one source of information. Paranormal investigation is like doing algebra. Things add up to be conclusive.'

'Gotcha.' William nodded, amusement sketched in the creases of his face. 'You need the ultimate proof.'

'Bob,' whispered Bunnie, her head down.

'But not Warwick.' Rosemary tilted her head. 'Why is that?'

'Warwick's death was a result of chronic health conditions,' Terrence said firmly. 'It was not unexpected.'

'Timely of him to die on a search for ghosts.'

Milly shifted Rufus so the little dog's head rested on her arm. 'Now he could be a ghost himself.'

'Not likely,' said Alicia. She pulled back sharply and clamped her mouth shut.

'Why not?' asked Milly. 'Why do some people become ghosts and others don't?'

'Roman has a theory,' said Jasper. 'You told us the other night.'

Roman's moustaches twitched as he thought. 'Yes. Ghosts are left behind when someone has unfinished business or they were taken suddenly.'

'So, Warwick's business was all wrapped up?' Milly asked.

'He was not a well man,' said Terrence. 'His doctors

didn't expect him to live a long life. He had his affairs sorted.'

Milly nodded. 'But you don't think Bob did?'

'Bob,' murmured Bunnie. 'My Bob.'

Milly took a sharp breath in. 'I'm so sorry, Bunnie. That was thoughtless of me. I remember when my husband died. We had a lot of time to prepare for his eventual passing, and I still found things not complete. It's very complicated.'

Whether Milly's words were any comfort to Bunnie, it was hard to tell. The little woman kept her head down. Milly bit her lip and started stroking Rufus rapidly.

Mrs Lionel broke the awkward silence. 'What a lovely dinner, Roman. A real tribute to the men whose lives we came to celebrate.' She raised her glass. 'To Bob and Warwick, dear friends of Bunnie, Terrence, Alicia, and Donald.'

Glasses clinked as muttered 'hear, hears' echoed around the room. Bunnie did not join in but at least lifted her head to gaze mournfully into the distance.

Terrence pushed his chair back and stood, dwarfing his companions beside him. 'Thank you, chef. We appreciate your efforts. It's getting late, though. We must go.' He glanced at Jasper. 'Don't want to have any other encounters with wildlife.'

'Drive slower then,' said Rosemary.

Terrence gave her a small smile. He clicked his fingers again and Donald turned to help Bunnie up. She allowed him to take her arm and he half-lifted her from the seat. Once she was up, she sagged, and Alicia gripped her other side. 'Bob?' said Bunnie, looking around. 'I can't see him.' Her gaze fell on Rakisha and her eyes widened. 'Raving Rakee, have you seen him?'

Rakisha shivered, her threaded beads clashing. 'No,

darling, just as I couldn't see Bumble or Oscar or Geraldine, our dear friends who died in the community.' She stood, chair scraping noisily. 'Once Mother Earth takes our darlings, they are enfolded in her arms and given back to the world. I told you that a long time ago.'

Bunnie shook her helpers off and brought her shoulders back, eyes fastened on Rakisha. 'And I've told you, lunatic, that souls live on around us. They appear when they want to but they're always there!'

Rakisha wiped hair from her face and put her hands on her hips. 'Bob isn't here, darling, face it. He returns to the Earth and you should be happy about it!'

Bunnie lunged across the table, making Rakisha scurry back, and was caught by Donald and Alicia. They pulled her off, and linked arms in hers. 'Thanks again,' said Terrence, as Bunnie was walked toward the exit. 'It really was...' The door shut behind them before the Mulburians could hear his conclusion.

Milly tucked the dog tighter in her arms and went to Rakisha who was trembling against the wall. 'Are you alright?'

Rakisha was quiet for a moment before reaching out a hand to stroke the little dog.

'He's a darling doggie,' she said quietly. 'I had a little doggie once.'

'Salty,' said Milly.

Rakisha went still. 'What was that, darling?'

Milly tickled Rufus behind his ear. 'You called this one Salty once. Is that what you meant?'

'Yes, darling. Salty. My little friend. I had forgotten how much...' Rakisha reached for Rufus and Milly handed him over.

'Well, Rufus is as much yours as he is mine, Rakisha.'

Milly put her arm around her friend. 'I'll take her home,' she said to the room. 'How about we leave any questions about tonight for tomorrow?'

'Thank you, Milly.' Jules hurried to the door so Milly could steer Rakisha through without stopping.

As it closed again, William laughed. 'Now I can see why you like it here, big brother! Never a dull moment, as they say. I bet you'll be sorry to leave.'

Heads swivelled to Robert at the news. He rapped the table with a nervous finger before he too rose and left the room. William swigged the rest of his drink and went after him.

'Well,' said Hannah when the room fell quiet. 'Tonight's stirred up a bit of mud, hasn't it?'

No one denied that.

NINETEEN

As Rosemary thought he would after their sombre exit from dinner the previous evening, Jasper came onto his balcony before eight the next morning, peering expectantly over the rail. She made two cups of tea and headed out, pausing to run her hand over Sunny's head as the cat settled on the back windowsill to watch. 'A bit of excitement last night,' said Rosemary.

Sunny's tail twitched. *Isn't there always?* it seemed to say.

Jasper reached for the mug as Rosemary stepped outside. 'Hey, thanks. I don't come out here just for the free tea.'

'Right.' Rosemary sipped the hot brew. 'Must be for the fresh air.'

'That, and Snowy needed a trip outside.' Jasper indicated the old dog ambling around the backyard. 'And maybe because I wanted your thoughts on what happened at the restaurant.'

'We had a very nice meal.'

'It was superb, wasn't it? But you know that's not what I

meant.' Jasper checked on Snowy again. 'We could have talked more last night but Roman moved us on.'

'He was wanting to clear up.'

'We could have helped him do that.'

'Part of Roman's immeasurable service is his generosity. He was in host mood. He would have been insulted if we'd done the dishes.'

'Yes, I guessed that.' Jasper drank his tea. 'So, what do you think of Bunnie?'

Rosemary stared out over her balcony. Her lavender needed pruning and Mr Cameron's trees were encroaching her yard. 'I think she's a grieving widow.'

'And what else?'

'I should do my butterfly bushes as well.'

'What?'

She pointed at the garden. 'Pruning. It's time.'

'Rosemary...'

She smiled at the exasperation in his voice. 'I think Bunnie's an *expectant* grieving widow.'

'What does that mean?'

'She is expecting Bob to reappear as a paranormal phenomenon.' Rosemary balanced her mug on the railing between the balconies. 'Her grief seems associated with the fact that he hasn't yet appeared, rather than the fact her husband is dead.'

'And what about the others in that group? Not particularly sad about Bob.'

'Or Warwick.'

'He hardly rated a mention.'

Rosemary nodded slowly. 'Did you note the lack of denial?'

'To what?'

'Roman's theory about who becomes a spectral being. No member of A-BTPI said anything to refute it.'

'You think Bob has unfinished business?'

'No doubt he has, but I don't think Roman's theory relates to whether Bob had his bills paid or his superannuation up to date.'

'You think *business* means something less financial.'

'Perhaps. Do you remember what else Roman said?'

'That someone taken suddenly might become a ghost.'

'Yes. Don't you think it strange?'

'What?'

'That the A-BTPI didn't refer to Bob's *murder* at all. It was as if he'd died like Warwick did, of medical complications.'

'I imagine that's not the case.'

'Do you think the rest of BTPI have the same expectation as Bunnie, that Bob will return in an ethereal form?'

'Yes.'

Jasper let his empty mug dangle from his fingers. 'Did you notice Terrence?'

'Of course.'

'I meant, did you notice Terrence's attention to Bunnie?'

'He was being a good friend.'

Jasper chuckled. 'That, and more.' He tapped his back pocket where his latest book usually was. 'You need to read the books I like.'

'I'm happy reading the books *I* like.' Rosemary took the mug from Jasper. 'Tell me, what am I missing?'

'All the romantic clues Terrence was giving out. His attention levels. His pandering to her mood. He could hardly eat his meal he was so busy helping her.'

Rosemary studied Jasper's dark sincere eyes. 'I'm not good at picking up romantic clues.'

Jasper's colour deepened but he said with a laugh, 'Don't I know it!'

'You also think Terrence is in love with Bunnie.'

'Yep.'

'Which means he'd do anything for her.'

'Like driving her to Mulbury in an endless search for her ghostly husband.' Jasper leaned his elbows on the rail. 'You saw them the night Bob was discovered. We saw them again. They come to dinner, not to eat but so Bunnie could moon into the shadows. He's by her side a lot.'

'What about the other members of the A-BTPI?'

'Terrence is the leader, I think. The others are followers.'

'Including Warwick?'

Jasper stretched back, letting his hands grip the rail. 'Maybe. Do you think Warwick was told to break into The Leftover Restaurant?'

'I have no idea.'

'It seems unlikely that he did it off his own bat.'

'We don't know his motives. We don't know the man at all.'

'We don't know any of them.' Jasper plunged his hands into his pockets. 'They're from Big Town but they aren't in the Agatha Christie Critics, the Historical Fiction Faction, or the Military Mamas.'

'Tell me they're book clubs and not bikie gangs.'

He nodded. 'Book clubs, or social groups made up of book people. So probably neither man were readers.'

'That leaves us none the wiser about their tribe.' Rosemary turned to go. 'I'm going to see Heather's ibis at ten o'clock. Keep an eye on my shop?'

'Sure will.' Jasper whistled to Snowy who began a slow climb up the wooden steps. 'Isn't the ibis in Heather's workshop?'

'Yes. Unless she's put it in the shed.'

'Odd.' He bent to pat the old dog before opening the back door for Snowy to go inside.

'What is? She does sell her creations from time to time.'

'Yes. But if the ibis is in her shed, why did she want to borrow my car?'

Rosemary frowned. 'Shopping, maybe?'

'Perhaps. Although she did say it was for something she had to do at ten o'clock.' He lifted a hand and went inside.

TWENTY

Rosemary had to wait longer than ten o'clock to find out what Heather was up to. An early people mover of grey-headed hikers appeared at nine thirty and pressed their faces up against her window until she let them in to stop the smudges. They bought jars of strawberry and jumbleberry jam which, according to one particularly garrulous man, was to sustain them through the three days of their hike. 'We don't walk very far,' he confided as he packed two jars away for himself. 'But we have faith the jam will see us through.'

His words gnawed at Rosemary long after the hikers scrambled into their car and drove away. Her jam was excellent but it was hardly going to supply the necessary nutrients for bushwalking. In fact, eating sugary jam before exercise was likely to induce a quick energy response leading to a crash after about ten minutes. But the hiker had faith in it, just as Bunnie Brownlee had faith in the return of her husband. How long would *that* belief sustain her?

Heather rapped at the door fifteen minutes later than expected. Rosemary had filled the shelves from the early morning deluge and was waiting at the counter. She gave Sunny a quick pat and strode to the door.

Heather smiled as she opened it. 'You'll need your jacket.'

Rosemary tested the air: chilly but bearable. 'We're only going to your shed where it's warm.'

Heather shook her head and held up what Rosemary recognised from the mini book enamel on the key ring was Jasper's car keys. 'No, I'm showing you my birds.'

Rosemary hesitated but Heather waited patiently, her bright blue eyes never leaving Rosemary, so she swung back inside to get her coat.

As she came out again, Heather pointed at the ground. 'You'll need your boots.'

This time, Rosemary didn't pause. She went back inside, slipped her sneakers off, and rammed her feet into her work boots. Sunny watched her from the back of the couch, tail flicking from side to side. 'I'll leave you in peace now, Sunny.'

The ginger tabby's tail tucked beside her body and she lowered her head as if in relief.

Rosemary headed for the door again and joined Heather on the pavement. The young woman grasped her arm and tugged her lightly towards Jasper's old car. Rosemary opened the passenger door and removed the pile of books on the seat before getting in. She balanced the books on her lap as Heather got in and started the car. 'Where are we going?'

'A short drive away.'

'I thought you were showing me your ibis.'

'This is where it came from. You'll see.'

Heather hummed as she drove, her hands firm on the wheel. The cascade of blonde curls around her shoulders prevented Rosemary from seeing her face. Heather drove steadily, her fingers beating to her own tune. It struck Rosemary she'd never been driven around by Heather, and she had the wrong image of her as a nervous driver. Like most things the youngest Hubbard sister did, driving was an easy skill. If not for the fact that Heather lived in her own world—one full of dead birds, garment creation, and haybale stacking—she would have been a highly valued member of any work team in the city.

They drove toward Big Town but once they left the small clusters of houses, Heather slowed and turned off the road to park the car on a grassy verge. 'Here we are.'

Rosemary looked around. Green tinged paddocks spread out in front of them, recovering from the summer. Areas of prickly wattles and hakeas clumped along the fence lines. A mob of sheep eyeballed them from about ten metres away, wondering whether they had hay. 'And this is where the ibis was?' asked Rosemary.

'Come with me,' said Heather, sliding out of the car. 'I'll show you.'

Rosemary followed the younger woman, hurrying a little to keep up with Heather's occasional skip. They climbed through a sagging wire fence and followed it towards the first clump of shrubs. The D-Day Development sign loomed overhead and Heather walked sideways to avoid it, her shoulders hunched.

Despite trying to be logical, Rosemary felt it, too. The sign was as big as two cars and thicker than a normal billboard. Steel posts anchored it to the ground. The display of cheery townhouses on its front did nothing to dispel the eerie feeling of gloom attached to it. If those houses went up, the undulating paddocks with their peaceful sheep and softly blooming wattles would be razed. No amount of artificial grass and chlorine-spiced pools could make up for ruining the country landscape.

'Over here, Rosie Rosemary.'

No one else in the world could get away with calling Rosemary *Rosie*, but Rosemary hardly heard it. She pulled her mind away from the Sparkling development signage and hurried to catch up to Heather who had disappeared among a thicket of young trees. 'Where are you?' called Rosemary softly, suddenly aware the noises of the day—chorusing magpies and cackling sulphur-crested cockatoos__were dulled in the leafy space created by the trees.

'Here,' said Heather. 'Quiet now.'

Rosemary stepped carefully on the leaf and twig debris beneath her feet. She ducked around some branches and saw Heather crouched on the ground. Rosemary lowered herself, somewhat awkwardly, as the space was only big enough for one. She had to squeeze up against Heather. 'Sorry,' she whispered.

Heather put a light hand on her arm, pressing gently as if turning Rosemary's sound down. With her other hand, she gestured to the ground about a metre in front of them. 'Wait,' she said, her voice scarcely louder than a gentle breeze.

They waited for about ten minutes, Rosemary's calves threatening to cramp. She shifted slightly and the move-ment disturbed something. In a frantic flutter of tiny wings, two birds came out from the trees in front of them and landed on the ground where they hopped around, alert for danger.

There was nothing spectacular about the birds, but something about their lively movements was captivating. Their bodies were the size of golf balls and covered in cocoa-coloured fluffy feathers. Tails as long and thin as pencils stuck in the air, their tips a brilliant blue. The same colour washed the tops of their stubby beaks, flashing as they darted here and there. As the women watched, three others joined them, and they began pecking at dried grass clumps.

'What are they?' breathed Rosemary. 'Definitely not ibis.'

'Blue beaked pixie wrens,' sighed Heather. 'Friends of the ibis.'

'Friends?'

'They gathered around my ibis. It's how I found the poor thing.'

'In here?'

Heather moved her head slightly. 'In the paddock. I followed them in here.'

They watched the little birds in silence for another five minutes before one flew into the trees, calling the others with a downward whistle. Within seconds, they were gone.

Rosemary crawled out of the thicket first, Heather on her heels. As they stepped back into the paddock, noise seemed to explode around them: bleating sheep, croaking crows, and a distant rumble of a car heading to Big Town. 'It certainly was quiet in there.'

Heather pushed her hair back over her shoulders. Her curls had caught several leaves and she stood still as Rosemary plucked them out. 'Blue beaked pixie wrens,' she repeated.

'I didn't even know they existed,' said Rosemary, extracting a last twig.

Heather smiled, her face tilting up to catch the sun's rays. 'Rare little birds and I found them.'

Rosemary frowned. 'Rare?'

'As hen's teeth.' Heather laughed, a sweet high sound

that momentarily silenced the crows. 'That's what Hannah would say.' She started back to the car.

Rosemary followed obediently. Two ibis stared at her from across the paddock before ducking their heads to concentrate on eating whatever was in that swampy patch of ground. One of their compatriots was now on the table in Heather's taxidermy room. 'Heather,' said Rosemary stepping quickly to come up beside the young woman. 'What were you doing in this paddock? To find the ibis in the first place?'

'I saw it.' Heather kept walking but pointed to the other large birds.

'From the road?'

Heather shook her head. 'From here.' She indicated a spot near the fence.

'I know you walk a lot but this area seems out of your usual circuit. What were you doing there? In the paddock?'

Heather shrugged. 'They called to me.'

'Who? The wildlife people?'

Heather laughed. 'No, the birds.'

Rosemary nodded. In the past, Heather had been known to communicate with the ravens at Ravenshome. How that happened was beyond Rosemary but she did know the younger Hubbard sister was highly sensitive to the mood and behaviour of others, including animals. Rosemary assumed birds had been acting oddly around the body of their lost one, and Heather had noticed when no one else would have glanced this way. 'And what about the blue beaked wrens? How did you know about them?'

Heather stopped and turned to Rosemary, the laughter gone from her face. 'I saw them fluttering around my ibis.' She wiggled her fingers. 'Then they went into the trees. It isn't normal to have a bird in there. I knew that.'

'But how do you know they're rare?'

'I did some research. There hasn't been a colony of pixie wrens reported anywhere since 1856.'

'The start of the gold rush.'

Heather smiled, the sudden brightness of it making Rosemary light up, too. 'This area was flattened by miners but now...' she touched Rosemary's arm with her fingertips '...now these trees have been allowed to grow back the way they were. Bird friendly. The wrens returned after all this time.'

They walked on, climbing through the wire fence to the car. Rosemary took a last look back at the paddock with its contented sheep and ibis in its middle, and the dark clumps of trees at its edge. As Heather started the car and did a U-turn to head back to the town centre, Rosemary shifted so she could look at her. 'Heather, have you told anyone about the birds?'

'Hannah knows my ibis is for Holly.'

'Not the ibis, the wrens. Have you told anyone about the blue beaked pixie wrens?'

Heather nodded, golden hair falling over her seat belt. 'Yes.'

'Who?'

Heather smiled again and shook her head before glancing at Rosemary. 'You.'

'Right.' Rosemary sat back. 'That's good. But why me?'

'Because.' Heather turned into Goldmarket Road and parked outside The Read Mulbury before answering. 'Because Rosemary Exeter always knows what to do with special information.'

TWENTY-ONE

Mulbury felt empty Monday morning. Tourists were few, arriving in their cars in pairs and quickly perusing the shops before taking off again without buying much more than a single cup of coffee. Rosemary peered out of her window at Goldmarket Square. No one sat underneath The Exceptional Tree or at any of the outdoor tables around the cafés. She couldn't hear the sign of the heavy door from The Read Mulbury or the croak of Mrs Lionel's motion sensor frog. 'It's as dull as dishwater out there,' she commented to Sunny.

The cat, her coat the colour of orange marmalade in the sunshine glowing through the skylight, rubbed her face on her mistress's leg. *Just the way I like it,* her happy purring seemed to say.

With nothing much else to do, Rosemary headed out to see Jasper. The silence of the bookshop was immediately explained: a note on the door said *Back at 12pm. Read something from your TBR pile until then.* She kept going to the tearoom and opened the door to the sight of Ronnie on his back in the middle of the floor with Tallulah sitting on his stomach gurgling happily.

Ronnie turned at the sound of the door, the broad smile on his face faltering as he saw Rosemary. 'Oh,' he said, laying the baby down on his chest. 'Hello, Rosemary.'

'No customers, either?'

'Not at the moment.' Ronnie struggled to a sitting position, Tallulah chuckling in his arms. 'We were having a bit of fun while it was quiet.'

'A sensible thing to do.'

'Really? Oh, I mean, yes.' He smiled, stood and shifted the baby so she faced outwards. The little girl drooled and chuckled, grabbing at her father's hands. 'Honey's out the back doing some bookwork.'

'Alright if I go to see her?'

'You don't have to ask.' Ronnie stepped aside. 'You're always welcome.'

Rosemary nodded and headed to the spare room where Honey had her desk. Ronnie's words touched her more than she wanted him to see. She had no doubt what he said was true as Ronnie was one of the sincerest people she knew. It was extraordinarily wonderful, she felt, to have her daughter's family so entwined in her own life.

Honey turned at the sound of a person entering the room. 'Mum, hi! Good to see you.'

'Are you having challenges with your books?'

'What?' Honey glanced back down at her work before shifting completely around in her chair to face her mother. 'No, everything's fine. Steady, I should say, which is comforting.' She put the pen she was holding down. 'Actually, I've finished my bookwork. I was doing a bit of something else.'

'What is that something else?'

'I'm trying to work out how we can help Robert so that...' She gestured at the walls.

'So, you can keep this place as Honey B's Teas.'

'Yeah.' Honey hooked her arm over the back of her chair. 'I don't want Patti and Gerry to think they can't have the shop back if they need it, even if it's far too small for how Patricia's has grown.'

'Right.'

'I think we need a plan to help Robert keep all his assets as, in a funny sort of way, it's turned out that they're our assets as well.'

'Yes. What have you come up with?'

Honey turned to take up the pen again. 'Not much, sadly. I started with what I think Mulbury Feeds would sell for and if it would cover Robert's loan from his father. I've been trawling rural real estate sites and I've got a rough idea. The trouble is business prices have gone down even in the time Robert has owned Mulbury Feeds. If he had borrowed the whole lot, he wouldn't get his money back.' She frowned at the notebook in front of her before pointing her pen at her mother. 'Unless you know of any savings he has that will top it up?'

'I'm not privy to Robert's state of wealth.'

'Didn't think you would be.' Honey threw the pen down and ran her hands over her head, smoothing hair back toward her ponytail. 'We made assumptions about Robert, didn't we?'

'What do you mean?'

'He is easily the richest man I know, but he's tied his wealth up in Mulbury. Asset rich, maybe. Cash poor.'

'Yes.' Rosemary sat on the spare bed and stretched her legs out. 'His other wealth is tied up in the father's will. If he gets his share of the family business, it will add to his assets.'

'Which he could then sell. The family business shares, I mean.'

'It would be up to him.'

'But in the meantime...'

'In the meantime, he has a problem to solve which means we do, too.'

Honey beamed. 'Exactly, Mum! Exactly what I was thinking.' She tipped her chair onto its two back legs. 'What do you know about William?'

Rosemary pursed her lips, thinking about her encounters with William. 'He's an entrepreneurial businessman, like his father. Even for fun, he engages in high-risk activities.'

Honey crashed her chair down and leaned forward. 'What does that mean, Mum?'

Rosemary met her daughter's intense gaze. 'There are many reasons why people do high-risk activities like he does. A love of adrenaline. A high tolerance of danger. Below normal frontal lobe development.'

Honey rolled her eyes. 'Perhaps that sums William up.'

'Or...'

'Or what? What are you thinking?'

'The activity might be an attempt to mask other emotions. Loneliness, for example.'

Honey sat straight. 'You think he does all those crazy things because he's lonely?'

'It's a theory.'

Honey laughed, her trademark deep chuckle making Rosemary smile. 'What makes you say that? I haven't seen one iota of emotion in William except sarcasm.' She stopped laughing and put a hand over her mouth. 'You know about loneliness. That's how you recognise it in others.'

Rosemary put a hand on her daughter's arm. 'I was very lonely when your father left but I haven't been for many years.'

Heavy footsteps sounded behind them and Ronnie appeared in the door. 'Rosemary, I think you have some customers. Mrs Lionel is looking for you.'

Honey stood at the same time as her mother. 'Mum, you can't leave me on that note.'

'I can and I will.' Rosemary squeezed Honey's arm.

'Well, okay then.' Honey leaned over to kiss her cheek. 'I love you, Mum. Always.'

Rosemary smiled. 'And that's why I'm not lonely at all. I'll see you later.'

She left for her own shop, not before tickling the happy baby under the chin which was met with smiles of delight and excessive saliva. Mrs Lionel was on the pavement under the veranda in between The Green Mulbury and The Preserved Mulbury, her stance like an elderly Beefeater guarding the tower. 'Sorry,' said Rosemary, rushing up to her friend. 'There was hardly a soul in town before.'

'A very suitable phrase.' Mrs Lionel tipped her curls towards the window display of three jars of strawberry jam among an array of CWA cookbooks. Crouched inside the shop, staring intently at a ruby red jar, was Bunnie Brownlee.

'Right.' Rosemary adjusted her jacket and smoothed her braid over her shoulder.

'You look like you're preparing for battle, dear,' said Mrs Lionel, walking away to her shop. 'Call me if you need more soldiers.'

Rosemary pushed her own jangling door open, not quite sure why she felt that meeting Bunnie Brownlee needed such preparation. The little woman didn't stand up as Rosemary entered but continued to stare at the jam. At the other end of the shop, Terrence stood with Alicia and Donald, hands clasped in front of them as if waiting for absolution. Rosemary spied Sunny standing just inside their living area, hair stiff along her back. 'Sorry about my absence,' Rosemary said to Bunnie's back. 'Can I help you with anything?'

Bunnie didn't answer. She stretched a hand out and touched a jar. 'Bob loves strawberry jam.'

'It's most people's favourite.'

Bunnie shot a look over her shoulder. 'It's *Bob's* favourite.'

Rosemary felt herself hunch and straightened with an effort. 'Right. Lovely.' She glanced back at the three people standing like statues behind them. 'Are you sure I can't help you?'

Terrence glanced at the others. 'We hear you're friends with the detective investigating Bob.'

Rosemary considered him for a moment. 'Geoffrey is a good friend of Mulbury.'

'So it seems.' Terrence took a step forward. 'Bunnie is waiting on the autopsy result for Bob.'

'Bob,' murmured Bunnie, stroking the jar.

'I'm sure she is.' Rosemary looked down at Bunnie but the woman was absorbed in her own thoughts. 'It must be a horrible wait.'

'Yes.' Terrence's cheek twitched. 'You understand how it is. If we knew the results, if Bunnie knew the results, we... she...could move on quicker.'

Rosemary stopped herself from commenting on how

people experiencing grief didn't *move on* but probably learned to live with it. Bunnie didn't seem to want to move on, whatever that meant. Even now she was muttering Bob's name in a rhythmic chant that was getting under Rosemary's skin. 'As terrible as the wait must be, autopsies and related coroner's findings can take some time.'

'Yes, we know, so we were wondering what you knew. From your friend. The detective.'

'Nothing that you don't.'

'Nothing? Not a hint?'

From outside, Rosemary could hear the cheerful voice of Jasper returning from wherever he'd been (probably buying one of Franco's pies), hailing Ronnie who had carried Tallulah outside. The happy exchange was a deep contrast to the bleakness of the conversation she was in and she suddenly wanted to finish it. 'No. No hints. Geoffrey is a professional. Now.' She walked to the shop counter. 'Can I help you decide on a pickle or two?'

Terrence followed her and leant his elbows on the bench. 'No hints, I understand. We were wondering, though, whether he'd said anything about Bob's time of death? Whether he, in fact, died before he arrived in Mulbury?'

Rosemary tapped at her computer in the guise of uninterest. 'Before? Do you mean, shortly after or perhaps before he ended up in the mannikin's case?'

'No. Yes.' Terrence plunged both hands into his trouser pockets. 'Poor fellow. I mean, we were wondering *where* exactly he had died.' He looked intently at Rosemary and when she didn't answer, added 'What location?'

'Does it matter?'

'Yes.' Terrence shook his head as if softening the forceful answer and lowered his voice. 'If the police thought he'd died before the case arrived in Mulbury, that would change things.'

Before Rosemary could ask why, Bunnie sprung up from her position on the floor and hobbled stiffly over to the shop counter. 'Bob? Bob's not here?' She glanced wildly around, checking the room. 'Bob is here somewhere! Aren't you Bob? Bob? Bob!' The last syllable was a shriek.

Alicia came forward and went to take Bunnie's arm but the little woman was hurrying to the door. 'She heard you,' Alicia hissed at Terrence before following. 'Idiot!'

Terrence's face darkened. He strode off without another word to Rosemary and crashed out the door after his friends.

Rosemary turned to Sunny whose hair was at last flat against her back. 'They think Bob's ghost can't be in Mulbury if he died somewhere else.'

Sunny blinked, lifted a foreleg and licked its length before walking back inside the living area, tail in the air. *Not our problem,* her back end indicated.

Rosemary silently agreed, but that didn't stop her ringing Geoffrey and inviting him to dinner.

TWENTY-TWO

Geoffrey's invitation to dinner had to be delayed. Rosemary heard the fatigue in the detective's voice as he outlined his busy week and thought it miraculous he accepted any invitation at all. She vowed to make as nutritious a meal as possible for him as she suspected his late working days meant snatched pieces of toast with an egg most evenings. 'You'll come along as well,' she said to Mrs Lionel as they caught up for a cup of morning tea.

'That sounds like a command, dear.'

'I didn't mean-'

Mrs Lionel chuckled and stretched a reassuring hand towards Rosemary. 'Of course you didn't and of course I'll come along. Geoffrey is a dear friend.'

Rosemary nodded. They were sitting at Mrs Lionel's long dining room table with its comforting array of drying herbs laid out at one end. The aromatic air represented wholesome freshness, and indeed Mrs Lionel looked particularly hale that morning, with a wicked sparkle in her eyes. Rosemary sipped her tea. 'What's going on?'

Mrs Lionel's attention was taken momentarily by something on the ground. 'What do you mean?'

'You're up to something.' Rosemary glanced under the table but saw nothing but the legs of chairs, the table and Mrs Lionel. 'Is Percy involved?'

'How suspicious you are.' Mrs Lionel sipped delicately at her tea. 'Nothing's going on. Something *went* on, though.'

'What?'

'I had our William over last night.'

'William? William Sparkling?'

'That very William.'

'Why?'

Mrs Lionel moved her cup on its saucer until the handle pointed directly to the right. 'Because no one has really talked to the man.'

'I've talked to him.'

'Have you, dear? Really?'

'I have an open invitation for anyone to come and see me.'

'Not good enough, in this case. Do you know he has two dogs that sleep on his bed at night?'

The idea of the smarmy William snuggling up to dogs at nighttime startled Rosemary. Her eyes widened. 'No, I-'

'No. Indeed. Did you know William has a photograph of his mother in his wallet?'

'No.'

'No. And then you won't know behind that photo is another of two boys and their father.'

Rosemary remembered the image on Robert's desk. 'One boy with wavy hair, the other with straight, and a grim man in between.'

'You've seen that photo?'

'Not from William's wallet. Robert has the same one.'

'I wonder if Robert knows William carries it around with him?'

'William and Robert don't talk...' Rosemary gestured at her friend.

'They don't talk like they would if they were talking with me.'

'You are easy to talk with. You're kind.'

Mrs Lionel moved her shoulders back and sighed. 'It's not kindness. It's genuine interest. We have two brothers in our town who seem completely different people from each other. We know siblings aren't always alike—just think about those lovely Hubbard girls—but to be so different? What happened to make them like that?'

'Nothing has to happen. They could be just different.'

'Perhaps.' Mrs Lionel leaned forward to pour herself more tea. 'No one will know that if we don't take the time to be interested in their lives.'

'We know Robert.'

Mrs Lionel sat the teapot down with a clunk. 'Do we? Think, Rosemary. Do we really know Robert? We know all about his generosity and goodness, and we suspected his relationship with his father wasn't tight. However, despite all the connections we have built, we didn't know he had a brother.'

Rosemary pursed her lips. She thought she'd been respectful of Robert by not asking too many questions about how he landed in Mulbury. Perhaps that had been a mistake? Surely he didn't want people probing his past life? She didn't like it when people asked about Alasdair. 'It isn't right to pry.'

'No, it isn't. But it is okay to ask gentle questions to see whether a person wants to talk.'

'This is what you did with William.'

Mrs Lionel shook her head. 'I merely asked him around for an after-dinner dessert. I eat far too early for a man used to a busy city life, so I thought a more relaxed offering would be better. I made a steamed chocolate pudding.'

'He wouldn't have been able to resist that. I know from experience.'

'Precisely. A bowl of pudding and cream, alongside a sweet little Madeira, and he was quite chatty.'

'You made him talk with sugary offerings.'

'I did no such thing. I was curious to find out more about him.'

'Right.' Rosemary put her elbows on the table so she could rest her chin in her hand. 'Besides his sleeping habits and the glimpse of unusual sentimentality, what did you find out?'

Mrs Lionel added a drop of milk to her cup. 'Oh, I'm not going to tell you everything. I will give you a summary and then tell you the best bit.'

'Oh, come on...'

'No, Rosemary, you don't need to know everything. Sometimes, with the combination of a warm room and a pleasantly full stomach, things are said that are confidential. I *will* say that those brothers did not have a close relationship with their father but they adored their mother. Her death caused an estrangement that was not reconciled. William may have been working with their father, but he was regarded more like an employee than a son. A *good* employee, that is. One that did what the boss said.'

'Which is one reason why he's advocating for the will's condition to be followed to a tee.'

'One reason, yes. Another, of course, is he is simply a son doing what his father has asked.'

Rosemary nodded. 'I can appreciate that. Perhaps he

needs counselling before he continues wreaking havoc on his brother.'

'That would not be timely.'

Rosemary leaned back. Mrs Lionel drank her tea as if it was the most delicious she'd ever had but she clearly hadn't finished the story she had to tell. The sparkle in her eye had yet to dull. 'There's something else, isn't there?'

'Yes.' Mrs Lionel pushed her empty cup aside and clasped her hands to rest on the table. 'You must not share this with anyone. Promise?'

'Of course.'

Mrs Lionel raised one eyebrow. 'Alright then. William Sparkling has a daughter.'

It hadn't crossed Rosemary's mind to associate the brash Sparkling sibling with being a father, but then again, she had known people who never fitted the parent mould. 'Right. I hope he knows how lucky he is.'

'I think he does.' Mrs Lionel smiled. 'It was the way he spoke of her.'

'In what way?'

'Proudly, dear. The way you talk about Honey.'

'Right. And that's the best bit you found out?'

'Well, of course. Don't you think it good news? It must mean he isn't just acting on his own behalf. Some of this he's doing for Vivienne.'

'How old is Vivienne?'

'Ten.' Mrs Lionel tugged her cardigan across her shoulders. 'I understand he hasn't seen her for a long time.'

'Robert has never mentioned a niece.'

'Robert had never mentioned a brother.'

'Good point.' Rosemary frowned and crossed her arms. 'I don't see how this really affects Robert's immediate issue of losing Ravenshome or Mulbury Feeds.'

'Perhaps not but it does add a complication to his actions.'

'Is Vivienne a beneficiary of the father's will?'

'I didn't ask and he didn't volunteer that information.'

Rosemary was quiet for a moment. 'Robert knows what's in the will. Maybe some of his dilemma is related to Vivienne.'

'In what way, dear?'

'Perhaps if Robert doesn't do what his father wanted, that is, to help run the business, it will be affected which in turn will affect Vivienne's inheritance.'

'That sounds complicated.'

'Yes, but you were the one who suggested more complications if Vivienne's in the picture.'

Mrs Lionel smoothed her skirt. 'Well, if that is the case, I hope she knows nothing about it. That would be too much for a ten-year-old.'

'I guess that will be up to her father. Did William say any more?'

Mrs Lionel shook her head. 'No. He told me she was bright, particularly excelling in maths, and then he clammed up. It wasn't long after that he left. I suspect he thought he'd said too much.' She sighed. 'I don't think it occurred to him that the way he spoke of his daughter showed a humanity we'd not seen before.'

'I'm sure he didn't. Or, if he did, he may have regarded it as a weakness.'

'Oh, how ridiculous that would be.' Mrs Lionel reached for the teapot again but it was empty. 'That's a signal I should get back to work.'

'What should we do next?'

'I've got some soap to cut into blocks and then-'

'No. What do we do about Robert and William now we know about Vivienne?'

'I'm not sure.' Mrs Lionel rose stiffly, using the table to help her straighten. 'Whatever it is you had planned, check it doesn't affect that little girl.'

Rosemary stood as well and stacked their cups and the teapot on a tray. 'I don't have anything planned.'

Mrs Lionel tugged her cardigan into place and started for the door of The Preserved Mulbury. '*Planned* is probably too strong a word but I know you had some ideas.'

Rosemary walked around the table to place the tray on the kitchen bench. 'You're right, I do.'

Mrs Lionel stopped and locked eyes with Rosemary. 'You won't do anything, will you, before you know...'

'...how it affects Vivienne. Of course not.'

'Thank you, dear.' The older woman bent to stroke Sunny before leaving. 'I'll see you soon.'

Rosemary scooped the cat into her arms and followed her friend to the door. She waited until she heard the frog croak before turning back to her own work. Helping Robert keep his assets now had an extra dimension. Perhaps the key was to find out more about Vivienne Sparkling?

TWENTY-THREE

Rosemary had deliberately left Robert and William to themselves since the younger brother had arrived. That hadn't stopped her automatically keeping tabs on William's day to day activities. Ravenshome, despite its position as Patricia's, was firstly quite a luxurious home. Robert had slowly renovated the upstairs area, keeping the area overlooking Mulbury as his bedroom, but turning the other rooms into spacious places for study or contemplation or, regarding the two other bedrooms, sleeping in. She doubted Robert had ever slept late during his time in Mulbury, but about William, she wasn't sure. One thing was clear: William didn't turn up in town each day until well after ten o'clock and he favoured Kelly's coffee with one of Franco's pastries for a mid-morning snack. It wasn't hard to beat him to the patisserie.

'Hello, William,' Rosemary said, holding a paper tray up. 'I've already got you a spanakopita. I took the liberty of getting one for myself as well. Will we sit over there?' She pointed to the seat under The Exceptional Tree.

William stopped more than a polite distance away. 'Rosemary. If I'd known, I would have got you coffee.'

Rosemary tried not to grimace thinking of Kelly's coffee. 'Thankfully, I'm full of tea. Shall we?' She walked to the seat and sat, settling the tray next to her.

William hesitated so long she thought her ruse had failed but, with the soft touch of the under branches of the enormous tree brushing his shoulders as a quiet breeze stirred them, he sat down stiffly and sipped his drink.

Rosemary spent a long moment carefully ripping open the paper bag surrounding the tray and picking up one pastry. She didn't have to feign contentment as she ate as the pastry was one of Franco's best: crispy and delicious, with a delicate mix of spinach and cheeses. William watched her for a moment before taking the second and devouring it.

'Good choice?' asked Rosemary, licking pastry flakes from her fingers.

'Yes. I usually have one of his sweet ones, but this is really hitting the spot.' William took a handkerchief from his pocket and wiped his fingers fastidiously. 'I have accepted your bribe.' He tucked the hanky away and looked at her. 'What do you want?'

'I want lots of things,' said Rosemary. 'Blue skies. Sweet apricots. The annihilation of fruit fly. But that's not what you're talking about.'

'No, although coming from the city, I concede the wont for blue skies.' William gave a flat smile. 'The women of Mulbury use food to pry out information from me.'

'If you're referring to Mrs Lionel offering you dessert, then you are mistaken. Her intentions are always honourable. She kindly fed you and expected nothing in return.' Rosemary brushed away some crumbs. 'I'm not Mrs Lionel.'

'You have dishonourable intentions?'

'No. But I do think it's time we spoke bluntly.'

'I understand you talk no other way.'

Rosemary shrugged. 'There's no point in speaking otherwise.'

Something passed over William's face. It was just a flicker, but in it Rosemary glimpsed the sort of pain experienced when talk was so blunt it hurt. She studied the man beside her. He was a slightly smaller version of his brother, but something had hardened him. He sat with one leg over the other, making his slim-fitting trousers slide up to bare a tight black sock. His shoes were unnecessarily pointy for spending the day in Mulbury, and polished to a clean, warm tan which was evidence that not much of any day was spent walking about any dusty country town. It was the slight jig of his foot that gave his discomfort away, a movement juxtaposed against the casual swing of his arm to rest along the bench's back. 'Go on,' he said, in an unconvincing bored tone.

'We need Robert to stay in Mulbury.'

William said nothing.

Rosemary held his gaze. 'We need Robert to stay in Mulbury with his assets here intact.'

'Ah.' William swapped his leg over and let his hand drop to the seat. 'You need Robert's assets.'

'Mulbury needs Robert's assets to keep functioning as it is.'

William put both his feet on the ground and leaned back. 'You need his *assets*, not Robert himself.'

Rosemary frowned. 'Are you saying that if Robert had to sell his assets, they would still form the basis of Mulbury

Feeds, Patricia's and the garage? That the new owner would keep them that way?' She paused, regarding his immobile face. 'That *you* would buy them?'

'What would it mean to Mulbury if I did buy them? They would be Sparkling properties just the same.'

'I don't trust you would buy them with the intention of keeping them as is.'

William laughed shortly, throwing up his hands. 'And there it is. Blunt as a hammerhead shark.'

'You asked me what I wanted. I want to know what will happen to those buildings people are dependent on.'

He nodded slowly, a smile playing on his face. 'And you don't give two hoots about Robert.'

Rosemary glanced back at Franco's Patisserie as a squeal of delight from a happy tourist told her they'd discovered one of his special Danishes. It gave her a moment to think. As she turned to look at William again, she saw his face unexpectedly tense. 'I give lots of hoots about Robert but I'm not worried about him. He doesn't see himself as a collection of real estate and he also knows his own investments will come due in the not-so-distant future. If Robert wants to stay in Mulbury with his properties gone, no doubt he'll find a modest lodging somewhere until he can buy his own place. Any one of us would offer him a spare room, but he'd be just as happy sleeping in a tent.' She shifted so she faced William squarely. 'Robert isn't fussed about himself but he cares deeply for the residents of Mulbury. He will want to keep his assets for the sake of them.'

William looked away so she couldn't see his face. She heard the slight strain in his voice, though, as he spoke. 'Our father's will is binding. If we don't follow what he's outlined, we won't see a cent of our inheritance and Robert won't have anything left. Which means...' he swivelled to Rosemary '...neither will your friends.'

She leaned back, brushing final crumbs from her legs before putting the empty paper tray on the bench. 'You're completely dependent on the contents of the will.'

'What?' He grinned but it was all teeth. 'I have my own portfolio.'

'No doubt. But I imagine, like Robert's, it's tied up for the long term. You're worried about what might happen in the short time.' She took a deep breath in and sent a silent apology to Mrs Lionel. 'To Vivienne.'

'Vivi? How...?' He shook his head. 'You've been talking to Mrs Lionel.'

'Always. She mentioned your daughter out of concern for you, not as gossip. Vivienne is why you're so determined to see your father's wishes through. I get it.'

'Do you?' William brushed a hand over his face. 'Do you really? Vivienne is my only child. I need this for her.'

'Children don't need money. They need love.'

He gave that terrible short laugh again. 'Well, you'd know all about that. You've had your daughter with you all her life.'

'And you haven't?'

He dropped his head and leaned forward so his elbows rested on his thighs. 'I haven't seen her since she was eight years old.'

'Why not?'

'She lives with her mother and stepfather in another state.'

'That's no reason.'

'Isn't it?' William put his head down further. 'She has a life with them. I'd only be interfering.'

Rosemary stared into the Square. A young couple

walked away from Franco's clutching pies in bags, laughing together as the woman directed her partner's hand to her rounded belly. The gesture reminded Rosemary of a time long ago when she also had a partner to share the early movements of their daughter. She sighed. 'It's not that hard, William.'

He straightened. 'What would you know about it?' He pointed across Goldmarket Road. 'Your daughter has always been in your life.'

'Her father chose not to be in her life.' Rosemary stood. 'I only hope he regrets it.' She looked down at where William sat with his hands on his knees and elbows straight. 'The only thing that would matter to your daughter is seeing you. The money is nothing.'

He stood as well but kept his gaze towards Honey B's Teas. 'What would you know about it?' he said again, but softly. 'The money is *everything*. And the will is airtight. Our father made sure of that. D-Day Development will continue with its plans or we won't see a penny.' He glanced at her. 'That means Vivi as well and, out of all of us, she needs it the most.' He tucked his fingers casually into the front pockets of his slim trousers. 'Thanks for the brunch. I need to go make some calls.'

He started off and Rosemary reached out a hand to stop him. 'You're always welcome, you know. For dessert or tea at The Preserved Mulbury.'

William paused before giving a brief nod and walking away. Rosemary watched him as he skirted around the happy couple and disappeared behind The Sweet Potato. He suddenly reappeared again, walking towards her with his hands still in his pockets. She blinked. No. As he came closer, she could see this man had a dark leather jacket on and, although his hair was the chestnut of William's, it was straight and slightly too long. He raised his hand as he saw her.

'Robert,' she said when he got closer. 'Are you looking for a cup of tea?'

He looked over to the garage across Low Road. 'Well, I was heading to work. I have a car to service.'

'Surely it can wait twenty minutes.' Rosemary set off for The Preserved Mulbury, hearing Robert's footsteps turn on the gravel behind her. She pushed in through the jangling door and went straight to the kitchen. Robert followed but paused to murmur a welcome to Sunny in the windowsill of the shop. The kettle had boiled by the time he arrived at her dining table. 'So,' he said, sliding off his jacket. 'Are you going to tell me why you were schmoozing with my brother?'

'I don't schmooze,' said Rosemary crossly, pouring water into a white teapot. 'We were talking.'

'Do you often eat Franco's pastries for morning tea?'

She didn't look at him as she brought the tea tray to the table. 'I thought I'd try them out.'

He didn't chuckle like she expected him to. Instead, he spread both hands onto the table. 'You can't change anything, Rosemary. The will is what it is.'

'As your father wrote it.'

'That's right.' He took a mug full of steaming tea. 'Thanks for this.'

She sat down opposite him. 'Your brother is thinking of Vivienne.'

Robert spluttered, tea dribbling down his chin. 'He told you about Vivienne?'

'No. He told Mrs Lionel.'

'Right, right, that makes more sense.' He wiped his face with a hanky, stopping when she widened her eyes at him.

'Oh, you know what I mean, Rosemary. Mrs Lionel is a good listener.'

'As am I.'

'In a different, sort of calculating, way.'

She opened her mouth to protest but reconsidered. Calculating was quite complimentary. 'However we found this out, it explains your brother more. He's trying to protect his daughter's inheritance.'

'Yes.' Robert put his mug down and sighed. 'Yes. I know. If we don't do what the will says, we'll be playing quite a different game. And I get it. If Vivi was my child, I'd want the will protected.'

Rosemary tweaked a loose strand of hair back in her braid. 'You say this as if there's more to Vivienne than I think.'

'He didn't tell you?'

She shook her head.

Robert let his head drop. 'Vivi has a neurological condition. A progressive one. She's not yet in a wheelchair but it won't be long. William wants things for her. A suitable house, the best technical aids she can have, a personal carer. He needs money for that and sooner rather than later.' He rubbed his face with both hands.

Rosemary was quiet as she sipped her tea. 'I'm guessing you have no choice but to do what legally must be done,' she said eventually. 'Morally, it's the right thing to do.'

Robert clasped his hands together and leaned forward. 'You think I have no choice but to sell something. Whatever I do, it will affect people.'

Rosemary folded her arms and regarded the man in front of her. He was staring at her sadly, his normal energy absent from his eyes. 'Do you have a copy of the will?'

'Yes, of course. I've spent most evenings poring over it

looking for any clause that would allow me to not sell a thing but keep the distribution of its contents the same.'

'Mind if I look, too?'

'No. In fact I'd like a second opinion. Well.' Robert closed his eyes and tipped his head back. 'Well, a fourth or fifth opinion. I've been to several lawyers.' He went back to looking at her. 'Is there anything in particular you're looking for?'

'Just the vibe.'

Robert's eyebrows shot up. 'The vibe?' When she didn't say anything more, he stood. 'Okay then. Come around later. I'll show it to you.'

Rosemary walked with him to the door and watched as he walked across the Square to the garage. Sunny pushed at her shins and she bent down to stroke the ginger stripes on the cat's head. 'I don't know what I'm looking for,' she whispered to the cat purring loudly. 'But I hope I find it anyhow.'

TWENTY-FOUR

Rosemary didn't get to Robert's that day, or the next. Tallulah developed a cold, and Rosemary spent her evenings in Honey and Ronnie's homely lounge room strung with drying washing, nursing the snuffling baby while her parents baked and cleaned furiously so one could stay with the little sickie during the day as the other worked. The preparation had almost worked, although Rosemary had helped during the busy morning and afternoon tea times, leaving Jasper to keep an ear out for any preserves customers jangling through the door.

Geoffrey drove into Mulbury just before five o'clock on Friday and parked carefully on Goldmarket Road outside The Green Mulbury to visit Mrs Lionel. Rosemary could hear their voices as she shut shop and started on dinner. The day had been quite warm, so her meal plan had changed from soup and casserole to spring rolls and chicken stir fry. As she chopped up the vegetables, she heard Mrs Lionel laugh, a pleasant sound through their adjoining walls. Geoffrey and the older woman had been friends for decades, starting from an incident of cattle rustling when

Mrs Lionel had run the dairy after her husband had died, and continuing (crimeless) ever since. 'It will be good to have him visiting here more often,' Rosemary remarked to Sunny.

At six-thirty, the door jangled open, and Rosemary heard multiple footsteps as a small crowd walked in. She had invited Jasper, Mrs Lionel, Honey and Ronnie, but the new parents had declined because of Tallulah. Rosemary had wanted to keep the evening intimate, and it had certainly turned out that way. Not that Geoffrey would mind. He smiled and nodded at her as he came into the dining area and sat at the table looking comfortably relaxed.

'I brought this,' said Jasper, brandishing a bottle of wine. 'The ladies from the Midnight Mystery Club gave it to me for helping them set up their book club.'

'What is a Midnight Mystery, dear?' asked Mrs Lionel, settling into a seat near the couch so she could tickle Sunny sitting along the back cushions under the chin.

'It's more to do with the time they meet.' Jasper offered the wine around. 'They all work night shift so their book club is literally at midnight.'

Geoffrey took a sip of his wine. 'I could have done with that when I was working night shift. All we had to look forward to during our midnight break were old newspapers and half-completed crossword puzzles.'

'I bet you won't miss that,' said Jasper. 'How are the plans for retirement going?'

'Slowly.' Geoffrey frowned. 'Although I've given notice, I still must keep going for now. It hasn't changed my work-load at all.'

'You work so hard,' said Mrs Lionel, shaking her head at Jasper's offering. 'You'll miss the action once you stop.'

'Perhaps.' Geoffrey sat up straighter as Rosemary put a

plate of spring rolls in the centre of the table. 'Although there always seems to be action in Mulbury.'

'Are you any closer to solving Bob Brownlee's murder?' Jasper paused with a roll suspended on his fork. 'Sorry, I shouldn't be asking. None of my business.'

'No, it isn't.' Geoffrey gave Jasper a brief look. 'But I understand your curiosity. You can't witness what you did without having questions about what happened. The thing is, we're really no closer to knowing, which doesn't mean we have nothing to go on. It means that these things take time.' He stabbed at a roll. 'They can take a lot of time.'

Rosemary sat opposite the police officer. 'Are you thinking you'll be retired before you find out?'

'It's possible.' Geoffrey shrugged as he ate. 'But that's the way it goes.'

'Poor Mrs Brownlee,' said Mrs Lionel. 'I can't imagine what she's going through.'

'Hmm,' said Geoffrey, putting his fork down. 'She's an interesting one.'

'In what way, dear?'

Geoffrey dabbed at his mouth with a serviette. 'I've seen many grieving people and I know everyone grieves in their own way, and there's no right or wrong, but I've never seen one like Bunnie Brownlee. She comes into the station every few days, doesn't ask for me or anyone in particular, looks around the waiting room as if expecting someone, and wanders off again, usually with her entourage in tow.'

'The A Team,' said Jasper.

'The A Team?'

'If it's who I'm thinking it is, the A Team is what they call themselves. They're part of the Big Town Paranormal Investigators but a *special* part of the Big Town Paranormal

Investigators.' Jasper tapped his chest. 'They wear a monogram: A-BTPI.'

'Okay.' Geoffrey nodded. 'Yes, I've seen that but didn't know they were a group apart from the others. Very interesting.'

Jasper looked puzzled. 'Is it interesting for a particular reason?'

'Quirks can add up to a bigger picture. We like to know everything we can about our suspects.'

'Are they suspects then?' asked Mrs Lionel, frowning.

'Everyone is a suspect until proven otherwise.'

Rosemary cleared the table and put dishes into the sink. 'Statistics show that most homicides are committed by family or at least people known to the victim.'

Geoffrey sat back in his chair. 'Yes, indeed. That's where we start.'

'So poor Bunnie Brownlee is a suspect.' Mrs Lionel tutted. 'She seems so upset.'

'She's upset, but in an odd way.' Jasper rubbed the top of his glass idly to make it sing, earning a scowl from Rosemary. 'Sorry,' he said, grinning sheepishly. 'I only mean she doesn't seem to think that Bob is dead. She keeps looking for him.'

'She's in shock, poor dear,' said Mrs Lionel. 'She won't accept the fact that he's gone.'

'She knows he's dead.' Rosemary put a bowl of steaming rice on the table and followed it up with one of the stir fry.

'But she keeps calling out for him.'

'Yes.' Rosemary gave her friend a look. 'Calling out to his spirit.'

Geoffrey hmphed. 'You think she's calling to his ghost?'

Rosemary shrugged as she sat back down. 'They are paranormal investigators.'

'Yes.' Geoffrey looked down at the table for a long moment. 'Yes, they are.'

'Have you had any encounters with, you know...' Jasper waved his fork around '... ghosts?'

Geoffrey lifted his head and studied the bookseller. 'In all my time in homicide, I have never witnessed, felt or otherwise noticed any spirit, ghoul or invisible presence at the crime scene. Or anywhere. I have my feet firmly on the ground when dead bodies are concerned.'

Jasper nodded. 'I would think that if anyone was going to see a troubled soul, it would be you.'

'Not necessarily, dear.' Mrs Lionel put her fork down gently. 'As grounded as I am, I do believe that some people experience phenomena others don't.'

'You're talking about Rakisha,' said Jasper. 'She sees auras.'

Mrs Lionel shrugged.

'Heather, then. She communicates with birds.'

Mrs Lionel took a polite sip of water.

'All very well,' said Rosemary, stopping Jasper before he could go through everyone's proclivities. 'Geoffrey and his team are no closer to getting justice for Bob.' She helped herself to more rice. 'There is one thing I'm curious about. Did the autopsy result in a conclusion about when Bob Brownlee died?'

Geoffrey put his fork down and cleared his throat. 'You know I can't talk about the case in detail, Rosemary.'

'I acknowledge that. The time of his death, however, could illuminate some thoughts about the case.'

Geoffrey frowned. 'Well, I can speak in general terms for now. Outline the forensic process if you like.'

Jasper stretched back in his chair. 'Not too gory, if you don't mind, Geoffrey.'

'Forensic science isn't gory, just facts.'

'To some,' Jasper muttered.

Rosemary patted Jasper's arm. 'You'll cope. Please, Geoffrey, go on.'

The old detective pushed his empty plate aside and clasped his hands together on the table. 'At any reported death, we call our crime scene specialists. They will include a team from forensic science but the body is then taken to the coroner's office where it is reviewed.'

Rosemary matched Geoffrey's posture. 'What sorts of things would tell you about the time of death?'

'Rigor mortis?' asked Jasper. 'That's what you always hear about.'

'Rigor mortis is part of what they call the "march of rigor" as the body changes and muscles stiffen over time,' said Geoffrey, tapping his hands on the table. 'The stages before that include body chemistry changes and cooling of body temperature. Then liver mortis sets in, where the body starts to discolour. But all these stages vary so much in time, it is very difficult to estimate exactly when someone died. It depends on the weather, the day's temperature, the surface the person is on, and how they died.'

'But there are rough windows of time?' Rosemary asked. 'For example, if someone was found in a confined box or something similar, with cool temperatures, and transported carefully in a car?'

Geoffrey's face grew stern.

Rosemary shrugged. 'Hypothetically speaking.'

'Right.' Geoffrey pulled his shoulders back. 'If someone was found in those circumstances, it might be possible to gauge a rough window of time.'

'For example...?'

'For example, and hypothetically speaking, the state of

the deceased in circumstances similar to that, discovered accidentally by members of the public, would allow an estimated time of death.'

'And in those circumstances, hypothetically?'

'In those broad circumstances, with the deceased in a complete state of rigor mortis with evident cellular changes, it could be estimated that time of death was about eight to ten hours before discovery.'

'Right.' Rosemary leaned back. 'I see.'

'What do you see, dear?' Mrs Lionel patted her mouth with her napkin and placed it on the table.

'I see that Bob Brownlee was long dead before he appeared in The Leftover Restaurant.' Rosemary smiled at Geoffrey. 'Hypothetically.'

TWENTY-FIVE

Saturday was one of those quirky autumn days where the sun shone fiercely as if trying to hang on to summer. Rosemary propped the door of The Preserved Mulbury open to let a breeze waft right through the shop and her living quarters to the balcony beyond. In Goldmarket Square, tourists fanned themselves with pie bags or napkins as they sat under The Exceptional Tree. Rakisha came out of The Sweet Potato and plonked herself down on one of her rickety outdoor chairs, brushing her recalcitrant hair away from her face. Rosemary regarded the empty preserves shop for a moment before wandering across the road to join her.

'Rosemary, darling.' Rakisha swatted listlessly at a fat fly. 'Would you like an earth blessed tuber coffee?'

Rosemary stopped herself from shuddering. 'No, thank you. I was wondering whether you could do me a favour?'

'You'd like a carob coffee?'

'No, thanks again.' She sat on the edge of the bench and faced Rakisha. 'Honey asked me whether I could make her some healthy snacks because she's so busy with Tallulah and the teas. Would you have some recipes for something healthy with fruit and nuts?'

Rakisha's eyes brightened. 'Oh yes, darling! I will put together some samples for your darling Honey Blossom and see what she thinks.'

'Thank you.' Rosemary settled back on the seat beside her. 'How are you? There's a lot going on as usual.'

'Oh, me?' Rakisha lifted her hair from her neck before letting it fall in a fluffy cascade. 'My chakras are balanced, darling. I am peaceful.'

'Your chakras were having a tough time at dinner last week.'

'Yes, yes.' Rakisha looked over Rosemary's shoulder and blinked her eyes rapidly. 'There are those who, with their very presence, disturb the rhythm of the universe.'

'Bunnie Brownlee.'

Rakisha's face twisted. 'Bunnie. She is not who she appears to be.'

'In what way?'

Rakisha turned to Rosemary and stretched out a bony hand to lay on her arm. 'Bunnie Lamont looks frail and bewildered.' She patted Rosemary's arm vigorously. 'But she is not, darling. She is neither frail nor bewildered. She is exactly as she wants to be.'

'Which is what? She gives the impression she wants to be a wife to a non-dead husband.'

Rakisha blew her breath out in an impressive raspberry. 'Bunnie has always preferred people who are not alive.'

'What do you mean?' Rosemary leaned towards the cotton-clad woman. 'Has she a penchant for ghosts?'

Rakisha shook her head, making her feathery earrings tangle in her hair. 'Bunnie does not understand the cycle of life, darling, the gift we give back to the earth at the end of our existence. She thinks we are better off as drifting souls rather than physical beings.' Rakisha rolled her eyes. 'That's why she spent years in a cemetery.'

'She worked in a cemetery?'

'No, darling.' Rakisha put her hands on her knees and looked grim. 'Bunnie does not *work*. She flows with whoever can look after her. Her first husband, Harry, was the groundskeeper at a cemetery. Her days were spent roaming its sites. There were complaints, of course. Especially when she started her nighttime vigils.' Rakisha shrugged. 'That was before I knew her, darling, so I don't know all that happened. Rumours, gossip, stories. They've always surrounded Bunnie.'

'What happened to her first husband, Rakisha?'

'He fell into a grave, hit his head on the coffin. They almost buried him accidentally.' Rakisha looked up at Rosemary. 'So I heard on the communal grapevine, darling.'

'How tragic.'

'Yes, tragic. Bunnie had to be extracted forcefully from the gravesite.'

'She must have been very upset.'

Rakisha eyed Rosemary. 'Darling, Bunnie had to be extracted forcefully *after* spending three months camped out at his grave. She had a tent full of smoky quartz and a gas stove. So the story went.'

'The way you said that tells me you don't think she was upset at her husband's death.'

'Oh, she was upset. No doubting her darkening aura, although I did not see her during that time. She was upset he didn't rejoin her.'

'Who?'

'Her husband, darling. The groundskeeper. According

to Bunnie, he should have been devoted enough to join her spiritually for the remainder of her days.'

Rosemary thought of Percy and shook her head. 'Devoted?'

'Yes, devoted. His life's work unfulfilled.' Rakisha shook her head, sending hair to cling to Rosemary's arms, and clutched at the seat. 'I forget, darling, you have difficulties.'

'Difficulties?'

Rakisha twisted in her seat and raised her arms. 'Oh, it's not your fault, Rosemary Exeter! You just don't have the aptitude for spiritual enhancement.' She waved her hand up and down Rosemary's body. 'It's not in your soul to connect with others. Your aura is very solid in that matter.'

'I don't see that as a difficulty.'

Rakisha chuckled and let her hands drop. 'No, darling, of course you don't.'

Rosemary took a few deep breaths and let the mirth die away. 'Just what am I missing?'

'Souls, darling. They stay with us if they haven't finished their flesh purpose.' Rakisha glanced at Rosemary. 'Do you understand?'

An image of Mrs Lionel bending over to talk to something on the floor flashed through Rosemary's mind. 'More than you think.' She paused. 'Roman said that ghosts are troubled souls, shadows of someone who has died early.'

'Oh, that darling moustached man!' Rakisha clapped her hands. 'He knows, darling. He is of my ilk. But he forgot to say souls may not be troubled, they may just have work to do.'

'How does this relate to Bunnie's first husband?'

'Well, you see.' Rakisha leaned towards Rosemary, her flyaway hair engulfing them both. 'She camped right next to where he died and not once did his soul reach out to her. Not once!'

'So, he had finished whatever it was he had to do on earth which probably had to do with keeping the grass down in the cemetery.'

'More than that, darling. He had finished with Bunnie!' Rakisha sat back, smiling. 'And she did not like that. No, not one little bit.'

'What did she do?'

'She joined us in our happy place.' The smile dropped away from Rakisha's face, replaced by a worried twist of her mouth. 'And there she spread her rumours and darkness until the happiness oozed out of our lives and we fell apart like an overcooked brownie.' She wriggled her fingers to show the falling of crumbs.

Rosemary nodded, trying hard not to remember one of Rakisha's tasteless brownies. 'That must have been hard.'

'Devastating, darling! Ever so devastating!' Rakisha lowered her head and sighed, making strands of her hair float around her head.

'The bright side is you landed here.' Rosemary put her hand on Rakisha's shoulder, feeling its knobbiness through the draped layers of tie-dyed cotton.

The older woman looked up, scraping her hair away from her face with long, turmeric-stained fingernails. 'I hear your words, Rosemary Exeter, and I see your aura. So much like the sky on a still winter's day.' She reached out a finger to trace a line around Rosemary's head. 'You cannot lie, not in the usual easy manner of some.'

'It's more of a downfall than a blessing sometimes.'

Rakisha huffed. 'But today it is a blessing. I feel your words are real and for that, darling, I am grateful.'

Rosemary shifted on the bench, giving Rakisha's

shoulder a final squeeze and letting her hand fall away. 'Can I ask what you think Bunnie Brownlee is up to? How do you see her wanderings and the way she calls out to Bob?'

'That?' Rakisha straightened and pushed her shoulders down. 'That, darling, is Bunnie once again getting it wrong. She's waiting for Bob to come back to her, in an ethereal sense. He is not here.'

'Do you think he is anywhere?'

'Oh, he may be. I am not the one to question the intentions of souls.'

'Do you think he still had work to do? Or maybe he was troubled?'

Rakisha rolled her shoulders. 'I did not know the man, Rosemary. But he is not here. Of that I'm certain.'

'You're certain. How can you be?'

Rakisha looked at Rosemary, clearing the hair away from her face to see better. 'It's hard to explain to one who is so...' She waved her hand around '...grounded. I just know.'

'But how, Rakisha?' Rosemary waved her hand around to match the seated woman's. 'How can you know when there's nothing there in the first place?'

'Oh, darling.' Rakisha clutched at Rosemary. 'There is never *nothing*. Never.' She leaned closer. 'We are surrounded by waspy wifts of everything. But Bob Brownlee?' She sat back. 'He is definitely not here.'

Rosemary nodded. 'Right. Bob's not here but Bunnie thinks he is. Does that mean she's going to camp under The Exceptional Tree for the rest of her life?'

Rakisha blinked rapidly. 'No. No, no, no.' She shivered. 'If she does that, darling, I will have to leave. I couldn't stand...' Her hands twisted together.

'It's okay, Rakisha. I don't think her friends will allow it.'

'Friends? She has friends?'

'The people that were with her the other night at Roman's. Terrence, Alicia and Donald.'

Rakisha shook her head, sending her hair flying. 'Friends? No, darling, they weren't friends.'

'They acted very protectively.'

'But, darling, protective of what? Bunnie doesn't allow friends, she never did. Too solid for her. She wants admiration, fawning, worship. It's what drives her.'

Rosemary studied the woman next to her. There had been no animosity in her voice. Rakisha stared at her lap, her fingers playing with a long length of cord tie dangling from her blouse. 'She played havoc with your lifestyle.'

'Yes, darling.' Rakisha sighed, gave the cord a final tug and raised her arms to the sky before lowering them into prayer hands. She breathed in deeply and exhaled loudly. 'And I let her affect me again this time. No more.'

Rosemary let the woman practice her deep breathing for a while. A soft breeze stirred the leaves on the massive tree nearby, cooling the air briefly in a reminder that the season was changing. She closed her eyes for a moment.

'Rosemary?'

'Yes?' She opened her eyes to find Rakisha staring directly into them. 'Are you alright?'

'I am perfectly aligned, thank you, darling. But look.' Rakisha stretched her arm out to point across the Square to the front of The Leftover Restaurant. 'That one. See?'

Rosemary swivelled around. Bunnie Brownlee stood gazing at the old bank building, the A-Team beside her at a respectful distance. All except Terrence, who clustered closely to the little woman, his hand seeking hers. He grasped it but Rosemary could tell by the way Bunnie's fingers hung loosely she wasn't returning the hold. 'That one? Terrence?'

'That man, that one. He wants something he won't get.' Rakisha shook her head and jumped up. 'Thank you for the little talk, Rosemary. I hope you feel better for it, darling.' She scooted away in a flurry of cotton, taking a wide berth back to The Sweet Potato in case, Rosemary assumed, Bunnie Lamont saw her.

Rosemary turned her attention back to the little group standing forlornly in front of the closed restaurant. As she watched, Terrence tucked his arm around Bunnie and hugged her close. She half-fell on him, settling her head on his chest, and he bent to kiss her hair. Even from the distance between them, Rosemary could discern the look on his face. Terrence Wright was very happy indeed.

TWENTY-SIX

Rosemary wasn't quite sure what she was going to do when she got there, but she stood and her feet started towards the group without thinking. She'd covered half the ground when Robert came around the side of The Sweet Potato and collided with her. They grabbed at each other for balance and said sorry at the same time.

'My fault,' Robert said, still holding her elbows.

'Most likely,' said Rosemary, extracting herself from his gentle grip. 'Where are you off to?'

He tilted his head slightly toward the road. 'The garage. Where I work. You know.'

She frowned. 'Yes, of course. Although why aren't you already there?'

'I take it a bit easier on a Saturday.' He grinned and brushed his hair from his eyes. 'Unlike you. Although you don't seem to be heading towards your business.'

Rosemary glanced at the restaurant, but the little group had moved on. She glimpsed Bunnie being helped into a car, the three A-Team members forming a horseshoe of assistance. 'I've been talking to Rakisha.'

'Is she okay?'

'Better now, I believe, so I will go back to work.'

'Are you having a busy day?'

She nodded toward the mostly empty Square. 'Clearly not.'

'Then you'll have time to make me a tea and feed me some of those ginger biscuits you keep so well hidden.'

'I do not hide biscuits.'

'Great.' He indicated The Preserved Mulbury. 'Let's go then.'

'I don't suppose you brought the will?'

'No. You were coming to get it from me, last we spoke.' He indicated the garage. 'I was going to work, remember?'

Rosemary glanced back at the car as it moved slowly away. Bunnie's face stared pale and unhappy from the window as it did a U-turn and headed up High Road towards the cemetery. It didn't pause as Rosemary suspected it might from hearing Rakisha's story but disappeared over the hill.

'Rosemary?'

Robert was at the edge of the Square, looking back with concern. 'Yes, you're right. I've been distracted.' She strode up to him and went past, leaving him to hurry to catch up.

Sunny was in the middle of the shop when Rosemary jangled open the door. She sat alert with her tail wrapped around her legs, the tip of it flicking like a snake's tongue. Before Rosemary could bend to pat her, a voice called from her living quarters. 'I've made myself at home.'

Robert heard it as he stepped inside. 'William?'

A chair scuffed back and Robert's brother appeared in the doorway. 'Robert. You're here as well.'

'By invitation.' Robert gave Rosemary a quick look. 'Sort

of. But you? Since when do you barge into someone's house when they aren't here?'

'It was by invitation.' It was William's turn to check Rosemary. 'Sort of.'

Rosemary forced herself to not roll her eyes. 'You are both welcome any time. And, yes, you both had invitations. *Sort of.*' She stooped to pick up Sunny and walked into her home, making William step quickly back. She settled the cat on the couch and went to make tea.

The men hadn't moved. She tried not to look but the silence was heavy. As the kettle boiled, Robert slowly made his way into the dining area, his gaze anywhere but on his brother. William slunk back into the room, taking great interest in the books lining one wall. Rosemary took her time gathering pots and plunger, and the tin of ginger biscuits, and placed them on the table with a thump. 'Sit,' she said. 'I'll get some milk.'

They sat, a brother each side of the table. She put the jug on the table and settled at the end. 'Coffee's there as well. I suspect you both need it.'

'Oh?' asked Robert as he reached for the plunger. 'Why would you say that?'

Rosemary crossed her arms. 'Because you both need warming up and being a little more energised than you are. You walk around like the bottom's falling out of your worlds.' She held up a finger as Robert went to speak. 'No. Don't start. There will be a logical solution to the issues you face but you won't arrive at it with attitudes like you've both been carrying.'

Robert shrugged. 'I just wanted a ginger biscuit.'

She eyeballed him. 'Really.'

His face warmed. 'Although a solution would be handy.'

She offered William the biscuit tin but he shook his

head. 'We already have a solution. My brother needs to pay back what he owes—one way or the other—and then our father's wishes will be fulfilled.'

Robert lifted his hand to decline the tin as well. 'I know what I have to do.' He ran his fingers along the table as if he was playing a swift piano number. 'I have to choose the lesser of two evils.'

'They aren't evil choices,' said William sharply. 'It's just good business.' He poured himself a coffee. 'You were telling me that none of your endeavours turn a big profit.'

Robert bent towards his brother. 'But they're profitable enough, economically and socially.'

'Yes, so you keep saying. What happens when the inevitable downturn comes along?' William waved his hand toward Rosemary's shop. 'This little town is no different to any other that relies on the tourist trade. Can't you see we're in an economic decline? People are struggling with the cost of living, let alone the funds to buy strawberry jam or elaborate pastries or...' he twirled his hand furiously '...a skirt made out of a theatre curtain.'

'Maybe so.' Robert spread his hands out on the table. 'Maybe so, although a well-made pot of jam can bring a lot of pleasure to a family on a tight income. But that's also the point. I can't pull the rug away from people who are heavily invested in this town. I can't destroy their livelihoods by selling off buildings!'

Rosemary waited for the noise of his words to die down. 'There's much at stake for both of you.'

The brothers glanced at each other and looked away.

'What I want to know,' Rosemary continued, 'is how much of a priority your intention is to make these events acceptable to both your circumstances.'

'It can't suit both of us,' said William, crossing his arms. 'That's impossible.'

Rosemary shifted her gaze to Robert. He flung his arms up. 'The only suitable solution for me is one that means my friends still have their businesses. That would seem impossible. The will has strict caveats.'

'Many wills have been contested in the past,' she said.

The sudden silence was not what she expected.

'You've both thought of contesting it.'

Robert looked at William. 'It would go against the wishes of our father.'

William raised his head to stare at his brother. 'Yes.'

'Is that a problem?' Rosemary took a biscuit. 'He's dead.' She took a large bite.

Robert blinked. 'Thank you, Rosemary. That's rather the point.'

'What I mean is, he's not going to know.'

'He won't know,' said William. 'But the business world will. It's not a good look.'

Rosemary chewed her biscuit thoughtfully. 'Surely it happens all the time.'

'Well, yes, but our father...'

'Your father what?'

Robert stretched back in his chair, tipping it on its back legs. 'Our father was regarded very differently by the outside world. He was *beloved*.'

'That's not how I imagined him after talking to you both.'

'No.' Robert let himself flop forward. 'It's not how he was with us.'

'He wasn't cruel, if that's what you are imagining.' William took a biscuit and toyed with it. 'He wasn't anything much. That's the problem.'

'Cold as ice.' Robert wrapped his hands around his mug as if the temperature had dropped. 'The moment he saw either of us, his face froze.'

'He was an absent father?' asked Rosemary.

'No, he was there. Physically, anyway.'

'He was there very much physically.' William crumbled an edge of the biscuit on to the table. 'He was intimidating but silent.' He gave a harsh chuckle. 'I remember one birthday when my mother begged him to join in singing happy birthday and he didn't open his mouth. He couldn't even *say* the words. It was...'

'Horrible,' said Robert. 'Embarrassing. Our mother was very upset although she tried not to show it.' He shrugged. 'Hard to hide tears from two sons aware of her every movement.'

'Sounds nasty.' Rosemary pushed a plate towards William who kept crumbling the biscuit, the fragments falling like rain. 'But all the more reason why you shouldn't care about contesting the will.'

'I can't do it to our mother,' said Robert.

'She's dead, too.'

'Yes, well, thank you, Rosemary. I do know that.'

'You know what I mean.'

'I can't do it to her memory or the legacy of kindness she left.' He shook his head violently. 'I just can't do it.'

'I can't either.' William dropped the remainder of the biscuit on top of the pile of crumbs. 'I know it sounds ridiculous, but there are some things even I draw the line at.' He pointed at his brother. 'You'll have to sell.'

'You'll have to wait.'

'Right.' Rosemary put her hands on the table. 'I can help.'

William shook his head. 'No, you can't. I've had several

lawyers look at the will and they all say there's no way out. He'll have to sell.'

Rosemary took a breath in. 'I really need to look at the will.'

William scoffed. 'Do you have a legal background?'

'I have a pickle background, as you know. Can I still look at it?'

Robert tapped the table. 'I said you could. William?'

William brushed his hand through his hair, settling it into its smart style. 'I have no problem with that. I can't see what harm or *good* it will do.' He reached into his jacket pocket. 'I have it here.'

Robert shook his head. 'You carry that thing around with you?'

'Yes.' William hesitated then pushed it towards Rosemary. 'It's just in case...'

'Just in case *what?*'

Rosemary glared at Robert and took the rectangular envelope. 'Thank you. I'll have a look to see if I can find anything.' She tucked the will into her fruit bowl. 'I imagine every word is etched into both your heads.'

Robert shrugged but William only stared at the envelope nestled among some Granny Smith apples. Rosemary pushed her chair back and stood.

Robert rose as well. 'Rosemary, thank you, but I don't think it will make any difference.' He wiped his face but the sadness on it didn't clear. 'None at all.'

'Then it won't hurt me reading it.' She pushed her chair in.

Robert took a step towards the door and stopped to stare at her. 'Hang on, just what are you thinking? You have that look on your face.'

'What look?'

'You know full well what look.' His face shifted into a small smile. 'You're up to something.'

She waved him on, indicating to William that he should go, as well. 'Robert, I'm never up to something.'

The brothers walked through the shop, William heading out to the street first. Robert did a half-turn as he left. 'Rosemary,' he called back through the doorway. 'You're always up to something.'

She smiled, closed the door behind them, and bent down to Sunny who'd followed them out. The tabby purred as Rosemary stroked her chin. 'He's so suspicious.'

The cat did a languid turn and stuck her tail in the air as she went back to the couch. *He has every reason to be,* the tail seemed to say.

TWENTY-SEVEN

Closing time. Rosemary's attention was grabbed by a muffled yelp coming from The Green Mulbury. She dashed next door to find Mrs Lionel sitting on a kitchen chair nursing bleeding knees. 'I tripped,' the older woman said firmly. 'It wasn't a fall.'

Rosemary nodded grimly as she fetched the well-stocked first aid kit from Mrs Lionel's laundry cupboard. A *fall* spelled quite a different future than a *trip*, as Mrs Lionel had often said from her experience as a nurse. Rosemary cleaned the wounds on her friend's legs. 'What did you trip on?'

'That.'

Rosemary followed the direction of Mrs Lionel's finger. Laying on the floor to the left of a display of rose geranium and lavender soaps was a cardboard box. It was slightly squashed on one side, evidence of Mrs Lionel's misadventure. 'What is it?'

'I don't know but something solid is in it.' Mrs Lionel took a sharp breath in as Rosemary dabbed antiseptic on one knee, and put a hand out to soothe something near the floor that Rosemary assumed was an anxious Percy. 'Otherwise, I wouldn't have gone down. I was too intent on refilling my display and didn't see it.' She sighed and clutched her leg just above her knee. 'I think I've ruined a day's work.'

Rosemary applied a square plaster to one knee, glancing back at the scatters of soap spread across the floor. 'We'll recut them. They'll be saleable.'

'Thank you.' Mrs Lionel put the back of her hand to her cheek and pressed hard, but when she took it away, there was no evidence of tears. 'You are a good friend.'

'As are you. Is that better?'

Mrs Lionel looked down at the neat patches on her knees. 'Very well done. I expect there'll be some bruising.'

'You might have to be extra careful for a few days.' Rosemary gathered the rubbish from the dressings and stood. 'Let's have a cup of tea and look at that box.'

Mrs Lionel stayed where she was, tentatively stretching her legs out in turn, as Rosemary tidied up, put the kettle on, and fetched the box. It was quite heavy and she understood how catching her toe on it had brought Mrs Lionel down. She placed the box on Mrs Lionel's lap and made tea. 'What is it?' she asked after a few moments of silence.

'It looks like a rock. Strangely familiar, though.'

Rosemary brought the tea things over and settled them on the table before coming around to peer in the box. It was indeed a rock, but she reached in and tipped it over.

'Ah,' said Mrs Lionel. 'Some sort of gemstone.'

The stone was attached to the rock's grey surface, its many surfaces glittering. 'You said it's strangely familiar?'

'Now that I see it like this, it's quite familiar. It's a type of olivine, probably peridot. I've seen a sample in a museum. It forms in lava.'

'Right.' Rosemary touched the gem's surface lightly. 'The question is, what was it doing on the floor of your shop? I'd hardly call it a museum.'

'Thanks for the reassurance.' Mrs Lionel lifted the heavy object out and put it on a place mat on the table. 'I have no idea how it got there although I know I certainly didn't have anything to do with it.'

'Have you had a lot of visitors today? I thought it had been quiet.'

Mrs Lionel nodded. 'Very quiet for a Saturday which was why I decided to do some rearrangements. I was in the spare room for quite some time, selecting soaps.'

'Can you hear your door frog from the spare room?'

Mrs Lionel smiled wryly. 'Most can hear my frog from across the Square, although I have to say I had my head in a cupboard and, you know...' She tapped her ear.

'I get it. I'm sure my hearing isn't as good as it was, either.' Rosemary frowned. 'If someone wanted you to have the gem, why didn't they put it on your counter?'

'Unless it was an accident, something left behind by someone in a rush.'

'Someone who didn't expect to be seen maybe.' Rosemary glanced back at the shop. 'Have you noticed anything else? Is anything missing, for example?'

'Oh.' Mrs Lionel used the table to help her stand and took a few test steps before walking more confidently to her shop. She tutted at the soaps on the floor, then started a scan of the shelves. 'Oh,' she said again, pointing to a rack of drying herbs. 'Where's my sage? And my rosemary? And my basil!'

The rack, usually full of aromatic herbs hanging to dry, was largely empty. As Rosemary looked further, she saw great gaps in the shelf usually housing bags of already dried plants. 'Anything else missing?'

Mrs Lionel took a moment to walk around the room. 'No. My lotions and creams are still there and they're the most expensive items I sell.'

'I don't think this thief was interested in expensive items. They were very focused.'

'But why? Mrs Lionel put her hands on her hips. 'Unless they're chefs or make their own potpourri, there's not a lot of interest in mass quantities of herbs.'

'Not for the average person.'

'So, we're looking for someone in particular?'

'Perhaps a group of people with a particular interest.' Rosemary unhooked a bunch of drying lavender from the rack. 'What are the medicinal properties of lavender?'

'There are many.' Mrs Lionel went to the shop counter and leaned on it, easing the pressure off each of her legs in turn. 'It's an anti-inflammatory agent, so some people rub a little oil on their temples if they have headaches. It may help reduce anxiety and get people some sleep. Some use the heads in cooking as it can aid digestion. Will I go on?'

'Why do you like it?'

Mrs Lionel smiled. 'The fragrance is lovely and reminds me of my mother.'

Rosemary nodded. 'So, the thief wasn't interested in assistance with headaches, anxiety or digestion. You say sage, rosemary and basil are missing?'

Mrs Lionel walked carefully over to the packets stashed on her shelf. 'Only the holy basil is gone, I see. That's interesting.'

'Would there be similar properties in sage, rosemary and holy basil?'

'That would depend on which reference you adhere to.

Herbalism is an ancient art, dating back to prehistoric times. Unfortunately, I don't have access to the writings of Hippocrates, Galen or Pliny.' She pointed to a shelf above the counter. 'My modern guru is not near as well known. For plant-related properties, I will always consult my herbal dictionary written by Mrs Beatrice Bantam in 1856.'

Rosemary reached up and found the old volume, a scruffy leather-bound book with yellowed, fragile papers. 'Well used, I see.'

'It was my mother's. Does it remind you of something?'

'Aunt Lilibeth's recipe book.'

'Yes. The wisdom of the women who went before us.' Mrs Lionel took the book from Rosemary and opened it at the index. 'She lists things in alphabetical order but uses the same keywords in their description so you can compare properties. If I look up sage and holy basil...'

Rosemary waited patiently as the older woman went back and forth through the book, nodding to herself and mouthing occasional words. When she finally looked up, Rosemary tilted her head. 'Well?'

Mrs Lionel adjusted her glasses and began to read aloud. '"Sage is widely celebrated for its protective qualities, often used to cleanse areas of negative energies and provide spiritual fortification. It is said to ward off evil spirits and purify the atmosphere, making it a staple in many ritualistic practices."' She took a breath and continued. '"Holy basil, on the other hand, is revered for its divine associations and is considered to possess a sacred essence. It is believed to promote harmony, dispel malevolent influences, and enhance spiritual clarity."' She looked up. 'Both herbs, says Mrs Bantam, offer significant supernatural benefits through slightly different routes—sage through its purifying and protective properties, and holy basil through its sanctifying and harmonising effects.'

'Mrs Beatrice Bantam says that?'

Mrs Lionel smiled. 'I took the liberty of rephrasing a little. But you get the drift.'

'And adding rosemary to this conversation?'

Mrs Lionel's eyes twinkled as she responded, 'Ah, rosemary. Another herb with its unique supernatural properties.' She cleared her throat and consulted the book again. '"Rosemary is cherished for its ability to enhance memory and mental clarity. It is often used in rituals to promote focus and insight. In addition to its cognitive benefits, rosemary is believed to offer strong protective qualities. It is said to ward off nightmares when placed under a pillow and to safeguard against negative influences when hung above doorways. Many also use it in purification rituals, like sage, to cleanse spaces of harmful energies."'

'There is a potential connection between them.'

'A blend of protection, sanctity, and clarity. Imagining combining them. To some people, this would triple the protection.'

Rosemary pondered this. 'Mrs Bantam certainly knew her herbs.'

'Indeed, she did.'

'But we know the situation.'

'We do?'

'Come and sit down again. We didn't finish our tea.'

As Mrs Lionel settled in her chair and poured herself more tea, Rosemary picked up the rock again. 'We have a group of paranormal investigators, the BTPI. They wear peridot accessories, did you know that?'

'I did not.' Mrs Lionel sipped her tea. 'What else?'

'We have a sub-group of BTPI called the A Team. They wear smoky quartz accessories.'

'Lovely. True gem lovers.'

Rosemary frowned at Mrs Lionel who grinned. 'The properties of each differ.'

'Mrs Bantam did not include gemstones in her book.'

'No, but the internet does.'

Mrs Lionel rolled her eyes. 'Tell me. What are the properties of each?'

'For what we're looking at, peridot is believed to be a powerful protective stone. It's said to shield its wearer from negative energies and psychic attacks. Paranormal investigators cherish it for its ability to clear the mind and enhance the perception of the unseen.'

Mrs Lionel raised an eyebrow. 'And smoky quartz?'

'Smoky quartz is renowned for its grounding properties,' Rosemary explained, holding the rock up to catch the light. 'It helps to anchor yourself and ward off negative influences, making it an essential tool for those delving into paranormal activities. It's also thought to assist in communicating with spirits, providing clarity and protection in such encounters.'

Mrs Lionel nodded. 'So quite different properties, if you believe that sort of thing. One wards off the spirts while the other helps you communicate.'

Rosemary smiled, placing the rock back on the table. 'Exactly.'

'You think the people that took my herbs are members of the BTPI but not the A Team.'

'I do.'

'And why do some people investigating paranormal activity want to keep spirits away while the other wants to keep them close?'

'Wouldn't that depend on who the spirit was?' Rosemary couldn't help but glance under the table where she saw nothing but chair and table legs. 'Or what?'

Mrs Lionel smiled and indicated an area of carpet near the window. 'If you're looking for Percy, he's asleep in the sun.'

Rosemary stared at where her friend was pointing but saw nothing but the floor. 'Percy sleeps? And he can feel the sun?'

'Who knows?' Mrs Lionel smiled fondly at her apparition. 'I imagine it's a habit more than anything. A doggie ritual.'

Rosemary sat straight. 'A ritual?'

'Yes, he always sleeps there at this time of the year.' Mrs Lionel frowned at her friend. 'Just what are you thinking, Rosemary Exeter?'

Rosemary tapped the rock on the table in front of her. 'I was thinking about rituals.' She stood, her chair rough against Mrs Lionel's floorboards. 'Are you up for a drive?'

TWENTY-EIGHT

Rosemary drove towards Big Town at a slightly slower speed than she would normally. The D-Day Development billboard cast a long shadow across its paddock in the early evening light, hiding the call to sophisticated living in its dimness. 'That's where Heather found her ibis,' she remarked to her passenger.

Mrs Lionel grunted, shifting her legs so they were as outstretched as possible. 'She likes to wander, does Heather. I sometimes wonder what else she discovers in her quest to rescue deceased birds.' She moved her legs again.

'Are you okay?'

'Yes, perhaps a little battered. I did come down heavily on that floor.' She shrugged. 'But I didn't break anything so my bones must be quite good.'

'You are tough.'

'Not tough, dear. Just sensible. No use whinging about my comfortable situation when so many others are doing it hard.'

Rosemary chewed her lip for a moment. 'Do you think

it's possible some people do it hard because they're so well provided for?'

'Are you thinking of Robert and William?'

'Yes. No matter what happens with their father's will, neither of them are going to be poverty-stricken.'

'I don't think that's the point of their conflict, dear.'

'No. They're both concerned about their responsibilities to other people.'

'That makes whatever happens next difficult.' Mrs Lionel smoothed her skirt. 'But whatever that is, I always think there's a silver lining somewhere.'

Rosemary glanced sharply at her friend. 'What do you mean?'

'Well.' Mrs Lionel folded her hands in her lap. 'Imagine that Robert had to sell Mulbury Feeds and the new owners didn't want Hannah, Heather or Millie.'

'I don't want to imagine that. It would be devastating.'

'Do you really think so?'

Rosemary was quiet for a moment. 'Heather would be okay. She's got another job with Patti and Gerry. In fact, it would give her more time to devote to her bespoke garments.'

'Yes, exactly. And Millie doesn't need the work. She needs occupation and I can see her helping Rakisha in the café, perhaps helping to turn it into something more profitable so it supports two women of few needs.'

'Right. But what about Hannah?'

'Hannah.' Mrs Lionel smiled fondly. 'Hannah, the middle sister. Hannah stuck at Mulbury Feeds as her sisters find other ways to make their mark on the world.' She sighed. 'Hannah is lively and curious. Freed of the business her father started and she's kept going, she could do anything. Learn a lost trade. Travel the world. Go visit her sister and swim in an ocean. Hannah would be perfectly fine.'

Rosemary adjusted her hands on the steering wheel. 'Are you saying you want Robert to sell the animal produce store?'

'I'm not saying that.' Mrs Lionel smiled. 'And you know I wasn't. I'm just putting alternative possibilities out.'

'What about if he sold Ravenshome?'

'Patti and Gerry would need to relocate Patricia's. They could return to their old premises, Honey B's Teas, but they moved because that building wasn't big enough for their showroom and their need to store un-upcycled garments.' Mrs Lionel frowned momentarily before widening her eyes. 'There're a few choices for them. I imagine they don't want to move from Mulbury so they might do a deal with Jules and Roman. The old bank building has an upstairs area rarely used that could house a creative venture or perhaps they could take over a smaller place and put their garments online as well.'

'What smaller space? You just said Patricia's wouldn't fit back into Honey B's Teas.'

'I might offer them my shop.'

Rosemary's hands twitched on the wheel, making the car wobble a little. She settled it back on the road. '*You* are in your shop,' she said firmly, looking straight ahead.

'I know, dear. But I won't be there forever.' The older woman moved her legs again and, from the edge of her vision, Rosemary glimpsed her grimace as her knees bent. 'I could offer them The Green Mulbury for a small rent.'

'That won't work at all. The shop wouldn't even hold Patti's range of skirts.' Rosemary shook her head. 'No. Anyway, Percy would hate it. Imagine the noise from a busload of teenagers intent on unusual graduation dresses.'

Mrs Lionel laughed quietly. 'Percy would be fine as long as he was with me.'

They drove for a moment in silence. 'You aren't serious, are you?' Rosemary asked finally.

Mrs Lionel took a while to answer. 'I don't know, dear. You've caught me on a bad day.'

'Never make decisions on a bad day.' Rosemary put a quick hand on her friend's forearm. 'I'm sure some philosopher said that at some stage.'

'Possibly.' Mrs Lionel patted her knees gently. 'Anyway, I don't think I've answered your original question very well.'

'You have. If Robert had to sell anything, it would be better to be Mulbury Feeds.'

'Yes, I think so. Although, to be honest, I think it would be easier and quicker in this market to sell a regal house like Ravenshome than it would an animal produce business. Wealthy people always seem to have money for large houses when business people can't rub two coins together.'

'Unless, of course, they are wealthy business people.'

Mrs Lionel chuckled. 'Not too many of them in my hometown.'

'Except for William.'

'He's only a visitor. And do you really think he's wealthy?'

'What do you mean?'

'Well,' said Mrs Lionel, easing her leg into a bent position. 'If he is, why is he so concerned his daughter won't be cared for unless the will's conditions are met?'

Rosemary chewed her lip for a moment. 'Vivienne has a progressive neurological disorder. Robert told me.'

'Oh no!' Mrs Lionel sighed. 'That's so tragic. Her father wants to provide for her every need, I'm imagining.'

'Yes.'

'This does put things in a different light.'

'Indeed.'

The car was in the outskirts of Big Town, where new developments leaked into empty paddocks. Rosemary felt a familiar sense of sadness at the growth that would eventually reach Mulbury and other towns nearby. It may not happen in my lifetime, she thought, but it will almost certainly happen.

'Are you alright, dear?'

Rosemary glanced over at her passenger. 'Yes. Just thinking. And wondering. William has an expensive car, smart clothes and a coiffure that drips wealth but beyond that, I imagine his richness might be confined to assets and investments rather than cash. It's pseudo-wealth to some extent.'

'I was wondering the same, which would make the expectation of further wealth in cash from the will very welcome as he needs it for a particular reason.' Mrs Lionel turned her head to watch a group of people gathering at a bus stop. 'Tell me again why we've come to town?'

'We're here to witness someone's rituals.'

Mrs Lionel only nodded as Rosemary pulled up in front of the building housing the rural insurance company. Streetlights flickered on as they got out of the car, although the early evening was bright with moonrise. The door to the building was closed but as Rosemary pushed, it swung open. A series of signs marked 'BTPI' and 'Silviana's Salutations' with arrows pointing the way decorated the walls. 'What are we doing here?' whispered Mrs Lionel as Rosemary followed the arrowed directions.

'We're going to be observers at a meeting.'

'A meeting of the BTPI?'

'Yes.'

'Are we allowed to be observers?'

Rosemary pointed to a sign that read 'New members welcome'. 'I think so.'

'Not sure that relates to the BTPI,' said Mrs Lionel, frowning at the picture of a yogi underneath the words. 'There are other classes run in this building.'

Rosemary looked back at her friend. 'Well, we're not townies so how are we meant to know?'

Mrs Lionel shook her head but kept following. 'Cheeky,' she muttered.

The arrows led them to the same area Rosemary had been to before. This time, though, the door was unlocked and wide open. She hoped Bern wasn't around to see it as she suspected he might have had a conniption. She put her hand out to slow Mrs Lionel. 'Can you smell that?' she asked quietly.

Instead of the bland odour of an office, a sweet earthy fragrance filtered its way along the corridor to where they stood. Mrs Lionel sniffed. 'White sage,' she said. 'My sage, at that.'

'How can you tell?'

'It's freshly dried and it has the right hint of camphor to it. If it gets too dry, the oils have gone.' She moved closer to Rosemary. 'These are the people who took my herbs? Have we come here to accuse them?'

'Yes and no. Yes, I think they have your herbs. No, I didn't think we would accuse them of anything. I just want to see how they behave.'

'In what way?'

'I'll show you.'

They crept towards the burning herbs. Voices spoke quietly ahead and when they reached the end of the corridor, Rosemary saw a group of about twenty people seated in a horseshoe looking out the enormous windows of the yoga room. Three pots stationed around the chairs held smouldering plant matter, smoke winding its skinny way up towards the roof, dissipating in the slight breeze coming from an open window.

'They look like they're watching a movie,' said Mrs Lionel quietly.

'In a way, they are.' Rosemary nodded towards the great expanse of glass. 'Watch.'

They waited a few minutes. The room dimmed, lit only by the hint of moon rising over the edge of town. A few more minutes and it blazed into full view, a great white circle with a soft corona stretching out into the sky. The voices quietened and Rosemary saw people clutch at their chests. 'Necklaces,' she said softly. 'Peridot necklaces.'

'What did you say, dear?' asked Mrs Lionel, a little too loudly in the hush.

A woman in a side chair turned to the voice, making others do the same. 'Oh, no!' she said, standing swiftly, making her chair scrape on the ground. 'Ghosts!'

TWENTY-NINE

Rosemary expected a crowd of paranormal investigators to be excited about seeing a ghost or two. At the very least, she wanted someone to frown and pull out a notebook ready to make notes. What she didn't think would happen was what was happening right in front of her.

'Ghosts!' screamed the woman again, and the group rose as one and scampered to the windows, pressing themselves against the glass as if they were hoping they could teleport away.

Rosemary glanced at Mrs Lionel who stood in the corridor entry lit by the white moonlight. She did look pale and ethereal, but she was also obviously an older woman in a sensible skirt and cardigan standing with arms crossed and mouth slightly open. 'What do you think?' asked Rosemary.

'I think they don't want to see ghosts. But they're ghost hunters.' Mrs Lionel shook her head. 'What's going on here?'

'Let's ask.'

Rosemary stepped forward, followed by Mrs Lionel who, out of the direct moonlight, looked even more like a shopkeeper, former nurse and dairy farmer. The crowd shrieked again but gradually the noise died away, a tiny eeeek! the last to go. 'What on earth is this all about?' asked Rosemary, putting on her headmistress voice Jasper was so keen to remind her she had.

'You're... you're... human?'

'Last time I looked.' Rosemary tipped her head at the man who'd spoken. 'Are you?'

The man put a hand on his head as if to check. 'Well, yes, of course.'

'You seem more like a plate of jellies to me.'

Rosemary felt Mrs Lionel's hand on her arm. 'Are you alright, dears? You are visibly terrified. I thought that ghost hunters would be more...'

'Ecstatic,' said Rosemary.

'Resilient,' added Mrs Lionel.

The crowd peeled itself off the glass but remained on the other side of the room. The man came warily forward until he was within arm's reach of the women, his slightly red eyes visible now. It dawned on Rosemary that she'd seen him before: Gadget Man from the BTPI. She watched him closely as he stretched a finger out and poked Rosemary rather savagely in the bicep.

'Watch it, sunshine,' said Rosemary.

'Sorry.' Gadget Man tumbled back a step. 'Just check-ing.' He blinked at Mrs Lionel.

Rosemary took a step towards him. 'Don't even think about.'

'No, no, of course not.' His hand went up to his head again. 'So sorry. But why did you think we were ghosthunters?'

'I recognise you from when you dined at the restaurant. You're part of the BTPI.'

'Yes, I'm Cameron Gilbert, the current team leader.' He glanced back at the group who were creeping forward timidly. 'You think we're paranormal investigators?'

'That's what BTPI stands for, doesn't it?'

'Originally, yes. Bunnie Brownlee started it with Terrence Wright. But we branched away once we realised Bunnie's...obsession.'

'Bunnie's obsession?'

'Yes.' Mr Gilbert looked back at a woman wearing a familiar brown tracksuit, who nodded encouragingly. 'She wants more than anything to have her own ghost.' He shook his head. 'It was making her do very strange things—sleeping on graves, going to strangers' funerals, hanging around the hospital morgue—so we branched away.'

'You aren't paranormal investigators then?'

'Not in the typical sense. We are the BTPI but it now stands for the "Body for Theoretical Paranormal Incidents".' He pushed his shoulders back and looked Rosemary in the eye. 'We hunt for ghosts to protect others. We keep ghosts *away* from people.'

'Right,' said Rosemary, frowning. 'You're exorcists?'

'No, no, just professional protectors. If we find a ghost, we can alert others to be aware of them.'

'Right.' Rosemary stared hard at the man. 'You said *if*. Does this mean you haven't found a ghost yet?'

'We can't be one hundred percent certain we have, despite our sensitive responses to possible encounters.' Mr Gilbert lowered his voice and clutched the stone strapped to his wrist. 'Not that we want to meet any.'

'You meet every month, every full moon, in order to be scared stiff that you'll find a ghost?'

'No, no, no.' Long strands of the man's hair flapped over his head as he shook it. 'No, we want to be able to warn people if there are supernatural beings about. We are *ghoul free vigilantes* for the rest of our community.'

'I don't quite understand, dear,' said Mrs Lionel, inching forward but keeping out of the man's range. 'You are terrified of ghosts, yet you seek them out. That doesn't sound very sensible to me.'

'It's our way of giving back to the community,' said Tracksuit Woman, coming to stand next to Mr Gilbert. 'Some people do voluntary work at thrift shops or animal rescue shelters. Our voluntary work is keeping people safe from the supernatural. It's what we did when Bob was alive and, now that he isn't, it's even more important.'

Rosemary studied the crowd who were nodding earnestly. 'What's Bob Brownlee got to do with it?'

'Oh, Bob was our founding member.'

'Hang on.' Rosemary crossed her arms. 'You said Bunnie and Terrence started BTPI.'

'They did.' The woman screwed up her face. 'But Bob founded the Body, *our* BTPI.'

'Why?'

'He had an...' the woman's voice hushed '...encounter.'

'An encounter?' Rosemary's voice was too loud for someone in the crowd who squeaked in protest. 'What sort of encounter?'

'It was just after he married Bunnie, you see.' Mr Gilbert looked to the others, some of whom nodded encouragingly. 'They were in a graveyard one night. No, don't ask me why but we figured it was Bunnie who led *that* particular expedition.' The man grimaced. 'Anyway, while they were there, a *thing* came out of the shadows and hurled itself at them. Bob threw himself across Bunnie to protect her. Not that she was pleased about that, by all accounts, because she says she didn't see anything and was worried it might have been a sign of something else.'

'Bob probably made it up,' said someone in the crowd. 'He was a trickster.'

Mr Gilbert frowned at the speaker. 'Bob was a generous man and he saw himself as a protector. He started BTPI to protect others by finding out where paranormal beings might be and hopefully keeping others away. And that's why we joined because we, too, want to protect people from nasty spectral encounters.'

Rosemary looked at the shivering crowd, shaking her head slightly before turning back to Mr Gilbert. 'Bob sounds like a ghost*buster*.'

'Exactly! Although not with lasers or containment boxes. The best Bob could do was to locate the problem and keep others away.'

'And you continue his work?'

The man nodded, glancing around at his colleagues as they joined in. 'Our hypersensitivity to paranormal happenings makes us excellent at what we do.'

'Not so excellent, dear,' said Mrs Lionel mildly. 'You thought I was a ghost.'

'Well, yes, but we quickly ascertained you weren't.' The man turned and indicated a large leatherbound journal on his chair. 'You wouldn't have made it into the book.'

'The book?'

'It's where we record our encounters.' He marched over and lifted the book from the chair, flipping it open so Rosemary and Mrs Lionel could see columns of spidery writing. 'Every moment goose pimples rise on the back of our neck, every shadow we see but can't account for, every movement in the corner of our eye...it's all in here.'

'I can see that.' Rosemary pointed at the last column which was mostly blank. 'What's recorded here?'

'Oh. That's our conclusion.' He snapped the book shut.

'So, not many of your feelings actually turn out to be specific encounters?'

'We're working on that.'

Rosemary glanced around the crowd. 'If Bob started this group, why isn't Bunnie here?'

Mrs Lionel nudged her friend 'She's grieving, dear.'

Tracksuit Woman gave Mrs Lionel a sharp look. 'You think? I'm not so sure. But Bunnie was never part of our group. Bob started the BTPI but Bunnie ruled the *A*-BTPI. Now, they're a weird lot.'

'What do you mean?'

'The A Team, as they call themselves, would rather have a community of ghosts than people. They think they're special. No.' Mr Gilbert shook his head. 'Bunnie thinks *she's* special. She has a need to be connected to people of the past.'

'The graveyard she took Bob to,' said Rosemary. 'That was where her previous husband is buried.'

'Yes! You knew? She thinks Bob scared him away that night and she's been angry with him ever since.'

'So, she started the A Team.'

'With Terrence, of course,' said someone in the crowd above a sudden whispering. 'Others joined them.'

'Alicia,' said another.

'Donald.'

'Others joined,' repeated Mr Gilbert. 'But it was Terrence who was immediately at her side.'

'Any particular reason?' asked Rosemary.

He gave a short laugh. 'What other reason could it be but the obvious?'

Rosemary frowned, staring at the man. Mrs Lionel tugged at her sleeve. 'Love, dear. Love is the reason, as they say.'

'Right.' Rosemary pursed her lips. 'Love. And does Bunnie Brownlee love Terrence back?'

The man's face darkened. Behind him, the crowd went silent. 'No. Bunnie Brownlee knows only one love and that is for herself.'

'Does Terrence know that?'

The crowd murmured sadly, shaking their heads and looking down at their feet. 'Unrequited love,' said Mrs Lionel. 'Love of the very worst kind.'

'Yes,' said Mr Gilbert. 'It brings out the very worst, too.'

Rosemary tipped her head at him. 'What does that mean?'

He wiped a hand over his reddening face. 'Oh, speaking out of turn, I am.'

'Too late,' said Rosemary. 'We get a picture of a man madly in love. Is that correct?'

'I think so.' The man glanced at the others, some of whom nodded. 'I don't have much time for Terrence, particularly as I thought his intentions very obvious when Bob was alive. Still...' he shrugged '...Bob didn't seem to notice. He was a bit naïve, really. Too ready with the jokes to see that this joke was on him.' He glanced around as if Bob may hear him.

'That's awkward.' Rosemary indicated the storeroom where the first aid equipment was stored. 'Does anyone frequent that room?'

'I don't think so.' The man confirmed his response with his friends. 'Why would we?'

'Who do you get the key from to use this room?'

'It's mine,' said a quiet voice from the back of the crowd.

'I use this area a few times a week but not the first aid room. My mats and bolsters are stacked in there.'

'You're Silviana the yoga teacher,' said Rosemary after checking the pile of pink objects in the room she pointed at.

'Yes, that's me.' A tiny woman stepped forward, her hands in a prayer position making her sleeves fall back to reveal bony arms and frail skin. 'Namaste.'

'Namaste,' said Rosemary, noting the woman's silvery hair and bright eyes. 'Did you normally go around taking herbs from cottage industries?'

Mr Gilbert's eyebrows shot up. 'What?'

'Mrs Lionel owns The Green Mulbury where you took these herbs.' Rosemary nodded towards the burning sage.

'We didn't steal them.' He turned to the woman who shook her head. 'We couldn't find the owner. We left money in an envelope under the computer keyboard.'

Rosemary and Mrs Lionel exchanged glances. 'We didn't check,' said Mrs Lionel.

'Oh, no, you thought we'd stolen them!' Mr Gilbert looked aghast. 'No, no. We were in a hurry, though. We had to get back for this.' He indicated the group.

'You left your peridot behind.'

He frowned, feeling the stone around his wrist. He tapped his finger on his lip before holding his finger straight. 'Ah! My raw material rock! I had placed it on the floor. I hope it wasn't a nuisance.'

'No,' said Mrs Lionel before Rosemary could respond. 'I'll keep it safe until you come and get it.'

'Thank you. So,' said the man, rummaging in his pocket for his phone and holding it up. 'It costs ten dollars to join and I can take electronic payments.'

'Join what, dear?' asked Mrs Lionel.

'The BTPI.' The man frowned. 'You surely didn't come all this way to check we paid for the herbs?'

'Not entirely,' said Rosemary, taking Mrs Lionel's elbow gently and starting to back away.

'Your first yoga class is free after you register,' said Silviana, whipping her phone out from her baggy trousers. 'If that's why you're here.'

'No, that's not it, either.'

'Hang on,' said the man, his face darkening. 'Just why are you here? Are you sneaky journalists looking to cash in on Bob's death?'

'We're shopkeepers,' said Mrs Lionel firmly. 'The only cashing in we want is when you buy our goods.'

'Now we've discovered you did pay for the herbs, we'll go.'

They continued a steady retreat from the moonlit room. No one came after them and, even if they had, Rosemary was pretty sure a simple ghostly wail would have sent them scurrying back into hiding.

As they started the drive back home, Mrs Lionel shuffled around to look at Rosemary. 'Did you get the information you needed?'

'I got more than I bargained for.'

'Which is...?'

Rosemary drove on for a bit before answering. 'The A-BTPI is not what we thought.'

THIRTY

Mrs Lionel went straight home after their adventure, texting Rosemary to say she'd found the envelope full of money to cover the costs of the missing herbs. It left Rosemary to have a quiet night with Sunny. The ginger tabby sat next to her on the couch, matching her mistress's stare at the wall in front of them. 'A few things still puzzle me, Sunny,' said Rosemary, gently stroking the cat's head. 'But it is getting clearer. I'll iron them out tomorrow.'

Sunny curled her tail around herself and put her head on the couch. *Good,* the gesture seemed to say. *Your loud thinking was keeping me awake.*

Rosemary left her companion to the couch and went to bed to stare at the ceiling instead.

SUNDAY DAWNED BRISKLY. The cold fresh air stung Rosemary's cheeks as she leaned on her balcony rail to drink a morning cup of green tea. The sun sent long shadows in front of it as it rose, and magpies sat hunched on branches talking quietly to each other. It was the perfect setting for someone to think things through quietly-

'Rosemary!'

The loudness made her jump although the voice was as familiar as toast and jam for breakfast. 'Jasper. Something I can do to help you?'

'No?' Jasper hooked his dark hair over one ear and looked at her, puzzled. 'Is there?'

Rosemary left her rail and went to the one shared by the balconies between dwellings. 'No. But there might be something you can do for me.'

Even in the low morning light, she could see Jasper's flushing face. 'What would that be, Rosemary?'

'It's those books. The paranormal ones.'

'Spectre Season? What about them?'

'You've read them all.'

'Yes, all twenty-seven. They're quite gripping, you know.'

'I'll take your word for it.' She reached over the rail and caught his hand. 'Can you remember any of the plots that featured ghosts?'

He had his eyes on her hand and took a moment to answer. 'Ghosts, specifically?'

'Yes. Ghosts, apparitions, manifestations: whatever you call them.'

'Yes, I think I can remember.' He closed his eyes for a moment. 'There's one where a haunted lighthouse keeper is tormented by the spirits of lost sailors seeking retribution.'

'No.'

'What?'

'Not what I want.' She let go his hand to wave hers around. 'More.'

'In another, a grieving widow discovers her late

husband's ghost inhabiting their old home, guiding her to uncover a hidden family secret.'

'Not bad. Another?'

'Then there's a plot about a group of teenagers who accidentally summon a vengeful spirit during a séance and must find a way to banish it.'

'Definitely not.'

'One story features an ancient castle where the ghost of a betrayed noblewoman helps a modern-day historian solve an age-old murder.'

'Too historic.'

'Okay, what about a tale of a ghostly detective who returns from the afterlife to solve his own mysterious death?'

'Mmmm.'

Jasper straightened, keeping his hands on the rail. 'You think we have a dead detective in the mix?'

'No. We have a dead farmer. Not the same.'

'I'm not sure what you're looking for.'

Rosemary finished her tea and swung the mug by its handle. 'I'm looking for a feasible reason for the events in Mulbury. We have the mysterious death of a man stuffed into a mannikin's case. We have a tragic, but not mysterious, death of a man in a storage room. We have two groups of people we thought were ghosthunters but it turns out one wants to repel them while the other wants to attract them. And we have a woman who appears more interested in her husband dead than alive.'

'Two groups? I thought there was only the BTPI?'

'Turns out the BTPI is the group who's scared of ghosts while the A-BTPI wants to see Bob in all his ethereal glory.' She filled him in on the visit last night.

Jasper gripped the rail tightly. 'That changes things, doesn't it?'

'Yes. It focuses the mystery on them.'

'But you haven't any further ideas.'

Rosemary shook her head.

'You know...' Jasper bent to acknowledge Snowy as the old dog clattered stiffly down the steps to the backyard. 'One of my favourite Spectre plots doesn't involve any ghosts at all.' He leaned over to rest his elbows on the rail.

Rosemary matched Jasper's position on the rail, her left elbow lightly touching his. 'Tell me more.'

'It's about one of the side characters, called Nell, who desperately wants to see a ghost because everyone else in her group says they have. They tease Nell, you see. Call her a boring sceptic.'

'She doesn't like that label?'

'No, because she believes in the supernatural even if she's never seen anything to boost that belief. Anyway, she's normally a quiet thing but inside she's really angry. She kills the boyfriend of the lead Spectre by pushing him down a well and then sits on the edge waiting for his ghost because everyone believes ghosts are ghosts because they are troubled souls. She waits for three days in the summer heat but it never comes.'

'What happens next?'

'Nell's so dehydrated that she tips into the well and dies.' Jasper gave an involuntary shiver. 'When the Spectre lead hunts for her boyfriend near the well, she sees the ghost of the girl who murdered him instead.'

'That doesn't make sense.'

'It does. Nell murders the boy and comes back as the ghost she wanted to see.' Jasper rolled his eyes. 'It's ironic.'

'You said they believed ghosts were troubled souls. Why didn't the boy appear as a ghost then? He was murdered.'

'Ah, yes, but he wasn't *troubled*. He was a happy boy, especially because of his girlfriend. The relationship they had saved him from the memories of a terrible childhood and he was at ease with himself for the first time in his life.'

Rosemary nodded slowly. 'So from what you're saying, he had reached ultimate happiness. The murder wasn't the troubling act the killer thought it was. Not to him anyway. It was to Nell.'

'Yep.' Jasper grinned. 'And that's the power of a book. A good storyline makes sense in the end.' He stopped smiling. 'What's the matter? You look like the cat who's got the cream.'

Rosemary couldn't help glancing inside where Sunny sat on the windowsill, eyeballing them. 'Cream has too much lactose for cats.'

'Rosemary...'

'Right. Sorry. Can't help myself sometimes.' She stretched back, letting her forearms slide on the rails until she could grip it. 'By all accounts, Bob Brownlee was a happy, generous man. He wasn't troubled, as far as we know.'

'Perhaps this is why Bunnie can't summon him.'

'It could also be that ghosts aren't a real phenomenon.'

Jasper laughed. 'Well, of course I hadn't thought of that! But it doesn't really matter what we think. Bunnie believes Bob will return as a ghost.'

'And why would she want Bob as a ghost rather than real life Bob?'

'Perhaps, like Nell, she's never seen one before.'

'So this is her opportunity to create the thing she's been wanting to see.'

He stiffened. 'Bunnie killed her husband?'

'And put him in that mannikin case? No, I don't think that happened. She's too small. Shifting a dead Bob would require a much bigger person.'

'You mean she had help to kill him and cart him away?'

Rosemary turned to lean on the rail. 'I don't know about that, either.'

'But you have a hypothesis.'

'It's growing.'

They were quiet until Jasper stood up, threw the dregs of his tea over the back of the balcony, and whistled for Snowy. 'I know better than to push you into a half-formed thesis. What about I make you dinner tonight and you can tell me your theory? By then it could be fully formed.'

'I'll take your offer up for dinner but I can't promise I'll have it worked out by then.'

'Doesn't matter.' Jasper went to the steps leading to the back garden to help Snowy up the last one. The old dog wagged his tail gratefully. 'Your company is really what I'm after.'

'You don't have to make dinner for me to get that.'

'No.' He opened the back door for Snowy. 'But your time seems to be more taken up than it used to be. I feel like I don't see as much of you.'

Rosemary watched as he pulled the door wider as the old dog ambled over the doorstep and inside. He half turned to her but didn't catch her eye. 'Your time has also been taken up in a way different to previously,' she said carefully. 'And this is a good thing.' He still didn't look at her. 'I'll see you at six-thirty,'

'Okay. That'll be good.' Jasper nodded, followed Snowy in and clicked the door shut.

Rosemary didn't move. The mug hung idly from her

fingertips as she considered Jasper's words. All his words, the ones about the fictional Nell and the others that had stung a little. She tried to think back over the time since they had sat in The Leftover Restaurant listening to Bern, and all that had happened since. So much, it seemed, had changed.

She went back inside and set about the day, letting the mundane tasks of washing breakfast dishes and sweeping the shop rest her mind. It was often during those everyday tasks that unexpected but helpful thoughts sprang into her head as if the rhythm of the broom or the drip of the tap unleashed them. It was while she cleaned the glass front windows—the swirl of her cloth a blur as she worked—that a particularly useful observation leapt out of her brain, making her stop with her hand extended to the top of the pane.

'It's not Bunnie we should be focusing on,' she said through the glass to where Sunny lay on her back in the middle of the shop's floor. 'It's the mannikin.'

Rosemary pulled her jangling door closed. It was a little early to head to Jasper's but the evening was too cool to hang around under the veranda. She swayed a moment on the spot, not willing to disturb Jasper if he was frantically browning onions. Instead, she crossed Goldmarket Road and walked through the Square to where the Exceptional Tree stood dark and mysterious in the twilight.

It had been a while since she'd purposely studied the tree. Its ancient branches stretched out and up, some covered in blue green leaves while others ended bluntly in amputation, providing hidey holes for insects, possums and birds. The Tree was an ecosystem of its own. If anything could house ghosts, it would be the enormous entity in front of her. It had witnessed more life and death over its hundreds of years than Rosemary could ever imagine.

She pulled her jacket more firmly around her as a cold breeze tickled the gum leaves over her head. She'd stood here when Bunnie and her friends had hustled past, leaving poor Warwick behind to die his sudden death alone. It was a selfish act, to leave a friend stranded, but Rosemary remembered the way they'd bundled Bunnie into the car, as if the woman couldn't use her own legs. At the time, she'd thought it caring but now she saw it differently. Had it been guilt driven?

'Rosemary?'

The voice came from the other side of the Tree's trunk. Rosemary bobbed down to peer around it, putting her hands on the Entanglement which acted as a fence bordering the tree's roots, and finally looking up. 'Rakisha. What are you doing?'

The café owner sat on a low branch, her bare feet swinging slightly a metre above the ground. 'Hello, darling. I'm connecting with the Tree. You know, darling.'

Rosemary felt she didn't quite know but nodded anyway. 'Do you usually sit on it to connect?'

'No, darling. Placing my palm on any aspect of this wise wood grounds me but tonight I feel the need for more.'

'Has something happened, Rakisha? Are you alright?'

In the dim light, Rakisha's teeth as she smiled were the brightest part of her. 'You are a darling, darling! I am alright now. I needed centring and my chants were being unhelpful. Sometimes you need to get out of your head and trust Mother Nature.' She swung her legs harder. 'So here I am.'

'How did you get up there?'

Rakisha waved her hand dismissively at the gravel surface of the Square and Rosemary saw a café chair set under the branch.

'I see. Was there anything in particular you felt the need to centre?'

Rakisha put her hands either side of her, palms down and fingers wide. 'I understand the ambience. I know the unrest. It is affecting everyone.'

'What ambience?'

Rakisha sighed. 'Robert Sparkling must sell and it will change everything.'

'You know?'

'Everyone knows, darling. Everyone.' The feet stopped. 'I will suggest everyone sits in the Tree.'

'I'm not sure the Tree will want the whole of Mulbury perched like birds along its branches.'

'I don't think she will mind.' Rakisha stroked the branch affectionately. 'She has a lot of wisdom to impart.'

'Right.' Rosemary climbed over the Entanglement to stand under Rakisha. 'Can I help you down before I leave? I'm going to Jasper's for dinner.'

'Jasper, Jasper...' Rakisha's voice blended with the hush of waving leaves. 'Such a lovely man. Reunited at last.'

'What do you mean, reunited?'

'His father, darling. Surely you've seen him with his father?'

Rosemary tensed. 'You know?'

'Oh, yes, of course. It's obvious. Doesn't everyone know?'

'No. Not even Jasper.'

'Yes, he does. He knows it here.' Rakisha thumped her chest so hard, Rosemary stepped forward in case she fell backwards. 'Ask him, darling. Ask him what he feels.'

'What do you think he feels?'

'Love, darling. The love of a son for a father.' Rakisha laughed, a happy tinkering that merged with the breeze. 'So easy to see.'

Rosemary frowned. She lifted a hand to say goodbye to the woman in the tree but Rakisha was intent on studying a beetle on the branch with her. 'Rakisha, you're quite amazing,' she said softly but got no reply but a faint chanty hum.

She went over the Entanglement and walked back across the Square.

Jasper opened the heavy door of The Read Mulbury the moment she got to it. 'I'm not waiting for you,' he said, the open book face down on a wicker chair near the doorway saying otherwise. 'I've still got a few things to do in the kitchen.'

'Let me help.' Rosemary stepped inside, glancing at the book as she did. 'I may not be as interesting as the Baroness but I'm quite useful.'

'Oh.' Jasper snatched the book up as they went through the bookshop and into his living area where Snowy wagged his tail from his position on the couch. 'This is not a book about a Baroness.'

'A kitchen maid, perhaps?' Rosemary asked as she trailed her hand along the dog's speckled grey coat as she passed.

'No? Oh, no, no. It's not a regency romance at all.'

'Really?' Rosemary paused at the door to the kitchen, taking in the bowl of salad and a plate of cutlets ready for frying. 'Is it another Spectre novel?'

'No.' Jasper sidled past her to turn on the stove top. He settled a pan on the element. 'It's a biography of Jose Granada.'

'Is he a football player?'

Jasper dolloped oil into the pan. 'No. He's a dancer.'

'You're reading the biography of a dancer.'

'Yes.' Jasper curled his hair behind his ear where it sprang back out. 'Is that any more believable than me reading a biography of a football player?'

'Come to think of it, no.' Rosemary plucked the book from the table where Jasper had placed it. 'He's a tango dancer.'

'A tanguero.' Jasper shrugged and turned up the heat. 'I got it from Ken.'

'Ah.'

He turned to her. 'What do you mean, *ah?*'

'Nothing.'

He went back to his cooking. 'Nothing is *nothing* to you, Rosemary Exeter.'

Rosemary glanced around the kitchen, noting some packets of excellent quality tea and a biscuit jar full of hearty shortbread. 'He's been giving you presents.'

'Presents?' Jasper shook his head. 'Not really. It's just that we've found a few things we like in common.' He gestured behind him and Rosemary saw a box on the floor. 'We're swapping books and bits.'

'Bits?'

'You know. I've borrowed a few tools from him to fix the boards on the deck and he's going to borrow some gardening tools for his new place.'

'He's shifting?'

'Well, he was living in his brother's old place near the car yard so he's sold his house in the city and bought elsewhere.'

'Where elsewhere?'

Jasper stirred for a moment before pointing the spatula out the back door without looking at Rosemary. 'Mr Cameron's place. The old man is moving in with his daughter in Big Town.'

'Mr Cameron's is the house that's right behind you.'

'Right behind *us*, you mean. We're all joined together.'

Rosemary watched as Jasper flipped the cutlets over, a hint of garlic wafting through the kitchen. 'What about the car yard?'

'He's leasing it. That means he'll need to go there every

now and then.' Jasper shrugged. 'He said he can help me with the shop. On a volunteer basis, of course. And only when I need it.'

'Great.' Rosemary gathered knives and forks together as he plated the cutlets and set the little round kitchen table. She sat, waiting for Jasper to deliver her meal and pour her a tall glass of sparkling lemon water. He eventually sat with a thump, a smile on his face that stayed even after he drank deeply from his glass. She picked up her knife and fork. 'And what else, Jasper?'

'What?'

'There's something else to this story. I've wondered for a while.'

Jasper cut his meat, speared it with his fork, but didn't eat. 'I've been talking to Helena.'

Rosemary knew his relationship with his sister was rocky at times. 'That's good.'

'Remember she said Mum had a longtime visitor who was a real estate agent.'

'Yes. Helena and you suspected he is your real father.'

Jasper nodded. 'Ken was a real estate agent.'

'And?'

'Well, it seems he knew my mother a long time ago.'

'Over fifty years' ago?'

'Yes.' The smile on Jasper's face broadened.

'And?'

He tipped his head back and raised his glass. 'I think Ken is my father.'

'Have you asked him?'

Jasper shook his head. 'No. No.' He put his glass down. 'I mean, what if he's not? What if I've got it wrong again?'

Rosemary shrugged. 'In a way, it doesn't matter. As

you've said before, he's like a father figure. More than that, he's a friend. Just ask him, Jasper. Ask-'

A bang on the front door stopped her. Someone pushed it open and came in, their footsteps slapping the boards as they ran. Snowy let out a small protest bark. Jasper was on his feet as Rakisha appeared in the kitchen, her layers rocking, and clutching a biscuit tin.

'Darlings, darlings, she's here and it's not good. No, not good.'

Rosemary stood. 'Who's here, Rakisha?'

The woman scraped hair from her face and, bangles clashing, said, 'That naughty Bunnie Lamont.'

THIRTY-TWO

Rosemary and Jasper followed Rakisha outside. In the dim light of evening, Rosemary saw a car parked opposite Robert's garage, Bunnie and Terrence standing next to it. Terrence held Bunnie's arm as she gazed across the Square. He leaned down and looked to be whispering fervently in her ear but it was as if she couldn't hear him. She tugged herself away from him and started a halting run across the gravel towards The Leftover Restaurant, Terrence at her heels.

'She's persistent,' said Jasper. 'I'll give her that.'

'It's not persistence, darling,' said Rakisha. She used one hand to shuck her layers back into place, the other occupied with the round tin. 'It's self-obsession.'

Jasper stuck his hands in his back jeans pockets. 'What do you mean?'

'She cannot believe she could be wrong about Bob. She thinks he wouldn't want to leave her, even if he's dead.' Rakisha tutted. 'It's a challenge for some people, darling, to let go but this isn't what Bunnie Boo is doing. She thinks the world has been created for her alone.'

Jasper nodded thoughtfully and dropped his shoulders so he was more at Rakisha's level. 'She worries you, doesn't she? I've never seen you so disturbed about another person before.'

Rakisha was quiet for a moment as Bunnie and Terrence came to a halt in front of the restaurant where Terrence resumed his crouched tirade. 'Bunnie Lamont is complicated, darling Jasper,' she whispered. 'She sucks people into her vortex. Those poor men she married.' She stiffened. 'Oh dear.'

Even where they stood under the veranda on Gold-market Road, they could hear Bunnie's shrieks. Terrence took a step back, his hands in the air. Bunnie lunged at him, pounding her small fists into his chest and he held still, letting her do it.

Jasper took a step forward. 'Should we help?'

Rosemary shook her head. 'I think it best to let her absorb the news.'

He turned to look at her. 'News? What news?'

She pointed briefly across the Square. 'The news that Bob didn't die in The Leftover Restaurant which, with Bunnie's reckoning, would mean his ghost is nowhere near Mulbury.'

Jasper shook his head. 'I'm not going to ask how you know that, but I know that you *do* know that. Where would she find Bob's ghost then?'

'Nowhere, would be my first answer.'

'Yes, but if you thought there was a possibility of Bob's ghost appearing where he died, where would that be?'

Rosemary watched as Bunnie ran clumsily back across the Square to the car, Terrence a few steps behind. 'In the storeroom where Bern keeps his equipment.' She waved her hand at the car as the pair climbed in. 'Which is where I think they're off to now.'

'Except they aren't.'

The car didn't want to start. It chugged momentarily, black smoke puffing in time with the noise, and died. Terrence tried again, each time with diminishing results, until nothing happened at all. Bunnie started screeching again, the noise bellowing from the car.

Robert came out of his garage wiping his hands on a rag that he stuck in his back pocket. He put a hand on the roof of the car and leaned down to talk to the driver.

'What's happening, dear?'

Rosemary smiled as Mrs Lionel came up beside them. 'Bunnie's back and she's not happy.'

'Won't the car start?' This from Hannah, strolling up with Heather's arm looped through hers. They went to stand on Mrs Lionel's other side.

'We were having dinner,' said Mrs Lionel. 'And heard an argument.' She indicated the veranda as Honey emerged from her café. 'As did others.'

Honey crossed the road and went to Rosemary. 'We were having a barbeque with Geoffrey and I went to pull the blinds down in the shop. What's all the noise, Mum?'

'That was Terrence telling Bunnie something she didn't want to hear.'

Honey's eyebrows shot up.

'And now what?' asked Mrs Lionel.

Hannah pushed her chin towards the scene. 'I think we're about to get dinner *and* a show.'

Bunnie was clambering out of the car, her diminutive figure scrambling to stand. The driver's door opened, propelling Robert back. He held his hands up but Terrence wasn't interested in him. He ran around the front of the car and tried to take Bunnie's arm. She slapped him away. 'Don't you come near me, Terrence Wright! Don't come near me with your lies!' she said, her voice carrying clearly across Goldmarket Road in the quiet.

'But it's not a lie, Bunnie. Bob can't be here so you've got to stop looking for him.'

'You want *me* to stop looking for *him*?' She clenched her fists. 'I am *not* looking for him! Bob is looking for me. For *me*, I tell you! He wants to be with me forever.' She rammed a fist into Terrence's chest and held it there. 'Everyone wants to be with me forever! Other people get in the way of their mission!'

'Bunnie, Bunnie.' Terrence took her tiny fist in his big hand. 'I'll be with you forever. *Me*. Have me instead of Bob.'

Bunnie pulled her hand out of his grasp. 'You do not understand. It will be *Bob* trying to be with *me*. I have no control over that. And you are blocking me.' She jabbed a finger towards the restaurant. 'Bob must have died in that building so there he will be. Waiting for me! For *me*!'

'But I keep telling you, Bunnie. Listen to me.' He grabbed her arm again. 'He didn't die in the restaurant.'

Bunnie went still. Her arms dropped loosely to her sides. Her gaze, though, must have been fierce as Terrence let go and took a step back. 'Why are you so sure he didn't dic in the restaurant? How, Terrence?' She raised herself to her full height. 'How would you know, Terrence, unless you had a hand in it?'

Night was creeping in. The lights from Robert's garage and Franco's Patisserie sent soft beams toward the pair so that their forms were silhouetted against the white of their car. Rosemary went to the edge of the pavement, the others following, but still Terrence said nothing.

The sudden squeal of a door opening behind them

made Jasper jump, knocking into Rosemary. She steadied him with one hand while turning to acknowledge the detective as he came out of Honey B's Teas.

'Mrs Lionel, Rosemary,' he said with a nod of acknowledgement towards each woman before staring across at the scene unravelling behind them. 'What's happening?'

'A little clarity,' said Rosemary. 'It's not going down well.'

Terrence still hadn't spoken. He raised his head and seemed about to until he noticed the crowd watching him. His head ducked down but instead of addressing Bunnie, he leapt towards the car, running around to where Robert stood at the driver's door. The mechanic stepped back but Terrence had remembered the car was going nowhere. He looked around frantically and spotted a car in the garage yard, bolting towards it. Robert followed him, but slowly, and as Terrence jumped in the front seat, pulled a set of keys from his pocket to jangle at the agitated man. Terrence hesitated then came out of the car growling, hurling himself at Robert and knocking him over as he grabbed at the keys. When Robert refused to let go, Terrence groped for a nearby tyre iron and started belting the mechanic with it.

Mrs Lionel gasped. 'Someone stop him!'

Geoffrey was already striding over the road but he wasn't as quick as William. With an angry shout, the businessman ran out of the garage and grabbed Terrence by the neck of his shirt, pulling him backwards. 'Don't hurt my brother, you animal!'

It was difficult to see the whole action in the low light, but after a dusty scuffle, Geoffrey held Terrence in an arm lock, leaving William kneeling beside Robert.

Jasper led the charge across the road as the concerned crowd surged towards the garage. By the time they got there,

Robert was sitting up, holding his left arm. He tried to smile at the group as they gathered around him, but his face was pale with pain. 'I'm fine,' he said shortly.

'You aren't.' William stood, scowling around at Terrence. Geoffrey stopped whatever William thought he was going to do with a stern look.

'It's my arm,' said Robert quietly as Rosemary crouched at his side. 'I fell on it when he pushed me down. And possibly my ribs. He swung that iron like a pro.'

Rosemary examined the odd angle of his wrist. 'It's fractured.'

'Thank you, Dr Exeter.' Robert gripped his arm more tightly, hugging it into his chest. 'Did you see William?' he asked quietly.

'Yes.' Rosemary shrugged. 'He stormed in to protect his brother.'

'That was unexpected.' Robert glanced up at where William glowered at Terrence, Geoffrey holding him back now with an outstretched hand.

'Not really. He's your brother.'

'But he's never acted like that.'

'He needs you like you need him.' Rosemary shifted so she was sitting on the ground. 'Why do you think he's hanging around Mulbury?'

Robert took a painfilled breath in and released it slowly. 'Because of the will. To see it executed.'

'He could do that from the city. He doesn't need to be here.'

'No.' Robert studied his younger brother. 'You're right, he doesn't.'

A flurry of gravel and Jasper knelt beside them. 'I've rung the ambulance and they're on their way. Geoffrey's calling for back-up. Mrs Lionel and Honey are calming

Rakisha. Hannah's gone to get a rope to tie Terrence up.' He craned his head back to look over Rosemary's shoulder. 'Heather's followed to stop her.'

Robert gave a short chuckle. 'Everyone is doing their bit in their own way.' He wriggled, stopping with a grimace. 'Do you think you could help me up? I don't want to stay down here.'

Jasper stood, holding out his hand to Robert who grasped it solidly. William rushed over and put an arm behind his brother's back. Together, they hauled Robert to his feet. He swayed a moment and William held him tighter. 'How about we go into the garage and sit you down?'

Robert raised his head, but instead of nodding, tilted his chin toward the road. 'Let's wait a moment. I don't think the action has stopped.'

Out of the shadows beside the dead car, a tiny figure emerged, brandishing what looked like a golf club.

'Oh, darlings!' called Rakisha, her hands on her mouth. 'Bunnie Boo is on the warpath!'

THIRTY-THREE

Geoffrey had his hands full with Terrence, and William and Jasper held Robert, so Rosemary stepped forward to stop Bunnie in her tracks. 'No need to do anything drastic, Mrs Brownlee. Terrence has shown his true colours by trying to run away.'

'True colours?' Bunnie lifted the thin object which revealed itself as a thick antenna. 'He has no colour, that Terrence Wright. He's as pallid as a...' She waved the antenna as she sought the words.

'Ghost?' Rosemary suggested.

Bunnie screwed up her face. 'When souls stay on Earth for love of another, they are vibrant with colour.'

'And you know that from experience?'

The little woman's face morphed into an angry scowl. 'I am still waiting for my Bob to appear but he....' She jabbed the antenna towards Terrence '...he insists Bob is not here and he is *so* insistent I think he *killed* him.'

Terrence took a step forward but Geoffrey's arm stopped him. 'No, Bunnie, no, I didn't lay a hand on him.'

'And yet he's dead.' Bunnie wobbled the antenna. 'Tell me, Terrence. Tell me what happened!'

Terrence shook his head. 'Bunnie, it was a joke. One of Bob's stupid pranks.'

'A joke?'

'Yes. You know Bob loved pranks, Bunnie.' Terrence held out an arm to Bunnie but let it drop when she didn't move. 'You know that he was always putting whoopee cushions under our seats, fake spiders behind the toilet door, salt in the sugar bowl. And the sheep costume he made from his coloured wool. I mean, it was ridiculous. It was so big he looked like a yeti.'

Bunnie dropped the antenna by her side. 'The spinners and weavers loved Bob dressing up as a sheep.'

Terrence grimaced. 'Yes, they did.'

Rosemary took the antenna from Bunnie's loose grip and turned to Terrence. 'But you didn't,' she said softly.

Terrence took a while to answer. His lip curled as he finally spoke. 'I didn't. I didn't like Bob dressed as a sheep and I didn't like Bob dressed as a man. He was a clown. I couldn't *stand* him.'

Bunnie gasped. 'My Bob! Did you kill him, Terrence?'

'No.' Terrence held her gaze. 'Not really.'

'Not really?' Jasper's eyes were wide. 'What does that mean?'

Terrence kept his eyes on Bunnie but her face was hard and narrow. He opened his mouth to talk but Geoffrey held his hand up. 'You don't have to say anything-'

Terrence stopped him with a mirrored hand. 'I know I don't but I owe it to Bunnie to explain.'

'You do,' said Bunnie coldly. 'You owe me so much, but you can start with this.'

Terrence took a deep breath in and let it out noisily. 'Alright.' He pushed his shoulders back and stared at Bunnie. 'Bob crept into the office on Tuesday evening dressed in his ridiculous sheep costume.' Terrence twitched uncomfortably. 'He scared the living daylights out of me. I thought he was...'

'A ghost?' asked Jasper.

'A ghoul, more like it. It was dark in the office. He crawled on all fours, bleating. Bleating! It sounded like moaning. I didn't know what it was.' Terrence shivered. 'It was the last straw. Here was a man who thought it fun to dress as a sheep. It was humiliating! He didn't deserve you, Bunnie. You are far too intelligent for that lump of a fool.'

Bunnie didn't move. 'What did you do?'

'I walked away in disgust but he followed.' Terrence walked his arms. 'On all fours, mind you, until I started to get ahead of him so he got up and ran after me.' He shook his head. 'I couldn't get rid of him. He knew I was angry but instead of apologising, he started to goof around even more.'

'How?'

'Oh.' Terrence waved his arms. 'Putting a metal office rubbish bin on his head and pretending to be Darth Vader, flicking rubber bands at the indoor plants, even pretending to be Silviana by chanting in a silly, high voice. I couldn't stand it. I walked out and tried to lose him by going into the big room. But...'

'He followed,' said Rosemary.

'Yes, he followed.' Terrence slumped. 'He got even worse in there. He raided Bern's supplies and started wrapping himself up like a mummy. I went into the storeroom to stop him and that's when he spotted the mannikin's case.'

Rosemary nodded. 'He knew about Cecil.'

'Everyone knew about Cecil ever since Bern raised the money to buy him. Bob opened the case and there was Cecil, all dressed up and ready to go. Bob had no respect for how much that dummy had cost. He heaved him out on the floor and climbed in to lie in the case just like Cecil. You know.' Terrence did a fair imitation of a mannikin with half closed eyes and mouth. 'It was then he asked when Bern was coming in.'

'Was he scared of being caught?'

'No! He was going to jump out when Bern came along and scare him.'

'A practical joke on Bern.'

'Well, you've seen Bern. Takes himself too seriously.' Terrence hunched his shoulders. 'It would have been funny.'

'But Bern wasn't coming back for a few days.'

'Bob didn't know that he'd already gone and wouldn't be back for a while.'

'You did?'

Terrence gave the smallest of nods. 'The roster was on the wall. Anyone could have seen it.'

'But Bob didn't.'

Terrence's face blanked.

'So, you closed the lid.'

'It wasn't my idea. Bob said, "Shut the lid, shut the lid!" So, I did.'

'You're saying you shut the lid,' said Geoffrey. 'As Bob requested.'

'Yes, Bob asked me to.'

'Did he say, "Latch the lid?"'

Terrence stared hard at the detective. 'No, he didn't.'

'But you latched the lid.'

Terrence shook his head unconvincingly. 'It was a joke

on Bob. I only meant to leave it like that for a few moments.' Terrence closed his eyes briefly. 'I left him there in the case to teach him a lesson.'

'For how long?'

'I went home.' Terrence squared his shoulders. 'But before I did, I unlatched the case so he could get out.'

'But he couldn't.' Rosemary tilted her head. 'He was already dead.'

'He couldn't have been because he delivered his wool around the countryside.' Terrence nodded earnestly at Geoffrey. 'That's what the spinning ladies said, didn't they?'

'Someone delivered the wool.' Rosemary swung the antenna lightly. 'Someone dressed as a sheep.'

'It was Bob.'

'So, you're saying that Bob climbed out of the case, delivered his wool, and climbed back in.'

Terrence had a hard glint to his eyes. 'The wool was delivered. I don't know when he died in the case.' He crossed his arms. 'I was working in my office the whole week.'

'That's not right.'

Geoffrey gave her a sharp look. 'What do you mean, Rosemary?'

Rosemary went closer to Terrence. 'First of all, you said to me that most of your week was spent on farms, presumably talking to farmers about their insurance.'

'Well, yes, but not every week. You know, there are times...'

Rosemary held her hand up to stop him. 'You're saying you were in the office all week, including Saturday?'

'That's exactly what I was saying. I was at my desk. Ask anyone.'

'There is no one to ask as you work alone.' Rosemary

narrowed her eyes at him. 'You weren't at your desk when I drove past Saturday afternoon so I'm assuming you weren't at your desk during the week either. Someone was at your desk, or should I say, some*thing*.' She paused as Terrence's mouth opened but he didn't speak. 'It was Cecil at your desk in the rural insurance office.'

Terrence stiffened. 'I don't know what you mean,' he said.

'You *do* know what I mean.' Rosemary leaned a little closer. 'When I went past your office on the day Bob was found, there was a spiky-haired silhouette of a man at your desk.' She pointed at his head. 'Your hair is flat, luxuriously so. Cecil's wig that day suited his smart business attire and was shaped into spikes. Bern had set him up like that. Cecil was at your desk when you said you were there. You used the mannikin as a replacement for yourself.'

Night had settled around them, leaving everyone in the shadows. Terrence's hand went to his hair, pushing it up but it refused to spike and fell flat against his scalp. Bunnie crept forward until she was in front of him, Geoffrey's arm still blocking his movements. 'Bob died in your office building?' she asked.

Terrence dropped his head and gave the smallest of nods.

Mrs Lionel started towards the diminutive woman but Rosemary caught her arm to stop her. 'I think it's alright.'

'But Mrs Brownlee...'

'Watch,' Rosemary whispered.

Bunnie had pulled herself up to her full height. The look on her face clearly terrified Terrence as he shifted to be slightly behind Geoffrey. 'You,' said Bunnie. 'You lied all along.'

'Bunnie...'

She held her hand up. 'You said he died in the restaurant.'

'Well, no, I didn't.'

'I've been wasting my time,' she hissed, stamping one foot. 'I should be at the office building!'

THIRTY-FOUR

No one had time to respond to Bunnie. Geoffrey bundled Terrence into Robert's garage as the distant sounds of police and an ambulance screamed louder. Jasper and William followed with Robert in between them, although he looked perfectly capable of walking on his own. He rolled his eyes at Rosemary as they went past but she saw the sudden pain in his eyes as he tried to move his arm. The sisters had returned, Hannah with a fistful of haybale twine. Heather linked her arm through Mrs Lionel's and steered her friend over the dark road back to The Green Mulbury, Hannah following in disgust as she realised tying up Terrence was no longer needed. That left Bunnie facing Rakisha, Rosemary and Honey, her face still screwed up angrily. She glanced at the car.

'It's not going to start, darling,' said Rakisha.

'I know that, you loony.' She swung her head to look at Rosemary. 'You could drive me. I need to find Bob.'

'Bob is at the morgue, sadly,' said Rosemary.

'Not his physical form, his soul! His spirit! His mischievousness! His...' Bunnie waved her hand around.

'His memory, Bunnie?'

Rakisha's words were soft, difficult to hear over the clammer of protesting voices from Terrence and Robert in the garage: Terrence trying to explain his actions, and Robert reassuring his brother that he was fine. Rakisha took a step towards Bunnie turned as she turned. 'His memory?' echoed Bunnie.

'Well, darling, I think that's what you're really chasing, isn't it? Memories of Bob and you together, the fun times you had. The *companionship*.' Rakisha extended her hand and rested it gently on Bunnie's shoulder. 'It's lonely sometimes by yourself. I know, darling.'

Rosemary tensed, unsure of Bunnie's reaction and ready to jump in front of Rakisha, but Bunnie's shoulders dropped under the weight of Rakisha's hand. 'Don't forget Harry. He didn't come back for me, either.'

'They don't come back, Bunnie darling. Not in the way you want.'

Bunnie tensed her arms by her side and closed her eyes. She looked ready to explode but, after a long minute of quivering, her body went still and she opened her eyes again and stared directly at Rakisha. 'They should come back. They loved me.'

Rakisha didn't move. Another extended moment, and Bunnie let her gaze drop away to the biscuit tin Rakisha was clutching. 'What is that?'

Rakisha blinked and held the tin up. 'Oh, darling, this is Milly's beautiful biscuit container.'

Bunnie eyed the tin. 'There's something about that tin. Is it glowing?'

Rakisha beamed. 'Oh, Bunnie Lamont, you can see the love oozing from every dent and mark on this!' She stroked the lid, running her fingers over the pressed pattern. 'This tin holds more than snacks. It has memories, darling. Milly's memories of her darling husband and the moments they shared together.'

Bunnie put a hand on her cheek. 'A tin holds memories?'

'Oh, yes. Any object can. Haven't you ever looked at something and been flooded with images of the past?'

The evening deepened a little as Bunnie thought. 'Bob's sheep costume,' she said softly.

'What's that, darling?'

Bunnie cleared her throat. 'Bob's sheep costume. We made it together over many winter nights in front of the fire.' She put her fingers in front of her nose. 'Even now, I can smell the lanolin. We laughed together more than we ever had making that costume.'

'There you are, darling. *Fleece* will always make you remember Bob.'

Bunnie nodded slowly, her eyes on the tin. 'What else is in there?'

'These are for Honey Blossom.' Rakisha glanced around at Rosemary. 'Snacks, darling. Healthy nibbles. Here.' She opened the container and thrust it under Bunnie's nose. 'Have one, darling. You'll feel better once you've eaten.'

Bunnie hesitated but took a small brown ball out and sniffed it cautiously. 'What is it made of, Raving Reeka? Horse manure? Dirt? Poison?'

Rakisha blinked and shook her head, making her flyaway curls lift and dance around her shoulders. 'Oh no, darling. They were grown in manure and dirt, if that's what you mean, but they aren't poisonous. Why would I offer anyone something poisonous?' She smiled kindly. 'I have hope for you, Bunnie Lamont. I have glimpsed your aura. It is changing. *You* are changing.'

Bunnie glared at Rakisha. 'People don't change. *You* haven't changed a bit.'

'Darling,' said Rakisha, offering the tin to Honey. 'I don't need to change.'

Rosemary shook her head as the snacks went to her, ducking her head so Rakisha couldn't see her grin.

Bunnie opened her mouth to say something but paused. Instead, she shoved the snack in and chewed noisily, her face wrinkled up as if thinking of the worst things she could say. Honey followed suit, chewing once or twice before backing away as Rakisha watched Bunnie happily. Rosemary saw her daughter cough subtlely into a handkerchief before shoving it into her pocket. Honey widened her eyes at her mother then pulled a brief face. Rosemary turned back to Bunnie to watch her do the same.

But she didn't. The foul expression on Bunnie's face had been replaced by surprise. She slowed her chewing and nodded. Rakisha was back in front of her now, the tin still extended. Bunnie took another snack. 'You,' she said, her mouth full. 'You are a force of nature, Rakisha.'

'No, darling,' said Rakisha. 'I take the force of nature and blossom it into a representation of goodness. You like my snacks?'

'No,' said Bunnie, swallowing. 'I *love* them.'

THIRTY-FIVE

After the excitement of the previous evening, Mulbury had a slow Monday start. The shops under the veranda on Gold-market Road opened on time, but Jasper's book barrow and Honey B's sandwich board didn't get out until an hour later. Even Rosemary stayed in the peace of her dining area, although she was busy. The phone calls she'd made had got results and there were things to organise. She rang Robert. 'Hi. Are you fixed?'

He laughed, but she detected a slight shakiness. 'My plaster is heavy and my ribs hurt but I'm patched up, if that's what you meant.'

'Terrence is a large man.'

'Don't I know it.' The phone hissed in the way it does when pushed across clothing. 'Large and strong. And I've learned not to leave tyre irons outside the garage.'

'You were in the wrong place at the wrong time.'

'Yes and no.' His voice dropped. 'William stayed at the hospital with me and brought me home. He hasn't left my side. I've had more offers of cups of tea than I've even had from you over my time in Mulbury.'

'He's concerned about you.'

'Yes.' Robert paused. 'Don't you think that's odd? He's never shown concern for me at all.'

Rosemary wandered into her shop, where long lengths of autumn light stretched across the floor from the skylight. Sunny stretched out in one beam, her illuminated fur nearly the colour of the floorboards. 'No, it's not odd. It's a product of the circumstances. Your father is no longer holding sway over your brother, and he's discovered Mulbury.'

'What do you mean by that last bit?'

She looked out over the Square where Rakisha was setting up her outdoor setting, her hand twirling around gently as she chatted with Milly who nodded and threw back her head to laugh. Behind them, Kelly plunked a chair into a table and adjusted the weatherproof umbrella over it, taking a moment to smooth her shirt and wave to Franco who was taking something out to his bin. He nodded, hurrying back into his shop where a queue of hungry tourists ogled his pastries. 'Mulbury is where you find peace. It happened to me, to Mrs Lionel, to Jasper. And Rakisha and Milly. And, of course, you. William has spent the last couple of weeks buying coffee and eating delicious fare and noticing how much you care about the people that live here. He's human, Robert. He wants the same peace as us.'

The phone was quiet for a long time, long enough, in fact, for Rosemary to rearrange a whole row of quince jelly so they lined up in rich ruby splendour in the shop's light. 'I've been too hard on him,' said Robert so quietly Rosemary had to pause to hear it.

'Yes. But you don't have to continue to be.'

'The will...'

The anguish in Robert's voice made Rosemary swallow. 'Don't worry. I've got that covered.'

'What on earth do you mean?'

She shuffled the phone to her other ear so she could use both hands to smooth a label on a pickle jar. 'Are you coming to Monday dinner tonight?'

'I guess so. I really hadn't thought that far ahead.'

'Bring William. We have a guest coming.'

'Who?'

'No one you know.'

'Rosemary, what's going on?'

'Just tying up some loose ends. Dinner's at the Hubbards.'

'It'll be crowded if we have extra people. There's not much room in their house.'

'That's okay. I'm helping them.'

'You sure you want me to bring William? Hannah might serve him up for dessert.'

'Bring William. He can help you across the road, you poor old thing.'

'Oh, ha ha.' The smile was back in Robert's voice. 'Right, I'll see you tonight.'

Rosemary ended the call and made another one straight away. 'Getting my ducks aligned,' she said to Sunny. The tabby pricked her ears up at *ducks* but gave her mistress a long stare and sauntered off to lie in a sunbeam.

THE DAY WENT BY, Rosemary speeding up as she went from one task to the next. The animal produce shed was perfect for a small crowd of diners. Hannah and Milly made quick work of arranging hay bales as seats and a stack of pallets as one big table. Heather made a huge macaroni cheese and Mrs Lionel contributed her apple and rhubarb crumble, so there was enough food for regular Monday dinner aficionados as well as a bit extra. Rosemary helped put out cutlery and plates before heading off to pick up her guest from the Big Town Railway Station. They took a while to return, and by the time they did, everyone had a bowl of macaroni in their hands as they sat chatting on the sweet smelling lucerne bales.

'You're back,' murmured Mrs Lionel as she stood to greet them.

'Yes.' Rosemary glanced around her friends, noting William sitting in the middle of Robert and Heather. 'This is Julius Brown.'

A small man wearing a multipocketed brown vest stepped forward eagerly to shake Mrs Lionel's hand, almost tripping on an undone shoelace. He righted himself, pushed tiny round glasses back up his nose, and beamed at the crowd. 'Hello,' he said. 'It's so exciting to be here.'

Hannah glanced at her meal. 'Well, Heather does make a mean macaroni cheese. It's the paprika, I think.'

Professor Brown blinked at her but took a bowl of pasta when Rakisha gave it to him and held it like an offering in front of him.

Rosemary stepped forward, bringing him with her with an outstretched arm. 'This is Professor Brown,' she said, looking straight at the Sparkling brothers. 'He's from the university's environmental department.'

'Oh, please,' said the man. 'Just call me Prof.'

'Prof,' said Rosemary. 'Could you tell my friends why you're here today?'

Professor Brown grinned broadly and jumped up and

down slightly on the balls of his feet. 'Yes, yes, it's so wonderful!' The bowl wobbled dangerously.

'What has made you so jubilant, dear?' asked Mrs Lionel when it was clear the Professor's excitement was taking time to be shared.

'Goodness, didn't I say?' He pushed his glasses back again. 'This is the first sighting in over twenty years and...' he blinked and raised his gaze to the sky '...I can't believe it's in my jurisdiction!'

Hannah swallowed her last mouthful and balanced her bowl on a pallet. 'Have you seen a UFO?'

Professor Brown brought his gaze to the puzzled Hubbard sister. 'A UFO? No, no, that's the stellar department. The environmental department is earthlier.' He laughed, rocking onto his toes. 'This is a sighting of something much more significant. Something so rare they were about to be labelled extinct. To discover them in such an inauspicious clump of trees makes this find like uncovering a jewel.' He rocked back on his heels, making his bowl tip and slopping macaroni on the floor where Rufus cleaned it up. 'Little blue jewels!'

'This man is crazy,' said Hannah to Mrs Lionel standing next to her. 'Do we have to wait all night to hear what he's got to say? The crumble is still warming in the oven.'

'Quiet, dear,' said Mrs Lionel, putting a hand on Hannah's arm. 'I think he's nearly there.'

'Right.' Hannah wriggled impatiently. 'Prof, what is it you've seen?'

'Why, pixie wrens! Blue beaked pixie wrens!'

The crowd kept silent. Heather stood, her golden curls bouncing about her shoulders as she clasped her hands together.

'That's lovely,' said Mrs Lionel, her hand still firmly on

Hannah. 'Besides acknowledging a species thought lost, what does it mean in a broader sense?'

'It means,' said Rosemary, 'that the area in which these little wrens reside is protected. No one can build there. It must be left alone, as well as a substantial area around it.'

Roman stood as well, his hand on Jules' shoulder. 'And where is it the little birds reside? Is it somewhere needing protection?'

The Mulburians all got it at once. They swivelled their stare to William Sparkling, who sat stiffly next to his brother. 'I think I know,' he said slowly. 'The wrens have been discovered on D-Day Development's land. The development can't go ahead.'

'Well, you can fight it,' said Rosemary. 'But it's not likely to win or at least not for some time.'

Robert looked down at his plaster cast and wriggled his fingertips as if checking they were still there. William kept staring at Professor Brown who had started on his pasta as if he hadn't eaten for days. 'Brilliant,' William said softly.

Robert raised his head. 'Brilliant?'

William nodded. 'Yes.' He grinned. 'Brilliant!'

'Brilliant?' said Kelly to no one in particular. 'He thinks it brilliant not to make a packet out of some old swampy paddock?'

Rosemary folded her arms and watched as William stood, running a hand through his short hair in a gesture that reminded her of his brother. 'The will,' he said, looking sideways at Robert. 'There's a clause in it.' He shifted his gaze to Rosemary. 'You found it.'

Rosemary nodded, '"*If circumstances are beyond control of the operator, caveats can be disregarded.*"'

Robert clambered up, momentarily clutching his side.

'If we aren't allowed to build, we can still meet the terms of our father's will.'

'Okay,' said Hannah. 'And what does that all mean?'

'It means,' said Heather, rocking slightly, 'that the pixie wrens have saved Mulbury Feeds.' She smiled at Robert who looked at her fondly. 'And Ravenshome is safe.'

'And Vivi has all that she needs,' said William quietly.

Robert gripped his brother's shoulder and nodded. 'It'll work out.'

'Yes.' William glanced at Rosemary. The tension eased from his face and she gave him a smile.

'No one has to sell?' Kelly rolled her eyes. 'So, this was all a storm in a teacup?'

'A storm in a teacup is still a storm,' said Mrs Lionel. 'Now, Professor Brown, would you like some dessert?'

It was very late before Rosemary could extract the Professor from the happy crowd. He was slapped heartily on the back by nearly everyone in the room and grinned every time. She'd never seen someone put away so much apple and rhubarb crumble but it was one of Mrs Lionel's best and every second person kept filling the Prof's bowl. On the way back to Big Town, he fell asleep, snoring gently with his head against her car window.

When she arrived home, Mulbury slumbered. The only light came from the single streetlight and the glow of Franco's fridges. No ghost hunters invaded the Square. The Exceptional Tree dipped a branch to her as she closed her car door quietly, and she gave a slight bow back. Mulbury was almost back to normal.

THERE WAS one outstanding thing to clear up.

Rosemary and Mrs Lionel stood in her shop contemplating the need for more laundry liquid when someone knocked on the door. Mrs Lionel beckoned, and a man stepped in, wincing at the cacophony of frog noise.

'Mr Gilbert,' said Rosemary loudly over the croaking. 'Are you back in search of more things supernatural?'

The man shook his head. 'I've come for the peridot,' he said. 'We're finishing up in Mulbury. You're safe, as there were no paranormal incidents recorded on our devices.' He patted the bag over his shoulder from which the EMF reader protruded. 'I need to go home to calibrate it as we do after every major investigation. Keeps it reliable, see.'

'Good to know, dear,' said Mrs Lionel. 'I've kept your rock safe. Do come right inside and that will shut the noise off.'

Mr Gilbert eyed the motion detector. 'It's a rather noisy frog, isn't it? Quite the alarm.'

'It does sound particularly noisy today.' Mrs Lionel hurried forward and closed the door behind him. 'Oh.'

The frog usually gave one last choking croaking and then was silent. This time, though, a high-pitched squeal sliced through the fragrant store. Mrs Lionel put her hands over her ears.

'It's not your frog.' Mr Gilbert pulled out his EMF detector. The dial was firmly in the red, and the squealing noise sounded from tiny speakers in its back.

Mrs Lionel backed away. 'Can you turn it off? It is truly a horrible sound.'

Cameron turned the gadget over hastily and found the switch. The noise died away, leaving both women looking at each other in relief. 'Oh dear,' he said. 'I do need to work on this one. I knew it needed a good service.' He laughed, pointing at the neat rows of soap. 'You don't have anything ghostly in this room full of natural goodies that would make it go right off like that.'

But Mrs Lionel didn't answer. She was staring at the doorway to her living quarters. As Rosemary watched, the older woman crouched down, using the counter to keep her balance, and clicked her tongue. Nothing happened, although Mrs Lionel was smiling.

Rosemary crossed over to the counter, picked up the box with the peridot rock, and gave it to Mr Gilbert. 'Here you are.'

'Thank you.' He stuffed the box into his bag and tipped his head. 'Goodbye, ladies.'

Rosemary showed him out, locking the door behind him, and stepping quickly away from the frog again. Mrs Lionel was still crouching on the floor, smiling at the floorboards.

Although she couldn't see him, had never seen him and most likely would never see him, Rosemary knew immediately what was holding Mrs Lionel's attention.

Percy, the ethereal terrier.

**Mulbury Mysteries**

#1: A Sticky Situation

Mulbury is a quiet place where visitors wander happily around Goldmarket Square. When the body of an old man is found under The Exceptional Tree, everyone assumes that he died peacefully. Everyone, that is, except Rosemary Exeter.

A small-town mystery with quirky residents and an unimpressed cat.

#2: A Pretty Pickle

Winter in Mulbury, and frost hardens the ground. The tourists still flock to the little town, going about their happy business with no hint of what's been discovered in Jasper Lu's backyard. Who do these bones belong to? Rosemary Exeter is determined to find out.

#3: A Tricky Treat

The Mulbury Gala is in full swing. Rosemary Exeter's pickles and marmalades are selling briskly at her stall, alongside Mrs Lionel's green cleaning products and Jasper Lu's secondhand books – until there are screams from across the road. Why has Mrs Caroline King hit the dust? She's not telling so it's up to Rosemary to find a reason.

#4: A Jaunty Jam

A quiet visit to Justin Gentleman's farm to select fruit and vegetables turns to tragic intrigue for Rosemary Exeter. As well as solving that mystery, there's also the puzzling behaviour of members of The Jaunty Jalopers, some of whom are up to more than simple treasure hunting.

Novella: One Christmas Pickle

Christmas time in Mulbury, Australia. Plum puddings, roast turkey and blistering hot days. Who overcooked the fire brigade's fund-raising Santa? With the team of fire-fighting volunteers stuck in Mulbury until their truck is fixed, and almost certainly one of them a murderer, Rosemary hides the one clue she has while searching for others.

A Mulbury Mystery Christmas novella with punch... and brandy sauce.

Two Christmas Pickles

A rainy Christmas time in Mulbury, but that won't deter the Cracker Christmas Kid's Charity Run. When a mob of motorcyclists roar into town with panniers full of donated presents, the last thing they want to discover is a pair of bodies in the Christmas sacks. Who'd want to kill Ted and Ned? Rosemary aims to find out.

Other books by Juno Harvey

Because I Know it's True

Since the car accident that altered her family's lives, Grace Worthington has always been a loner. Now, with her father's death, she is truly alone. When she reads about Alexander Cameron's search for his missing sister, she sees an answer for both their problems. She has no family: he has no sister. Grace follows Alexander back to Scotland, and becomes involved in the biggest act of her life.

ABOUT THE AUTHOR

Juno Harvey lives in Victoria, Australia, with her family. She makes jam on the weekends and works in a university during the week.

Want to join Juno's Reader's Team?
Click here (or go to www.junoharvey.com) and receive a free story!

https://www.junoharvey.com/

Books of light...and shade.

www.ingramcontent.com/pod-product-compliance
Lightning Source LLC
Chambersburg PA
CBHW020351120726
47904CB00002B/539